SOL CANYON

A "What Would Marlow Do?" Mystery

Michael Wolf

Published by Famous Shamus Books

ISBN:979-8-218-76103-5
LCCN: 2025917142

Edited by: Heidi Stangeland
Cover Art and Design by: Guy Vasilovich

For Norma —
-who instilled in me a love of books

Acknowledgements

Some writers can lock themselves in a room for hours a day and crank out a book in a few months. I am not that guy. I spend more time thinking about my story than putting it to paper. But I have my friend and sometime writing partner, **Guy Vasilovich,** to thank for his endless prodding and encouragement to "finish the damn book!" Also, a heartfelt thank you to the famous **Stephy Cha** for reading my first draft. Her notes and suggestions were most appreciated. And a big thank you to my editor, **Heidi Stangeland**, who helped me get this book to print.

AUTHOR'S NOTE

This, my first foray into writing a detective novel, started ten years ago. It began with an image that was lodged in my head of a young man, hands in the pockets of a trench coat with the collar up, wearing a fedora with the brim pulled down, standing in the amber glow of an old-fashioned streetlight, on a skateboard.

I was intrigued by the notion of a twenty-something lad who was romanced by a library of pulp fiction stories of hard-boiled detectives. He becomes embroiled in a case, and the harsh reality of events forces him to quickly grow from an immature youth to a somewhat more mature man. He must solve the mystery to save his own skin and, along the way, learns a few hard lessons and – spoiler alert – manages to not get killed in the process.

I plunged in and began writing. The skateboard went away, replaced, I guess, by a set of golf clubs. But the symbolism of the toys, if you want to call them that, remains.

Certainly, I see a lot of myself in this young detective. I, too, have read hundreds of stories over the years, from early Tey, LeBlanc, Christie, and Doyle to modern-day authors like Michael Connelly. I sought out various writers of Norse Noir, and authors from Ireland to Australia, Korea, and China, but my favorites were always those that brought to life the gritty adventures in post-war Los Angeles – like Mosley, Ellroy, and Chandler. Their savage writing skills set a high bar.

Unlike my protagonist, I am far from my twenties, but I still feel as green as he is venturing forth, and in some ways just as over-confident. "I can do this." I keep telling myself. I've done it before – if you count the half dozen or more unproduced screenplays or the drawer full of unpublished short stories. I've never been one to let a lack of experience stand in my way. So, I read how-to books and attended writers' panels and book fair lectures, consulted friends and colleagues, and I plowed ahead.

As I said at the top, I've been worrying this novel to death for ten years.

Books can be like paintings in that they are never finished; at some point, you just stop. So here it is.

Enjoy.

Mike

CHAPTER

ONE

The glorious and somewhat notorious Chateau Marmont is a seven-story French Gothic hotel, perched on a hill in West Hollywood. An old-fashioned manor, styled with separate cottages off to the side, she was built in the 1920s, with an off-white stucco façade, grey tile roofs, and towered above the eastern end of Sunset Boulevard like an aging, jaded movie star.

It was not yet six-thirty in the morning. I was standing out on one of her balconies, naked as a jaybird, letting the balmy late summer air cool my sweat. It felt great. The view wasn't bad either. The sun was just starting to peak over the San Gabriels in the east, throwing narrow shafts of light between the hotels and condominium towers and painting the street with bands of gold.

South, over the cities of Santa Monica, Beverly Hills, and the rest of the basin, the fog of a marine layer had settled in from the Pacific like a rumpled, dirty grey sheet on a broken spring bed in a rent-by-the-hour motel, not that I knew of such places personally. I wagered these clouds wouldn't last long. The forecast was for low nineties that day, low hundreds again in the valleys. This poor excuse for weather would maybe last until eight or nine this morning at the latest.

It used to be that the view from here, looking westward, was blocked by the Marlboro Man, a seventy-foot-tall plywood monument to smoking and looking manly in a ten-gallon hat and plaid flannel shirt. He wasn't your typical billboard.

He was a cut-out wooden silhouette without a frame, and he lorded over the street like the bigger-than-life Hollywood celebrity he was. He guarded the entrance to The Strip like one of Tolkien's Argonath guarding the River Anduin. But even his iconic status couldn't save him from the onslaught of the anti-tobacco Orcs who felled him at the end of the last century.

On the positive side, though, from my balcony perch now I could almost see this section of Sunset in its entirety as it wound its way around the curves of the Santa Monica Mountains, cutting a path about mid-way up the slope separating the flat-roofed apartment buildings of West Hollywood from the hilltop celebrity mansions on the crest.

The Strip, as the locals called it, started from this hotel and meandered past a slew of other hotels, bars, restaurants, and more than a few famous nightclubs like The Whiskey, The Roxy, The Viper Room, and House of Blues, until it ran out of gas at the eastern border of Beverly Hills. It had always been the heart of Hollywood nightlife from its earliest beginnings as the main thoroughfare for celebrities travelling from Beverly Hills to work in Hollywood and back again.

As Hollywood was dry in those days, lots of taverns and gambling clubs sprouted along the way. Prohibition made this stretch of county land even more attractive to the speakeasy owners.

By the 30s and 40s, when Ciro's and the Trocadéro were all the rage, this was where a gal could be pumping egg creams behind a soda fountain at Schwab's one day and become a movie star the next, or where F. Scott Fitzgerald and Robert Benchley would share a cocktail by the pool at the Garden of Allah and discuss their latest screenplays at the same time, bemoaning having to write such tripe just for the money. Here also toiled the likes of MacDonald, Cain, and Chandler. These were the streets and sidewalks where Archer, Spade, and Marlowe prowled.

My name is James Gardiner, Private Investigator. Like my forerunners, I work in the shadows, shining a light on the dirty little secrets and bringing the criminals to justice.

On the street down below, I spied some late-night revelers rolling home with the sunrise, a guy in a late model Mustang rag top with a couple birds, one in the passenger seat and another in the back. The driver pulled a quick U-turn and slid, drifted into the driveway of The Sunset Hotel across the way. Tires squealed against the pavement, piercing the morning quiet, intentionally, no doubt.

With a quick peck on the cheek, the dolls hopped out without opening the door, barefoot, carrying their heels, giggling, drunk. Right about then, some cherry lights flashed, and a siren burped but once. It looked like some copper was going to get to write one more ticket before his shift was up.

I turned around and rested the small of my back against the rail. The cement was cold against my skin. Inside the suite, stretched out beneath the silks, was my latest client, now, officially, former client, Glenda, a forty-five-year-old chestnut brunette with a body you could ache for. She had a rat for a husband who was too busy plowing his twenty-something secretary to pay his Mrs. enough attention.

So, she had me tail him for a couple of weeks, stake out his love nest, snap a couple of incriminating pics, and boom, her lawyer got her a seven-figure settlement.

Me, I got four grand a week plus expenses and a bonus. Tonight was my bonus. Truth be known, I worked for the bonuses, didn't need the money all that much.

It looked like the former Mrs. Brown was waking up. She was stretching and reaching for my empty side of the bed. Finding nothing but pillows woke her up. Aw, look at that pout.

Next, she was getting up, wrapping that white silk sheet around her like a princess wedding gown and dragging her train across the yellow, blue, and white fleur-de-lis-patterned carpet to the balcony, kicking aside the empty bottles of Dom that littered the floor. She clutched the sheets to her chest so modestly. She was five foot two with a hard yoga mom body and a pixie do. She looked up at me with her long, sharp nose and slightly jutting chin that she held a little too high. It gave her that aristocratic appearance of disdain.

"Come on back to bed, cowboy," she purred. "Let's get you back in the saddle again."

"No. I'd love to, but I've got to go. You know how it is. It's Monday, a workday, got to get to the office. Punch the ol' time clock." I mimed.

"But it's still so early. The sun's not even up. What are you, the milkman?" she teased. "Surely you have time for a quickie."

"I might have the time, but really, I don't have the energy. You've used me all up."

"You can't tell me a handsome, virile young stud like yourself can't keep up with an old broad like me." She pouted as she scratched a design on my chest with her fingernail. "I'm beginning to think maybe you don't like me anymore."

"Oh, I think I showed you how much I liked you all night last night, but I'm done, finished, kaput. This soldier ain't gonna salute anymore today, Sarge."

"Oh, I think I could get your private to stand at attention again."

She reached for me, but I dodged and hurried past, off the balcony, into the room. I grabbed my slacks off the back of the chair. I wasn't going to waste time looking for my shorts; I was going to have to go commando.

As I jumped into my pants and hopped my way towards my shirt, which lay crumpled on the floor, she stood in the doorway to the balcony, sucking on her finger, letting the sheets fall around her ankles in one last temptation. I finished dressing and slipped bare feet into my Italian loafers.

"You'll call me?" she asked plaintively.

I took a deep sigh and grabbed my charcoal fedora with a black satin band, size seven and three-quarters. I've got a big head. As I donned the hat and pulled it down at a rakish angle, I gave her my most earnest look. "I've got you on speed dial." I lied and left.

The elevator at the Chateau is old and small. I hadn't gone down even one floor when it stopped again, and an older man got on.

He was dressed for the office, in a dark grey suit, white shirt, and conservative tie.

He glanced at me briefly and then took a more surreptitious survey from my sockless shoes up to my rakishly tilted fedora. His dismissive eye roll said it all, but then I noticed a barely suppressed smile sneak across his face. Yeah, he was jealous.

I was sure I looked quite a sight to the valet, too, what with my shirt tail still hanging out, but the help doesn't judge here. They've seen too many A-listers waltz in and out looking much worse, I was sure. Anyway, this morning I kind of felt like a celebrity. I had that post-coital glow of confidence and swagger. I felt I belonged here. The Chateau was an old hotel by Los Angeles standards, and a very popular hideout for the Hollywood types with its private soundproofed bungalows, discreet entries, and zipper-lipped staff. It was also a bit notorious for the elite who had stayed here, misbehaved here, and sometimes died here.

When the kid brought my best girl, my real true love, around the corner, I was sure my eyes lit up. I never got tired of looking at her, long and lean with those sexy curves.

"They just don't make 'em like that anymore." The kid said as he took my valet ticket, wrapped in a fin for the tip. He gave her fender a loving caress, but I didn't mind.

My old gal was a shiny two-toned, turquoise and cream Mercury Marquis convertible with matching vinyl interior, glistening white wall tires, and chrome in all the right places. A 368 V-8 purred to me from under the hood. I had picked her up for a mere twenty grand, though I probably spent at least that much getting her cherried out. Her name was Lola.

This was starting to be a good day. I had a check for ten grand in my pocket, and I didn't really have to rush to the office. It was not like there was another job waiting for me to jump on. Work was pretty slow these days, and I was looking forward to maybe taking a little solo golf vacation up the coast.

I slid into the front seat, punched in my *Best of Billie Holiday* CD, and eased my baby down the long curving drive to the Boulevard. The raspy yet fragile strains of *Them There Eyes* floated up to me.

While this stretch of the Strip may be just turning in for the night, Sunset was still a major east/west artery, so morning rush hour traffic was already picking up. I hung a left, east, into the blinding morning sun and groped for my shades on the dash, then popped open the glove compartment. I kept a flask of rye in there. I could use a snort to wash away last night and get myself set for a new day.

At the first traffic light, I screwed off the top, tilted it back, and took a long swig, finishing the last of it. It was smooth and warming going down. I capped the flask and slipped it into my coat pocket. I had to remember to refill it back home.

They call this town the city of broken dreams. I would say it's more like the city of crushed dreams, ground into dust dreams, or the ever-popular 'I'm gonna make it or bust' dreams. Now, me, I have no dreams really, at least none that I cop to. Then again, maybe everything in my life is nothing but a dream.

That must explain the affinity I have for this place, for 'El Ay', City of Angels, Tinsel Town, La-La-Land. It's not all palm trees and freeways; it's not beaches and beach bums, nor diners and dives. There are those of us who live here and like it for what it is, a big sprawling city in the sun.

It's a place where a food truck pushing tacos might get a Michelin star. And, when you inevitably run into a celebrity at the grocery store at two in the morning, you make quiet eye contact, give 'em a discreet nod of acknowledgement, but don't make a scene, don't ask for an autograph or a selfie. You can save the name-dropping for the water cooler.

Sure, everybody likes to knock this place, but she's a tough old broad, tough like Bacall with a 38-snub nose pressed against the back of your head, or better yet, like Stanwyck with a big old 44 pointed at your balls.

You see, L.A. has no patience for the innocent. You get wise real fast, or you pay the consequences. September can be the hottest month of the year here in Southern California. The days reach triple digits. The cities bake all day, and that heat lingers through the night.

On nights like that, people get irritable because they can't sleep. So, they stay up late, and they stay out late, and they drink a little too much to slake their thirst. They get a little drunk, and they make mistakes.

And then there are those Santa Ana's, the devil winds. They come blowing through the mountain passes, adding yet another layer of misery to the heat, like a dry sauna turned up too high. It causes the hair on your arms to stand up. Pre-dawn is about the only comfortable time of day anymore, especially in a convertible with the top down.

I don't remember when I first got hooked on this whole L.A. noir thing of mine. Maybe it was watching old classic movies with my mom, like *Double Indemnity* or *Sunset Boulevard*. Movies that, in turn, lead me to authors like Cain, Chandler, and Mosley. Maybe it was a yearning for the historical Southland, that era when the region was a little rough around the edges, when it was suffering the growing pains of becoming a truly big city.

I liked this stretch of the Boulevard heading into Hollywood; it brought to mind those good/bad old days. It hadn't been all gentrified yet. The Director's Guild Building was pretty new, I guess, but the rest was at least fifty years old or more; still, some nice midcentury architecture left here and there.

I made a little detour through a drive-thru Starbucks and got my usual: two venti black coffees and a tall mocha Frappuccino. Then, with a wink to the barista, it was back on the road. This big old barge of mine was a little wide in the beam and wouldn't negotiate the corners of the underground garage in my building, so I parked at a lot a block away. Hector, the attendant there, loved my car even more than I did, and took good care of both of us.

I always enjoyed the short walk from the lot to my office. I grabbed copies of the Journal and the Times at the newsstand, then stopped by to see my old buddy at his usual spot on the corner of Hollywood Boulevard.

He was another Jimmy, like me. Hollywood Jimmy had been down on his luck lately; his trademark black and red serape was more of a muddy grey these days that matched his long and matted beard. He sold goldfish in little plastic bags for a buck a piece. I usually buy one a week from him because I had a hard time keeping the little suckers alive. One of my coffees was for him.

"Jimmy." I called out.

"James, my man. Muchas gracias for the coffee, bro. You are most righteous." He said in his raspy reefer rap. He handed me a little orange fish in a baggie of water in exchange for the coffee and a couple of bucks. I placed it in the empty slot of my cardboard coffee carrier.

"De nada, dude." I replied with a knuckle bump for punctuation. "I don't know what it is about your fish, Jimmy. They keep dying on me."

"It's not the fish, man," he said between sips. "They are healthy, guaranteed. You must be overfeeding them, or maybe your tank is fouled. Have you been changing the filter?"

"What tank? I've got a goldfish bowl."

"That's your problem, amigo. You aren't providing these little dudes with the proper holistic habitat. Your personal environment is an important element for your total well-being, as I can attest from personal experience."

He gestured to his immediate surroundings. "You had better get with the program. Do right by my little buddies."

"I'll do that, Jimmy. Promise." I gave him a tip of my hat and then crossed the stree

CHAPTER

TWO

The Cahuenga Building was another one of those great old Dames of Hollywood, a hundred years old if she was a day. Perched on Hollywood Boulevard, she was a classic, and her offices inside were classier still. She had the old Otis elevators with the birdcage frame and accordion gates. The outer office doors and windows were dark mahogany with opaque pebbled glass. James Gardiner – Private Investigations: that's what it said on my door, stenciled in black with a little gold drop shadow.

It was not yet eight, but I tried to get into the office early when I could. Yana, my part-time receptionist, secretary, bookkeeper, and all-around girl, usually had a class to get to on Monday mornings, so she liked for me to show up before she had to rush out. Yana was great, if a bit weird, with her all-black wardrobe, ironed straight black hair, a touch of Goth make-up, and black vintage cat eyeglasses; she reminded me of that little girl from the Addams Family all grown up.

She also nagged me like a fishwife, but I guess I needed it. Yana was a law student at USC and, despite her unconventional appearance, was the most no-nonsense, detail-oriented person I had ever met - a real type A to my type B. I always imagined she had a pretty lean bod under those baggy black sweatshirts, being that she claimed to be a weekend mountain biker.

But there was nothing going on there between us, strictly business.

"Morning, Yana," I said, handing her the Frappuccino.

"I'll be damned. You're actually in early today, James." Then she lowered her glasses caught an eyeful of how slovenly I was dressed. She shook her head with disappointment.

"I guess I don't need to ask about your weekend. Mrs. Brown? Honestly, she's old enough to be your mother."

"No, she isn't." I scoffed, taking a sip of my own coffee. "Well, maybe if she had gotten knocked up in high school, she could be." I argued, calculating the years quickly on my fingers.

"What is it with you and older women? What happened to you? Did you get dumped or dumped on by some young cutie and now you're gun-shy?"

"Nothing happened to me. Does something have to have happened to make me appreciate adult women? Anyway, she's divorced, or divorcing. So, no harm, no foul."

"Is it all just animal sex to you?" She continued, busily packing up her textbook and notebooks into her backpack. "You've never shown interest in maintaining a relationship with any of these women."

"Relationship?" I laughed. "They're old enough to be my mother. And what's so wrong with just animal sex?"

Yana picked up a couple of message slips and stuck them in front of my face. "Your mom called over the weekend, twice. Says you must have turned off your phone again or something because she's sure you wouldn't be intentionally avoiding her calls. And another woman called, also several times, won't leave a name or a number, just says she'll try and run you to ground later. Her words."

I was glancing at the headlines in this morning's Times, half ignoring Yana as she ran through a couple of other calls, I wouldn't be returning.

The front page was all election stuff this time of year, the mayoral race, various ballot propositions, and a controversial bond measure for an Indian casino near downtown.

"Also, there's a nice lady waiting in your office, a Mrs. Kim. I'm guessing new business. And she's right in your wheelhouse." She added with a smirk.

"This early? What are our business hours anyway?"

"You don't have regular business hours. She was waiting at the door when I got here, so I felt I had to let her in."

"Hmmm. Whatever she needs from me, she must be desperate. You could have told me she was here when I first walked in." I gave her a dirty look. "I really wasn't planning on working today. I need to get home and take a shower and change clothes." I pulled at the front of my shirt and took a cautious sniff before heading to my office.

"You smell fine, but tuck your shirt in," Yana called after me. "You look like a bum."

As I tucked in my shirttail, I realized I was still wearing my hat, so I hurriedly flung it on the hat tree on top of my trench coat. I loved that trench coat, but this is L.A. When was I ever going to get a chance to wear it?

I opened the door to my private office to see her seated primly in my guest chair, engrossed in her cell phone. She looked up, startled.

"Ah, Mrs. Kim, so sorry to keep you waiting. *Mi an ham ni da.*" I blurted out slowly and a little too loudly in my best attempt at Korean as I did a polite bow. "*An yang ha say oh.*"

I always like to at least try to speak to foreigners in their native language at least a few words. I think it shows respect.

Mrs. Kim gave me a blank look, perhaps a bit taken aback at my mastery of the tongue, or maybe because I was butchering the pronunciation beyond all recognition.

"I speak English," she answered back with a bit of an annoyed look. I see that look a lot for some reason. But Yana was right. She was indeed a very attractive woman, in her mid-forties, I guessed, slight, maybe five foot two or three. She obviously had been a knock-out when she was younger, with her big, wide-set eyes and high cheekbones like an Asian Audrey Hepburn. She wore a cute asymmetrical bob haircut, was dressed very stylishly, if a bit conservatively, in a navy-blue dress and jacket, Armani maybe, with a single strand of pearls, old money style.

"I'm sure you do, Mrs. Kim. Which is good because I'm afraid that's about the extent of my Korean. I can say hello and I love you in about twenty languages, but not much more than those few words in any of them." I laughed.

I then flashed her my best, most disarming smile. I couldn't help myself; it was instinctual.

She politely smiled back. "You are quite young for a private detective, Mr. Gardiner," she said a bit coquettishly.

"Please, call me James." I said as I got comfortable behind my desk.

"And you may call me Mimi."

"I look younger than I am. But I have been licensed and practicing for over five years." I said, gesturing offhandedly to the framed license hanging on the wall behind me. "If you would like referrals, I would be happy to provide you with some."

"Oh, no need, Mister James." She tilted her head so that she looked at me through her heavy eyelashes. "I was already referred to you by an acquaintance of a friend of mine at the club. It can be so awkward asking around about this sort of thing, you know, delicate matters."

She pulled out one of my business cards and pushed it across the desk. It was well-traveled, creased, and smudged.

"I understand perfectly. Most of my business is through friend-of-a-friend referrals. Let me give you a new card." I said as I grabbed a few from the cardholder. "Here, take several, they're cheap. Give them to your friends."

I leaned back in my chair, waiting for her to begin, which she didn't. "So, what brings you here today?" I finally prompted.
She smiled and took a moment to collect her thoughts, opening and closing her clutch as she put her phone and my business cards away.

"My husband is having me followed," she said, looking up at last. "He probably thinks I am cheating on him, and he has hired a man to follow me around wherever I go." She said 'man' as if men were something distasteful to her.

I waited for her to continue. "Are you?" I finally prompted.
She looked around furtively and then back at me. A wild gleam sprang into her eyes as she leaned closer and whispered, "No, but it might seem to be true that I could be having an affair." She giggled conspiratorially. "One's never too old to party, right?"

Now it was my turn to be taken aback.

"Mrs. Kim, as a professional investigator, I hold everything you tell me in the strictest confidence. But you probably shouldn't be confiding these kinds of secrets with me."

"Oh, Mr. Gardiner," she said coyly. "A woman never really tells."

I laughed. "Well, believe me, I am not one to judge. What would you like me to do for you?"

"I want you to help me shake my tail. Is that the correct word?" She said, suddenly, all business.

A smile snuck across my face. "Yes. That is the slang all right." I assured her.

"And you can do that for me?"

Now it was my turn to pause. This was not really my line of work, but a job is a job.

"I suppose I can help you do that, yes. I've been hired to tail people before, though never to help someone lose one. Have you tried taking an Uber?"

"Oh, yes. I thought I was so clever taking the Uber. We live in a gated neighborhood, so I know he cannot see me take a different car. But somehow, he knew and still followed me even in Uber."

"Hmm. He must have paid off your gate man to give him the high sign if you called for a car. Let me think about this for a few and I'll come up with a plan. You just tell me when and where you plan to go out again, and I will arrange it so this 'man' doesn't follow you. Why don't you give me your cell phone number, and I'll give you mine?"

"Oh, no, you mustn't call me on my hand phone. I think my husband has put a bug in it."

"I see. Okay, then I will give you a clean phone; it's a prepaid cell phone. And you can call me when you want to go out, and I will run interference for you. How does that sound?"

"Okay. You have one of those phones for me now?"

I reached down and pulled open the bottom drawer of my desk, where I kept such tools of the trade, only to find it empty save a few unused notepads. Damn, what a time to not notice I was out.

"No, I guess not. I'll have to get you one later today. If you want to come back, or I can deliver one to you somewhere."

"Oh, I don't think I should come back here." She said it a little too loudly. She leaned forward again as if to avoid being overheard.

"Being followed, remember." She said in an exaggerated whisper and knowing nod. "I am having lunch today at Founder's Club. Do you know the place? It is downtown."

"I do know it. My parents are members. That would be perfect. I will bring you a phone at lunch."

"Should I pay you something now?"

"A retainer is customary. My usual fees are eight hundred a day plus expenses. But this doesn't sound like more than a few hours at most."
"No problem-o. I'll pay you for one day. Does that sound suitable?" She giggled again as she set her purse on the desk with a strangely loud clunk and proceeded to pull out her checkbook and a gold-trimmed Mont Blanc.

Piqued by the hard noise of her soft leather handbag on my old desk, I stealthily reached across the desk with a pencil and lifted a corner of her Hermes bag open for a peek inside.
Mimi, busily writing her check, didn't notice as I tilted my head for a better look at the small automatic pistol with a wooden grip she had stowed inside.

"Are you packing?" I asked, surprised.

"What did you say?" she said, looking up.

"You're carrying a gun. Isn't that a bit of an overreaction?"

I had only one previous experience, which I knew of, where my client was carrying. It didn't turn out well. Getting between a man and his wife is risky enough without introducing guns to the mix.

"A gentleman never looks through a woman's purse." She said with a bit of a huff as she snatched her bag off the desk. "Besides, you can never be too careful. I am being stalked; you know. By a strange man!"

"Yes, and I am going to take care of that for you. But I would recommend that you leave the piece at home in the future. Unless you really know what you're doing, it can be more of a liability than security. Just my advice."

"I think I can handle myself." She said with a huff.

"Just the same, statistics show that people who have guns around are twice as likely to get shot than people who don't have guns."

"I appreciate your concern." She suddenly stood, handed me the check, and gathered her things back into her bag.

"I believe you made a mistake here," I said, looking at the check. "I said eight hundred a day. This is for eight thousand."

"Oh, this will not be a one-time deal." She said, cocking her head mischievously. "This man following me is most annoying. I'm sure I will need you again. Trust me, Mr. Gardiner. You will earn it. *Anyang*." She said with a quick bow, then turned and walked out, her heels tattooing the floor in a brisk rhythm that died along the corridor.

After she left, I sat for a minute at the desk, playing with my favorite fidget toy, an old $5000 Flamingo Casino chip.
I watched it spin on the desktop and noticed that I was already getting warm. I took off my jacket and got up to turn on the A/C.

The old window unit shuddered to life with a racket, like an old Model T going up a mountain road. I gave it a bang on the side with my fist, and it settled down to a dull whine.

Looking out the window, I noticed a new BMW, royal blue convertible with the top down, pulling out of the building garage. I splayed the venetian blinds with my fingers. There was my newest client at the wheel, a fellow ragtop lover. I liked her better already.

As she turned and drove off down Cahuenga, I noticed an older model Buick pull away from a red curb and follow.

"Well, I guess she's not imagining things." I said aloud to no one in particular. "What an amateur, though." He should be driving a Civic or a Camry if he wants to remain inconspicuous, I thought. Not some old tank like that. No wonder she spotted him.

As the A/C was still blowing warm air, I stepped away from the window and turned on an old oscillating fan, which was perched on the file cabinet. Maybe that would help.
At least its sweet hum would drown out the racket of the air conditioner. During hot spells like this, I questioned the virtues of having an authentic-looking office versus the comfort of central air.

In the outer office, Yana was still packing her black backpack and getting ready to head for class. I handed her the check, which she promptly filed in her desk drawer.

"She seems nice." Yana snarked.

"Ha, Ha. Now you know why I never bring any of my girlfriends by the house for mother's approval."

I spied my goldfish in a bag, still sitting on Yana's desk. I grabbed it and walked over to my mini aquarium, really just a glass bowl with about a gallon of water and a little Yoda figurine in some colored gravel at the bottom.

I scooped out last week's goldie with a net and handed it to Yana.

"Seriously, James, what do you see in these older women? I mean, I'm going to be their age one day, and I may want a boy toy for myself then. I need to know their secret," she said as she took the netted orange corpse to the bathroom toilet for burial.

"Well, sweetheart," I said in my best Bogart baritone. "If it's secrets you want…" I teased as I introduced the latest little guy to his new home. I gave him a pinch of food and watched him for a moment, ignoring my offering.

"I'm not your bro, James. I don't want the dirty details." Yana shouted back from the bathroom, punctuated by a toilet flush.

"I don't know why I can't keep these little fellows alive for more than a week."

"Maybe you feed them too much." Yana said, returning from the bathroom, wiping her hands a little too vigorously.

"I only fed it once a day. Say, you weren't feeding it, too, were you?"

"No, the fish are your responsibility. Do you ever change the water or clean the bowl?"

"That's what Jimmy asked me." I said as I watched my newest office mate tentatively investigate the fish food floating on the surface.

"Does the water look cloudy to you?"

"I was going to say, older women have a certain class to them." I continued. "They aren't looking for commitments, so no one is trying to tie me down."

"Who are you kidding? These dowagers are even more clingy than teenagers."

"Well then, I don't know. Maybe I'm just bored with life."

"Then quit pretending you're some 40s shamus and stop living life through your clients. Go out and do something for yourself. When I took this job, I thought you were a real detective."

"I am a real detective. It says so on my door."

"Real detectives don't spy on philandering husbands. They catch murderers."

"People just don't commit murder like they did in the old days. There's no sinister plotting; no diabolical thoughts go into it at all these days, it seems; there's no finesse. It's all on impulse today. It doesn't take a Sherlock Holmes to catch a killer anymore."

"Well, then, they solve problems in other ways; they help people who can't help themselves."

"Where have I heard that before?"

"Those are your words. When you first hired me. You told me that's why you got into this business. To help the poor unfortunate who needed a hero."

"I guess then I should have studied criminal science in college like those other guys, those real detectives."

"You don't need excuses. You have a lot more opportunities than the average guy your age. Just do something."

She threw her backpack over her shoulder and walked out. "And call your mother!" she hollered back as she closed the door behind her.

CHAPTER

THREE

I walked back into my office, grabbing my Canon off the file cabinet. Flipping through all the photos I had taken of Mr. Brown and his young paramour/secretary, I couldn't help but notice that she was not nearly as pretty as his now ex-wife. Guess it wasn't all about a lust for youth and beauty.

Who knows what drives a guy away from a willing wife?

I yanked the SD card out and scribbled the name "Brown" on the label and filed it with the other papers. I made a mental note to not forget to back it up on my cloud account later, always good to have backup.

I then pulled out a new shirt from a Nordstrom shopping bag that I had tossed in the corner a few days earlier, a black and red Hawaiian print. Having given up on the idea of going home to shower, I put it on, grabbed my hat and the paper, and headed out. The sidewalks were a little bit livelier now with tourists and homeless people jockeying for space and various costumed characters from the movies looking to pose for selfies for a few bucks. Sometimes it was hard to tell the Captain Jack Sparrows from the down on his luck beggar who was talking to himself. I gave a nod to 'Rick from Casablanca'.

"Nice hat!" I called out to him.

"Here's looking at you, kid." He called back as he gave me the signature index finger along the brim salute.

The number of unsheltered on the sidewalks had steadily increased as the morning had progressed. The tents and cardboard boxes had all disappeared, stowed away in secret caches down alleys and under stairs.

They had been replaced by bits of carpet and sleeping bags, pots and hats to collect a few coins, and inventive cardboard signs competing to attract the attention of passersby with wit and irony. There were maybe more than a few out-of-work Hollywood writers among the bunch. Somewhere, someone started playing a little Coltrane.

I stepped over some outstretched legs and weaved around others as I made my way a few blocks uphill to Franklin Avenue. There was a coffee shop that I liked there called *The 101*, named for the freeway that loomed nearby.

The 101 was an old-fashioned diner - dark brown vinyl, now faded and cracked, covered booths and benches, matching brown vinyl and chrome swivel stools at the counter, light brown tile mosaic wall coverings, and 60s space age light fixtures that probably used to be white but were now melding into the beige/brown motif of the place. I remembered they called this style Googie. It was not all that attractive anymore.

I pushed open the door and was immediately hit by the sweet aroma of coffee and bacon, the cool blast of air-conditioned air, and the loud clatter of dishes and shouts from the kitchen – "two over, piggies and a short stack!"

I could hear the fireworks as more grease hit the griddle. My mouth was already watering.

The place was usually busy for this time in the morning, but no line, thank goodness. The hostess directed me to a just vacated corner booth by the window.

Ah, diners! What I liked most about this joint was the wait staff.

They were great. Some of those gals had been working here since the 70s, I think. One of them, Norma, gave me a familiar nod as I headed toward my designated booth.

She strolled over to intercept me, with a mug in one hand and a fresh pot of coffee in the other. She set the mug down and filled it to the brim almost before my butt touched the seat. She set the pot on the table and fished her order pad out of her apron pocket.

"What are we having today, hun?" She asked as she scooped up the tip money and flipped the page on her order pad.

"Well, I'm feeling pretty good today; maybe I'll be adventurous and try the vegan scramble, rye toast with…"

"Extra butter. Got it." Norma just shook her head as that's what I order every time.

Okay, so I'm pretty predictable, but I wouldn't say I was in a rut. A fellow has got to eat proper if he wants to feel his best. I guess only the real tough guys can eat raw meat for breakfast. At least I was drinking real coffee and not that chicory or mushroom shit.

"How's our rocket scientist these days?" I asked.

Norma's son, her pride and joy, had worked his way through community college and then a few more years at the local state university to earn an engineering degree. One of Norma's regulars worked at JPL and had held out the promise of a job there to her son if he could get his degree.

"Oh, he spends more time talking to robots on Mars than he does with his own mother," she complained not very convincingly. "But you know how these career men are. They never know the value of a simple phone call." She continued with her humble brag as she walked away.

Suddenly feeling guilty, I decided to call up my own mother, but no sooner did she answer the phone than I was trying to wrap up the conversation.

"I'm sorry, Mother. Yes, I know I said I would call, but I've been on a stakeout for the last few days, and I just couldn't be making phone calls." I lied.

"A stakeout? That's the best story you can come up with to tell your mother?" She replied. When I was a kid, she used to twist my ear. Now her tone of voice did that for her.

"Yes, really, I was. You know what kind of business I'm in." I couldn't abandon the lie now; I was in too deep. "And I really can't meet today for lunch. I've just got a part-time gal at the office, and I am swamped with paperwork I have to do myself."

"James, if you don't want to have lunch with your mother, I understand. I guess you have your priorities." She sniffed.

"But I do want to have lunch with you. I promise I'll come by the house later in the week. For sure. Love you. Bye."

With that, I hung up. I didn't know why I dreaded talking to her sometimes. It wasn't like she was always riding me about my life choices, only every time I called.

In the booth next to me, I figured was a family of tourists – a young couple, didn't look older than myself, and two pre-school squealers. Their voices could break glass.

I barely heard my phone ring again with my custom Peter Gunn-themed ringtone. It was Jack.

"Hey dude. What's up?"

"Nothing special, just having breakfast." I glared menacingly at the little girl peeking at me over the back of her booth through her coke bottle glasses. She stuck her tongue out at me before ducking down behind the seat.

"You at the 101? I'll join you, I'm close by."

I loved Jack; we went back as far as high school, back when his folks still had money. We stayed best friends through his hard times. He was about the only guy I still knew from those days. It's funny how some lives intersect and, in that moment, seemed so vital and permanent, and then, for no reason at all, just drifted apart. The ones that didn't became all the more special.

The thing about Jack was that he knew I was at the 101 before he even called. I was always there around this time of day for breakfast, at least on weekdays. He always popped over, and I always really enjoyed talking with him, even if I had just seen him the day before. And I never minded picking up the check. Jack had to struggle, and I hadn't.
Why should I let a few bucks get in the way of one of the few good friendships I had remaining?

Norma brought my tofu, spinach, and a faux ham scramble and gave me a fill-up while I scrolled through the photos from my Mrs. Brown case. Her guy was such a dick, tossing over a hot wife like her for that screechy, whiney gold digger he was banging. His little girlfriend wasn't even all that pretty. He deserved what he got, or rather what he lost.

I had this great Canon 100-400 telephoto lens that put me right in the bedroom sometimes. Unfortunately, I didn't have the best angle on that night, and only one or two pics really were recognizable.
But they were good enough for her lawyer, I guess. I busied myself uploading the lot of them to my cloud account and then deleting the originals from the phone. I noticed the raucous out-of-towners were leaving and whispered a little thank you to the powers that be.

Jack waltzed in, dancing around the two little ones who were chasing each other in circles near the entrance while daddy paid the bill.

With his cargo pants and flannel shirt, he looked a little overdressed for the hot one we had in store for today. He plopped down in my booth, dropping his camo-green Patagonia backpack next to him on the seat. Jack was a hipster before it was not cool. There was always a big smile parked over that chin-strap beard of his. Norma was right there with his coffee, almond milk, and raw sugar.

"What'll it be, today, hun, the usual?"

"Naw, I'm kinda hungry today, Norma. Better give me the John Wayne, with double bacon and English muffins. No butter." He added.

"On a diet, Jack?" I asked.

"Ha, ha. Maybe I am. But you know what the Chinese say, 'Good appetite means good health' or something like that. I don't know how you make it to lunch on that appetizer you call breakfast." He picked up my paper. "How are my Dodgers doing? Oh, sorry." He feigned mock embarrassment. "That's right, you don't like sports."

"That's not true."

"Golf doesn't count. It's not a real sport."

"I like to watch sports as much as anyone else. I just only play golf."

"Okay, okay. So, how's my guy Bobby Jones doing this year?"

"Just great. He won the grand slam of golf this year. Never been done before."

"Really?"

I could only shake my head in despair. Why doesn't anybody my age like golf anymore?

"You go out last night?" I asked.

"Yeah, I kinda bounced from club to club. Pretty slow, you know, Sunday nights. The young ones have school in the morning."

I was confused. "We are talking poker, right?"

Jack had the poker bug, bad. He had been going down to Gardena once or twice a week for a game. Gardena, a small town a few miles south of the city, had always been known for their poker parlors all the way back to the thirties. Gambling had been outlawed in the state back then, but an exception had been made for poker.

Some legislator with a big campaign donation in his back pocket argued successfully that poker was a game of skill, not chance. Over the years, the card parlors proved very popular for those who didn't want to make the trek to Las Vegas. The clubs survived repeated attempts to close them down and still thrived today, even with the proliferation of Indian gaming. They were not as fancy as those casinos, but I think the hard-core players liked it that way. Plus, the Indian casinos were still an inconvenient hour or two drive out of town.

"Nah man, I'm laying off that for a while," Jack grumbled. "I'm kinda going through a cold spell lately. Cards just aren't falling my way."

"It's not supposed to be about luck. I thought poker was a game of skill." I said, quoting the aforementioned legislator.

"Actually, it's a game of bluff, psychology, but if everybody knows you're ice, all the game face in the world isn't going to save your bacon. You get called out on every hand."

"I see. Maybe you should try a different club. One where they don't know you're jinxed."

"You think I haven't tried that? No, it's best to just lay off for a spell. I've been hanging out at the Rainbow these days, instead."

"You're not still chasing the jailbait, are you?"

"No, and I'm not chasing their mothers, either. Burn." He said, poking my arm with his finger.

"I like my ladies like I like my whiskey." I countered.

"Eighteen years old?"

"Nicely aged." I dawdled over a third cup of coffee.

"I'm telling ya. You got to watch out for them older chicks, Jimmy, my boy. You show them too much of a good time, and they go and fall in love whether you're ready or not. Then you've got your own Fatal Attraction rabbit stew to eat."

"Yeah, that's what Yana was saying earlier. I think you're both wrong."

Norma showed up with two plates of food, both for Jack. He put the paper down as his breakfast arrived.

"Nothing more for you today, James?"

"No, thanks. I guess compared to my sumo friend here, I'm not that hungry."

Jack dove into his breakfast like a Labrador retriever. You could almost see his tail wagging. I didn't know where he put it; he was really not all that big.

"By the way, Jack, do you happen to have any extra phones on you?"

Without pausing in his attack on a stack of pancakes, he fished around in his backpack with his free hand and pulled a new disposable flip phone still in its blister pack.

"Thanks." I said. "Can you get me another dozen of these burners in a day or two? I'm all out."

"Sure, Jimbo. You want them all pre-loaded with those tracking apps, again?" He said with a mouthful of food.

"Yeah, same as last time. And don't forget to turn them on this time. That can be very vital in my line of work. Did I ever tell you about the time that one client, I think her name was Williamson, surprised me while I was surveilling her husband? Totally blew my cover and almost got me killed!"

"Only about a hundred times." He replied through a mouthful of pancake. I left him to his breakfast, grabbed my hat, and got up to pay the tab. Seemed like the only friends I had these days were on the payroll, one way or another.

"Bro!" Jack called out to me as I started for the cashier.

"Yeah?"

"You got a thing." He motioned with his finger at my shirt. "Store tag. Hanging off your collar."

I looked. Sure enough, there was. I hate those dangly things, attached by a plastic thread, more like a fishing line, punched through the fabric. You can't break them off with your hands; you need to cut them with scissors.

I headed home with my price tag dangling behind. I felt like Minnie Pearl.

CHAPTER

FOUR

Home for me was a tidy little bungalow in Beachwood Canyon, not even half a mile from where I had been eating breakfast with Jack.

I wasn't so lazy that I wouldn't walk there now and then. It was a nice walk, even though it was uphill most of the way. The neighborhood streets were lined with crepe myrtles, which were in bloom this time of year, hot pinks and eye-popping purples. The usual song of sparrows that filled the morning air had lately been drowned out by the awful screeching of a flock of green parrots that had taken up residence around here. Since I wasn't going to make it to the gym this morning, I thought maybe I would power walk to the house and call it my workout.

Mine was a classic L.A. house, I thought; white, Streamline Moderne style with lots of glass brick, Jalousie windows with a couple of round portals thrown in for effect, curved walls, and crisp accent lines here and there. I thought of it as my three-bedroom, two-bath cruise ship, sailing over a sea of neatly trimmed privet hedges and an undulating, almost green lawn. I even had a couple of nautical flags flying from a little pole on the roof.

I had a nice sweat by the time I hit the front door. As I fumbled for my keys, I noticed two lovely ladies my age, maybe a little older, smartly dressed in slacks and matching blazers, standing in front of the house next door.

I saw that the "For Sale" sign was gone. I guessed the place had either been sold or had been taken off the market. I also guessed that those two must have been real estate agents. One was yakking away on her phone, while the other was reading messages on hers.

The Real Estate game in California, especially the Los Angeles area, was bat shit crazy these days. It was one boom and bust cycle after another. But you could make a lot of money, fast, just like Vegas, or unexpectedly lose it all. Guess that was why so many people played.

I was tempted to ask what they got for the place, but I didn't. Instead, I gave the girls a friendly doff of my hat and pushed on in through the door. It was time to take a shower, shave, and get into some fresh clothes. I had a newer little black Prius in the garage that I used when I was not pretending to be a forties private dick.

After I was presentable again, I hopped in and headed for downtown. The Founder's Club was in the heart of downtown Flower Street. It was an old yellow brick building, eight stories tall and dressed up with manicured Ficus trees and holly hedges, and surrounded by towering modern glass skyscrapers.

The Club dated back to the nineteenth century; the building was almost that old. It was one of those private clubs for old white men to sit around in overstuffed leather chairs, smoking pipes, sipping port, and deciding the fate of the world. It had since changed with the times and was not so exclusively white, but it was still pretty stuffy. Mostly bankers, businessmen, and government types belonged now. The other elite in this town, the Entertainment Industry heavyweights, didn't come downtown much except for the occasional Laker's game. I didn't come much myself unless my mother dragged me here to lunch.

I left my car with the valet, ran up the stairs two at a time, and headed for the dining room. Henry, the maître de, saw me coming and gave me a nod, grabbing a menu.

"Hey, Henry. I'm not staying." I quickly explained. "I just ran by to deliver a package for Mrs. Kim. She's here for lunch. Do you know where she's sitting?"

Henry didn't seem to recognize the name. As he scanned his reservation book, I glanced around the dining room. I spotted her across the way by the windows, still in her blue suit and pearls. I waved my hand, but she was looking the other way and didn't see me. When I pointed her out, Henry recognized her.

"That would be Mrs. Lachlan."

"Her married name, I guess." I offered as I tried to catch her eye again. She was sitting with another lovely young lady, maybe a younger sister, more likely her daughter, who gave me a strange look before burying her head in her menu. She clearly didn't want to be there.

"Been there." I thought out loud, shaking my head. "Henry, would you please give Mrs. Lachlan this envelope for me?" I handed him one of those quilted yellow postal envelopes with the burn phone inside. "Certainly, sir."

As Henry left his post to deliver my envelope with the phone, I was suddenly surrounded by half a dozen men in tailored suits, arriving for lunch. The alpha male of this little group was tall and handsome with those sharply chiseled features women love, fifty-ish, and ex-military, I surmised from his ramrod posture and his high and tight haircut.

The other men, all thirtyish, pre-maturely balding and wearing rimless eyeglasses, jockeyed for position around him, chatting incessantly, and checking their phones for probably unimportant texts from their wives.

The General, my instant nickname for him, just nodded, lips pressed, jaw set, eyes a narrow slit scanning the field of battle, just like they teach at officer school.

Our gazes locked, briefly, but apparently, I wasn't worth more than a moment's hesitation as his eyes soldiered on.

Henry made for the table and handed over my package, indicating the sender with a nod back to me. Mimi looked up with a smile and then had the strangest reaction, startled, like a deer in headlights. I gave her a slight wave and turned to leave, pushing my way through the crowd that now surrounded the reception station.

I started to go, but a twinge of curiosity made me hang back. As Henry returned to lead the General's group of men to a table, they momentarily blocked my view.

When they had cleared, Mimi was gone. I made brief eye contact with the daughter as she peeked over the top of her menu, a cute eighteen-year-old, maybe, and gave her a smile and a little head nod.
She gave me nothing but an unseeing half-lidded glare.

"Kids." I muttered.

A minute later, Mimi reappeared, sitting up into view; she had bent down to put the phone in her purse on the floor or something.

I tried again to catch her attention but gave up after a few minutes.

The thought crossed my mind that maybe someone in the General's entourage was Mimi's secret paramour, and she didn't want to be seen there or then. She didn't need me in that case. The club had rooms upstairs, though not really for that sort of thing. But you never know what goes on up there sometimes.

I gave the dining room another once-over, making sure my own mother didn't happen to be here today. It wouldn't do to run into her here, now, not after blowing her off for lunch this morning. I had lucked out. There was nobody I knew here today but the staff.

Mimi called that evening. "Can we do this tail-shaking business tomorrow afternoon?" She cooed.

"Um, sure," I replied. "I've given it some thought, and I think I have a plan that will work. Where do you live?"

"On Freemont Place in Hancock Park."

I knew that place, a cozy little gated community, south of Wilshire, technically not part of Hancock Park. It was an island fortress asea in the big city. You wouldn't even know it was there unless you were looking for it.

"Probably better if I don't ask you to leave my name with the guard," I suggested. "I'll wait outside on Wilshire. You'll be driving your little blue BMW again?"

"Oh!" Mimi sounded a little surprised I knew her car. "Yes, I suppose I can drive that."

"It's the guy in an old silver LeSabre that's been following you, right?"

"I wouldn't know. I don't know anything about cars."

"Doesn't matter. I spotted him when you left my office this morning. So, what's your usual routine for tomorrow?"

"I always go to the Tennis Club on Tuesday afternoons. Do you know the one? It's up near Mulholland Drive. I usually take tennis lessons from Herve at one o'clock, but I can cancel if you want."

"No, don't cancel. I mean, yes, cancel the lesson, but go anyway. This will work. Stick to your usual routine. What do you do after your lesson?"

"I go to the spa there, then get a massage. I like to pamper myself now and then, so Tuesdays are my "me day". After that, I have a late lunch and go home around four."

"Okay. Pretend you are going to your lesson. When you get to Laurel Canyon, I'll be behind you, and I'll umm, I'll do something to allow you to get to the club without this guy following you. He probably knows where you're going, but this will give you time to sneak away. Before you leave the house, call for an Uber to pick you up from the club. You know how to do that?"

"Yes."

"Have them pick you up, leave your car in the club parking lot where it can be easily seen. When this guy who's tailing you finally shows up, he'll think you're inside playing. You should be free for the rest of the day."

"Oh, that sounds very sneaky. You are a clever young man, Mr. Gardiner." She gushed.

CHAPTER

FIVE

I opted to go in disguise for the operation the next day. I wore my vintage Dodger ball-cap and shades, and a faded Dodger jersey. To top it off, I wore one of my fake moustaches. This wasn't the first time I had gone incognito, and I had splurged before on a couple of high-quality hair pieces. Then I drove down to the lot on Cahuenga to pick up my Merc. I put the top down, dialed up my Dave Brubeck playlist on Spotify, and hit the road. It was a bright sunny day. This should be fun, I thought.

I had been parked on a side street across from the guard gate for about fifteen minutes when Mimi pulled out of her enclave right on schedule. With her white tennis visor and oversized Francois Pentons, I could see she had also dressed the part. The old Buick wasn't hard to pick up. The guy was an amateur, pulling away from the curb way too soon.

I hung back and followed them both as they wound their way through traffic toward the Hollywood Hills. I already had the spot for my diversion picked out in my mind.

I managed to pass the Buick on La Brea and place myself somewhere between the two cars before Mimi got to Laurel Canyon. Laurel's an iconic canyon in L.A. with a storied history. In the 60s and 70s, it homed a who's who of the music industry's top talent, the Beach Boys, The Animals, Mamas and Papas, Crosby Stills, and Nash, the list goes on and on.

Now it's a refuge for a lot of music and film industry workers who love the country vibe and the proximity to the city where they work. Laurel Canyon Boulevard is a winding little road that snakes its way up to the top of the hills and down the other side into the Valley. It's only two lanes, but it is a popular shortcut and thus always busy. A lot of people live in the canyon now, and there are at least half a dozen traffic lights.

It was at one of these lights that I pretended to stall my car; easy to do with an old model like mine. I made a good show of trying to restart it, to a chorus of beeping horns.

No one was getting around me as there was an unending stream of cars coming the other way. Finally, I got out and popped the hood. After giving myself a few minutes to stare stupidly at the engine, I reached in, pretending to jiggle a wire and shut the hood. I smiled sheepishly at the irate drivers behind me.

A break in the traffic allowed most of them to get around me, and I finally got a good look at the guy tailing Mimi. He was an old guy with short white hair cut in a flat top crew cut style. It looked like he wore a cheap suit, a white shirt, and a black tie. When he glared at me, the thought flew through my head that he was a dead ringer for the hitman/driver in 'Bullitt', the one who chased McQueen around the hills of San Francisco. Probably ex-cop, I thought, or maybe ex-Fed. I took a snap of his plates with my phone as he drove by for later research. I climbed back in, started the car up, and proceeded leisurely up the canyon to the tennis club. I took an early detour, wound around the back roads, and came in from the north.

I parked well up the street from the club and walked down the last few blocks. This neighborhood was a lot like my own, mostly 50s ranch style houses with a little yard in front, maybe a pool in the back, and lots and lots of trees.

I came up behind the private shamus, already in position, leaning against his old rust bucket on a neighboring street, smoking a cigarette. Beyond him, in the fenced-in parking lot, I could see Mimi's blue convertible sitting away from the others in the half-empty stretch of asphalt - no problem noticing it. Good girl, I thought. I wondered how many hours he would sit there before he became suspicious. I hoped the poor guy didn't sit there all night. But I thought they did have lights on the courts.

I watched for a minute or two, being careful to always keep a big eucalyptus tree between him and me in case he turned
around, which he did. But it was only to grab a camera from his car. He wandered over to the courts, looking for a spot where he might be able to see in through a gap in the green canvas coverings.

I took advantage of his absence to check out his car. It was a dump inside, among the expensive camera and lens cases were empty coffee cups, fast food cartons, bags, and several crushed empty cigarette packs. This guy lived in his car, obviously, or did a lot of stakeouts. I could relate to that.

For reading material, there was a copy of *Field and Stream* on the passenger seat.

"Yes, Alex, I'll take 'Rub-a-dub-dub' for one hundred."

"These three professions require a lot of patience."

"What are snipers, fishermen, and private detectives?"

When you spend too much time on a stakeout, you start talking to yourself. I wondered, is this going to be me in twenty or thirty years, lurking around trying to snap incriminating pics for a living. How depressing was that?

I snapped a pic of the magazine cover with the mailing address. There was nothing else to learn in this guy's little dinghy. I headed home. Mission accomplished.

CHAPTER

SIX

So that was an easy eight bills. I put my clubs in the car and headed out for a couple of days of golf along the coast and a chance to escape the late summer heat. I decided to take the scenic route. With the top down, the sun in my face, and the wind in my hair, I drove down Sunset towards Santa Monica, then turned up the Pacific Coast Highway for a drive along the ocean through Malibu, Ventura, and a few smaller towns to Santa Barbara. It was a good day for a drive. The sun sparkled off the ocean waves. A nice set was coming in at County Line, dotted with quite a few surfers looking for a late morning ride. Past Santa Barbara, I turned up towards the mountain pass which wound past Lake Cachuma and into the Sant Ynez valley. Horse ranches alternated with ostrich and emu farms lining either side of the highway. This was also wine country.

Tomorrow, if I teed off at the crack of dawn, I could get in thirty-six holes with a nice lunch between rounds. I didn't always play alone, but often enough. I could probably put in a little more effort in establishing a foursome of friends, but you sometimes meet interesting people when you're a single.

After a hard day on the links, I would be hitting a few of the many wine-tasting rooms there. I didn't hear again from Mimi for the rest of the week.

She finally called again late Friday afternoon as I was driving home.

At first, I didn't recognize the number, having forgotten that she still had one of my phones.

"I need to go out again, Mister James." She said in a forced whisper. "Can you shake my tail again for me?"

I couldn't tell if she was flirting or just didn't have a good grasp of English. I stifled a laugh, then explained to her, "Mimi, look, no matter how innocent I make this look, pulling the same stunt twice will be suspicious to anyone, even a dumb retired flatfoot like Mr. LeSabre."

"Who?"

"The private dick who's been following you around lately. Listen, we need to formulate a long-term plan if you want to continue to go out unnoticed."

As I explained it all, I imagined her stretched out on a chaise lounge, poolside, her hair wrapped in a white terry towel and wearing matching robe and sunglasses a la Audrey Hepburn, all the while whispering desperately to me on that pitiful little cell phone between sips from her Cosmo.

"Long-term plans can wait. This is serious. Life and death, if you must know." She said melodramatically. "You're a clever young man. I'm sure you will think of something. This Mr. Sabre, as you call him, follows me everywhere, day and night. He makes me terrified. I need to go out again on Sunday. It's very important. I believe I paid you for ten days, so you still owe me. Like I said. You will earn it."

Then she giggled nervously. Involuntarily, I wondered? She sounded like a little mouse.

"Okay." I agreed. "Give me a day to think of something.

I will call back tomorrow and give you instructions. Got that?"

"You're my hero, James Gardiner."

Yeah, I'm everybody's hero, I thought as I rang off. I was suddenly having mixed feelings about this job. Mimi was certainly charming, perhaps too charming – femme fatale charming. And I did still owe her nine more days of tail-busting, but I had a growing sense this woman was going to turn out to be a pest. Well, at least I could enjoy the drive home. I cranked up the volume on the speakers and listened to Chuck Mangione's "Feels So Good" as I tooled down the highway.

After ducking Mother for days, I finally had to make good on my promise to meet her for lunch. Of course, that's easier said than done. After half a dozen back-and-forth calls, Mother finally managed to rearrange her schedule to make two hours of room for me on Sunday. I swore her calendar was more tightly packed than the President's. She didn't work, mind you; her divorce settlement from my father was enough to keep her in the style to which she had become accustomed for life. Father lives in Manhattan now, and she is in Holmby Hills. And heaven forbid she should ever be idle. If it was not gallery openings or political fundraisers, it was this committee meeting or that charity luncheon.

When I arrived at the Riviera courtside grill, Mother was already there waiting, a queen in her court. With her high forehead, high cheekbones, and slightly upward tilt to her nose, she was every inch the patrician matriarch. Before I even sat down, and without asking, she quickly ordered food for both of us.

"I'll have the crab salad and an iced tea, and James will have the kale salad with quinoa." She barked.

"And a Bloody Mary," I managed to get in. "Make it a double, spicy, and an Espresso to start."

"Why do you even bother trying to eat healthy if you're just going to throw it all away with your drinking?" Mother started in.

She was always critical of how much I drank. Maybe she was right to be. Addictive behavior seemed to run in our family. She, herself, started each day with one pill and ended it with another, and in between smoked a dime of weed to get her through the day. The emergence of the legal marijuana industry had been a gift to her mother, no more sneaking her buys from the gardener. The waiter hurried away.

It was a postcard kind of day, blue sky, green grass, the idle rich in their tennis whites. The staccato thwack-thwock of tennis balls on rackets backed up the tinkling of ice cubes in tea glasses like some kind of minimalist Phillip Glass piece.

"So, how are you, son? You look well, I guess, considering."

"Considering what?"

"Well, considering that you have no one to look after you, that's what."

"I seem to manage just fine on my own."

"Never mind that. I have some exciting news. I have lined up a job interview."

"You're getting a job?" I asked incredulously.

"Not for me, for you. This is a real job, a junior executive position at a top investment bank."

"I don't have any experience for that kind of position." I protested.

"Oh, they know that. But you have your degree in banking, and this is really an executive trainee program."

"Economics," I interjected.

"Same thing. The money is nothing to write home about, but you've got your father's smarts and your MBA from Stanford. You could move up quickly if you put your mind to it."

"I don't need the money."

"You're not going to be one of those boys who just live off of their inheritance and amount to nothing, are you? Now, I called in a big favor to set this up, so please don't you go screwing it up like last time."

"I'm not interested. I already have a job."

"Don't start on about that. I've heard all about your little detective business from a few of your clients." She used air quotes for the word clients. "Not friends of mine, mind you, but friends of friends. It all gets back to me anyway, whether I want to hear about it or not." She added with a huff.

"Friends of friends? Really?" I said, with mock surprise.

"And the extracurricular." She rolled her eyes and shook her head in that universally disappointed mom gesture.

"That's so unethical, James, not to mention borderline indecent. I can only imagine what they say about us at the club."

"That's only one small part of my business." I lied. "I do lots of other detecting work. It's much better than sitting around an office all day filling out my ledger like some modern-day Bob Cratchit. What I do is fascinating, really. I get to use my wits to solve mysteries and bring bad people to justice."

Mother just looked at me over the top of her glasses, not believing a word I said. I wondered which she found more distasteful: that I made a living as a professional Peeping Tom, or that I was screwing women, she might have been having tea with in the afternoon. Probably both.

I continued to nod like I was listening, but my mind began to wander from thought to thought. Did she think I was doing this to get back at her, to get back at my dad? Or did she think I was just being rebellious?

I was a little old to be rebellious, and both my parents have done right by me. I couldn't complain. They even had the good manners to wait until I went off to college to get divorced.

The waiter brought our drinks as Mom segued from job prospects to girlfriend prospects. I snapped out of my brief reverie and gulped down my snappy tomato juice.

"I think you'd like Maxine's daughter. She finished Law school at Stanford in June, passed the Bar in July, and already has a position at a top firm in Century City." As Mother rattled off her bona fides, I stifled an attempt to be snarky.

"Don't think I don't know what you're up to, James. I see how you're avoiding commitment by limiting your relationships to women so much older than yourself."

"This girl you've picked out probably wouldn't be interested in a shiftless layabout like myself."

"That's why I am trying to help you out on that score." She said earnestly.

As she talked, I watched some women playing tennis. They were even older than Mother, easily in their sixties, but fit and nicely tanned. I would give them that. So, where were all these young girls I was supposed to be dating? School? I finished school years ago. Work? I had only Yana at the office, and our relationship was strictly business. Nightclubs? Yeah, right. I could see Jack and myself cruising the Rainbow Club. No, I was not into that scene, and most likely too old already for that crowd. I suppose I could try an internet dating site.

"James! Are you even listening to me?"

"Yes. No. You were saying?"

"I said, I've invited Rachel over for dinner next Saturday night, and

I expect you to be there. No excuses."

"Who's Rachel?"

"The girl I've been telling you about." She replied with no small amount of exasperation.

"Oh, right." I checked my watch. Not even twenty minutes had passed. Our salads arrived, and I quickly ordered another Bloody Mary.

After lunch, I needed a mental cleanse, so I took in a triple feature at Tarantino's New Beverly Cinema – three Orson Wells pics: *Stranger*, *Lady from Shanghai*, and *A Touch of Evil*.

I got home late and noticed that there was a white truck in the driveway next door, one of those contractors' jobs, heavy-duty, extended cab model with those built-in toolboxes on both sides and a rack over the bed and cab, but this one had no signage on the door panel.
I couldn't tell if it was a plumber or an electrician, but either way, it seemed pretty late for a service call.

The house was also dark, but as I walked over to it for a closer look, I noticed now that there were lights on inside.

Thin slivers of illumination bled out around the blackout curtains that had been hung over all the windows. Some unintelligible low talking echoed out from inside. Curious, I thought, and then put it out of my mind and went back to my own house and my own business.'

CHAPTER

SEVEN

Monday morning, I arranged for Mimi to drive over to MacArthur Park. It's about a mile from her house. It is a nice big park, if a bit seedy these days, with a little lake in it.

In the summertime, you can rent paddleboats and paddle around with your lover. One end is choked with lily pads if you're feeling like Monet that day. The park had certainly seen better days, but it was usually crowded, mostly with locals picnicking or barbecuing. Parking isn't as much of a problem on weekdays.

"Park your car and walk into the park near the lake," I told her. "Mr. Buick will surely follow because he will think you are meeting someone. He will want to see who that someone is."

"While you are in the park, pretend to make a phone call on your cell phone. Make your call last five to ten minutes or so. If you can pretend to act agitated, do that. While he is watching you, I will disable his car."

I'm not much of a car guy, but you can find anything on the internet these days. I had researched his old gas guzzler and figured out a way to do it that wouldn't look like deliberate tampering. Well, maybe a little bit of tampering.

"When you come back to your car," I continued. "Wait for a minute or two and then just drive away. His car won't start, and he won't be able to follow you."

Mimi did her part, amazingly without overacting it. I had arrived early and was sitting in my Prius, hat pulled down low, pretending to be asleep.

I watched as she arrived in her cute little convertible with the top down. She had her hair pinned up and was wearing her favorite oversized sunglasses. She climbed out, wearing a black sleeveless sheath dress, my own Holly Golightly, and sashayed into the park.

I wondered if she might be the muse to my Marlow. Next, the Buick pulled up and parked at a red curb, and Mr. Ex-cop hopped out and followed her into the park. Once he was out of sight, I crossed over to his car, popped the hood, and was loosening the starter wire when a voice from behind caused me to stand up too quickly and bang my head.

"That your car, Mister?"

"Yeah. Who's asking as if it's any of your business?" I said, rubbing the new bump on my head. I didn't have time for an interruption.

That's when he flashed his badge. "Sir, step away from the car and keep your hands where I can see them."

If he was a cop, he was a plainclothes detective. He had a cop haircut and was wearing a brown suit. I mean, who wears brown suits anymore? He never really gave me a chance to get a good look at his badge, so I just had to play the averages and figure this was legit. Then I noticed his partner a few yards away, a younger guy with a no-nonsense stare, hands on his hips with his jacket pulled back just enough to show the butt of his revolver in his shoulder holster.

I couldn't believe it. This wasn't happening to me, not now!

"You have any ID on you?" Detective Brown Suit asked.

"Of course, in my wallet, in my back pocket."

As I wasn't wearing a jacket, he could see I wasn't armed.

"Hand it over."

As this sergeant, detective, whatever, flipped through my wallet, reading my driver's license and other cards, he came across my investigator's license and badge.

"You've got a P.I. button here. Is that for real?"

"Yes, it is real. I'm a licensed investigator and I'm working. Here. Now."

"Vandalizing cars on the street. Is that what P.I.s do nowadays, Karl?" he called to his partner without so much as a glance back.

His partner only replied with a smirk and a slow shake of his head. "Times are tough. I guess maybe some do." He replied.

"You think this is a get out of jail free card?" the first detective addressed me. "Maybe he thinks he's playing Monopoly." He added to his partner.

"I guess maybe he does." The partner replied, still slowly shaking his head.

"The guy who owns this heap has been stalking and harassing my client. I'm just temporarily disabling his engine so my client will not be followed anymore. No permanent damage." I argued.

"Is that so? Sounds pretty far-fetched to me. You buy his story, Karl?" He said to his partner.

"Don't buy it for a nickel. Maybe he's the guy from Triple A." Karl says.

"You guys work up this routine by yourself? It's pretty good. You should take it to the clubs." I said.

"You like it? We'll show you the rest of our act down at the station. You can cut the bluff. We've been waiting for you to pull another fast one after that last stunt you pulled a week ago on Laurel Canyon."

"You guys tag-teaming my client?"

"On the force, we call it back up."

"That guy's a cop! I should have guessed." I muttered to myself. This was not going well.

"I'm thinking I'm going to have to take you in. Let's go." He said, grabbing me by the elbow.

"Am I being arrested?"

"You're being detained for questioning. Get in the car."

He didn't cuff me, and he didn't put me in a marked squad car, but it was pretty apparent to Mimi, who was now watching all this from the park, that the scheme was not working as planned. I looked across the street at her. She just cocked her head at an odd angle, then raised her hand to cover her mouth.

Mr. Le Sabre was nowhere to be seen, and the bump on my head was now giving me a headache.

Well, this was a first for me, I thought as I sat in the interrogation room, wondering all the while why I was being interrogated anyway. Yellowing walls that were once white reflected a harsh fluorescent light from nearly dead tubes that buzzed annoyingly. The smell of thirty-year-old cigarette smoke still lingered in the air. My metal chair was particularly uncomfortable, intentionally, I guess. I leaned forward, resting my arms on the table, chin in hand, and stared at the mirrored one-way window. I tried to imagine how many people were staring back at me, a regular line-up of hard-boiled coppers with the requisite bald one at the end sucking on a lollipop. I gave them a sheepish smile.

I had always known that my tactics of taking clandestine pictures bordered on the illegal. I always had a couple of well-practiced alibis at the ready with some fake IDs as backup.

I never allowed myself to contemplate the possible consequences of getting busted though. Now I didn't need to contemplate that anymore, I was staring it in the face or the mirror anyway.

After what seemed like an eternity, a Detective Sam Mejia came in. He tossed a manila folder on the worn metal table but didn't sit. He was an ugly son of a bitch. Shiny black hair lay flat on his head uncombed, like he'd just stepped in from the gym. His face had more pockmarks, crags, and lines than some old boxer who'd lost more fights than he'd won. Buried in two of the deeper crevices were the blackest of eyes you would never want to meet in a dark alley.

He wore a blue shirt with too many buttons unbuttoned and that oversized white collar that went out of fashion with Disco. All he needed was a gold chain. An unlit cigarette dangled from his lips and bounced up and down as he talked.

"You're in a lot of trouble, son." He started. "Interfering with a police investigation."

"What interference?" I snapped back indignantly. "They had me in their car thirty seconds after they flashed their badges."

"Not them. Officer Bowman. You were caught vandalizing his vehicle."

I was surprised. "Really? He's a cop?"

"Retired."

"So, he's not a cop. Why do you call him Officer Bowman, then, and why's he following my client around?"

"That's police business."

"You just said he was retired. Which is it?"

"Whichever it is, it ain't your business."

"She's my client. That makes it my business."

"Then why don't you ask your client?"

Having never been interrogated before, I was not sure how a hardboiled detective was supposed to act. I tried continuing with belligerence.

"Well, if he's not a cop, then I'm not interfering in police business. So, that charge won't fly."

"Vandalism is still a crime last I checked. Or wasn't that on your P.I. test?"

"That wasn't vandalism." I countered. "I didn't actually do anything yet except pop the hood."

"You think you're pretty clever, don't you? But really, you're just a smart-ass college kid with a store-bought badge. I can write up all the charges I need to see you locked up for a good, long time. You know how that works, don't you?"

"Then why haven't you booked me?" I said, not backing down. "What am I really doing down here? Or did you just brace me for shits and giggles?"

"I'll book you soon enough, boy. I want to see if I like the answers to my questions first. Then I'll decide how hard to throw the book at you. For starters, why don't you tell me what you were up to?"

"Well, as I told the arresting officer." I began politely. "Your 'retired' officer has been stalking and harassing my client. She hired me to get him off her tail."

"So, you fake car troubles one day, cut his wires the next. What then, shoot out his tires on the third try, or maybe take it to him personally?"

"I was kinda taking it day to day," I replied with a forced

nonchalance. "I figured eventually whoever hired this amateur would figure out that my client was on to him and call it off."

"This amateur happens to be my old partner, and a thirty-eight-year veteran with distinguished service. He taught me everything I know." He said calmly and quietly, pacing back and forth before the mirrored window.

I suspected if he wasn't still tailing my client, Officer Bowman would be back there, lapping up the praise. Then the detective turned and looked at me.

"You think just because you spotted the surveillance, you're some bad ass private detective, right? It never occurred to you that maybe Officer Bowman was being intentionally obvious in his methods in order to send a message to your client. And who do you think hired him?"

"Well, my client thinks it was her husband."

"Besides running interference, what else did she hire you to do?"

"That was it; lose the shadow on her so she could go about her business."

"And what business would that be?"

"I didn't ask. None of my business."

"She was having an affair, wasn't she? And you were to run interference."

"Well, yeah, she joked about having an affair, but I took it as a joke. Whatever her real reasons were, your guess is as good as mine. As I said, it was none of my business. I don't ask extraneous questions."

Det. Mejia picked up my folder and flipped through it. "That's your area of expertise, isn't it, facilitating marriage break-ups?"

"I like to think I help level the playing field."

"Isn't a shamus like yourself usually working for the cuck, not the cheater?"

"Most times, but you take the jobs that come your way."

"So, where were you and your client supposed to meet up after you disposed of Officer Bowman?"

"It didn't work that way. She called when she needed to go out. I ran interference. She went on her merry way, and I went home. When she needed me again, she would call."

"So, where is your client now, then?"

"Well, since I'm in here, I wouldn't know. Why don't you ask your partner? He's probably still on her tail if she hasn't already lost him all by herself."

"I think we both know who the real amateur is here. For your information, her husband did not hire Detective Bowman to follow her. Your client is involved in things you obviously know nothing about. But why would you? You're just a trust fund baby pretending to be a dime novel detective."

He reached into a manila envelope and pulled out my cell phone and tossed it onto the table.

"Call your mommy and tell her to come pick you up. I don't want to see or hear from you again. Find yourself another career. This is no business for a kid who wears two-hundred-dollar sunglasses." He said, looking at my Oakleys that had also spilled onto the table. Then he turned and left the room.

For good measure, the cops had me cooling my heels in lock-up for another hour or so until Yana arrived to get me. She watched without comment as I collected my things from the property window. The officer there poured my belongings into my hat before sliding it across the counter.

I didn't expect Yana to be all comforting and supportive. She usually liked to fence with me at the office. That's what I liked about her. So, of course, she came down on Detective Mejia's side.

"Is this one of my duties? I don't remember you mentioning this in my interview?" She asked.

"If I didn't mention it, it's because this is a first for me, too."

"Why does someone with your background and education keep slumming around with losers in bad marriages?" She snapped while aggressively steering her old Civic in and out of lanes, squeezing in at the last second onto the access ramp onto the North 101 to the salute of an angry car horn behind us.

I braced myself against the dash. "I don't think that's the situation here."

"You said her husband's having her followed." She downshifted to second abruptly, throwing me forward. "What would you call it?"

We zipped into the Four Level Interchange, or "the Stack" as the locals called it. It had to be the most convoluted freeway interchange in America. I hated it. Yana negotiated it like a Grand Prix driver with a bladder problem.

"That turned out not to be the case, I found out. At this time, I should remind you that my parents had a bad marriage, not that one thing equals another." My fingers dug deeper into the dashboard vinyl. "And let's not give the cops another excuse to drag us back to the station. Okay?"

Picking me up was causing Yana to miss a class, or so it seemed, as she drove like Mr. Toad on his Wild Ride, either to vent her frustration with me or in some vain attempt to actually make the class. Although I had it on good authority that she always drove that way.

I apologized for being a nuisance as she dropped me off at the curb. She just dismissed my apology with a disappointed shake of her head, popped the clutch, and squealed back into traffic almost before I had closed the car door.

Unlocking the office, I stared again at the name stenciled on the pebbled glass door and wondered if this was all just a goof, a meaningless lark of someone with nothing more useful to do with his life. My office was a fine replica of Sam Spade's or Jake Gittes': dark wood paneling, matching venetian blinds, a ceiling fan that didn't work, a rotary phone on the desk that wasn't hooked up, and a black statue of the famous bird of prey on the bookshelf. I kept an old wood-shafted putter leaning against the bookcase with a couple of vintage balata balls for practice and a few bottles of whiskey in one of several empty old green metal filing cabinets for when I wasn't in the mood for golf. I grabbed the latter and a glass from my Flintstones jelly glass collection on the bookcase shelf.

Those I usually saved for company. I poured myself a drink, plopped into my stuffed black leather swivel, and put my feet on the desk. Maybe I was just kidding myself. I certainly hadn't been following my own protocols. Rule number one: always check out your client first.
You don't want to be wading into a situation without knowing the score. Was she just after the guy's money? Was she setting me up? How much juice did her husband have? Did I really want to tangle with this guy? Mimi had come at me from a different angle, and I let all those precautions fall by the wayside.

She hadn't flat-out said she was having an affair. She was coy and danced around the subject, but it didn't quite ring true.
I didn't believe her and didn't care, really, what she was up to. Was I a patsy? Had I been played? Detective Mejia said I should ask my client, so that's what I was going to do.

I flipped open my laptop. When Jack got me the prepaid cell phones, I always had him load a tracking app on it so, if need be, I could locate my clients. He liked to hide the icon behind the calculator.

So far, no one had found it. I typed in the phone's ID that I gave Mimi just to see what she might be up to. Even though I had gotten busted, I imagined the commotion was enough to allow her to slip away unnoticed. So, in that sense, I accomplished what I was paid to do. I pinged her phone, and there she was, near downtown, a little north of Chinatown.

Maybe she was taking in a Dodger game. I had no idea if they were in town or on the road right now. Mimi didn't strike me as a baseball fan anyway.

My Prius would still be down at MacArthur Park if it hadn't been towed yet, but the Merc was in the lot down the street. No time to be discreet. I grabbed my hat and headed for the door.

L.A.'s Chinatown was situated north and east of downtown. It mostly catered to the tourist crowd, with its red painted pagoda roofs and curio shops, but I liked to go there to get Dim Sum. The area was only about half a dozen blocks long and a few wide, a triangular neighborhood bound by two freeways and what we Angelinos euphemistically called the L.A. River. It ran out at its northern point into Solano Canyon. Solano was the only neighborhood left in Chavez Ravine, a large group of hills that overlooked downtown.

The city had bulldozed the rest to make room for the Brooklyn Dodger's new stadium back in the Fifties. This was the neighborhood where Mimi's phone had led me, not what would immediately come to my mind as a rendezvous site for a little tryst, if, as Detective Mejia had suggested, that was her real agenda. Maybe, her paramour owned a little love nest here.

It was a working-class neighborhood. As I drove up the street, I noticed a big discrepancy from house to house. Some were more disheveled than others, and more than a few were boarded up and looked abandoned. Graffiti was in abundance. Others were in nice condition, if modest.

They were freshly painted, and yards were attended. One even had nicely painted gingerbread details along the porch roof.

Is this how gentrification takes root?

The street was lined with a lot of older model cars like mine, some with the suspensions altered so they sat low to the ground. Low riders, they called them. It occurred to me to be on the lookout for a particular Buick LeSabre. If Mimi were here, I figured he would be, too.

I passed a house with four young guys in white tees and blue jeans sitting on the stoop. They didn't look like they were working. They all gave me the eye as I drove slowly past. Another block down, I pulled over and got out in front of a house with a 'For Sale' sign. I could pretend at least to have some business here while I checked things out.

I climbed the stone steps to the porch and opened the screen door. The front door was locked, of course. A realtor's lock box hung from the handle. I picked up a bunch of papers that had been stuffed between the screen and the door, all solicitations, from contractors, other agents, termite companies – the usual, plus a bunch of campaign flyers for the upcoming elections.

It was now late in the afternoon, and the sun had already dipped below the ridge of hills that formed the western edge of this canyon. The streets were gradually sliding into shadow.

I returned to the sidewalk and continued up the street. There were a bunch of flyers blowing around in the breeze, which I, being a good citizen, collected they, more real estate solicitations – "We Buy Houses!" they shouted in English, Spanish, and, I guessed, Chinese.

I spotted Mimi's BMW up ahead, parked outside one of the nicer Craftsman-style homes, one that was well-maintained. It had that signature look with the peaked roofline held up by fat stone columns on a big porch that covered the whole front, all in dark brown wood shingles siding with forest green trim. I stopped, not walking any closer.

I was looking for my friend, Mr. Buick, but saw no sign of him. I stepped behind an old VW van parked under a big eucalyptus, where I could watch out of sight. I decided to wait and see if I could spot who she might be visiting.

I was debating whether or not to find a better place for a presumably long stakeout when the door to the house opened, throwing a shaft of light onto the walkway and yard.

Mimi stormed out, waving her arms and speaking angrily and animatedly to someone on her cell phone. She was followed by an older Asian man, bald and considerably taller than her. Mimi stopped at her car and continued her phone call, ignoring the man behind her. He also stopped at a polite distance away, waiting for her to finish, I supposed. Finally, she ended her call, turned, and seemed to be yelling and waving at still another person that I could not see inside the house. I thought I heard what sounded like a door slam inside.

Normally, I have my camera equipment with me at all times, but as luck would have it, that was a block or two back in my car. I did have my cell phone camera, though, better than nothing.

I stepped out of my car to get an unobstructed view. Mimi and the older man were now talking next to her car. Mimi still looked very agitated, so I started snapping photos, being careful to stay out of their line of sight. What was not in my line of sight were those four local boys coming my direction.

"Yo, guero! What you doing here?"

I looked up at four rather menacing Latino boys in their late teens or early twenties who were walking in my direction. One was maybe six foot four, three hundred pounds. Two others weren't quite as big and had handfuls of papers that they were picking off the parked cars. The one talking was short but had that Tommy Devito from Goodfellas crazy wide-eyed look.

I didn't want to lose my cell phone, not that it was particularly expensive, but I didn't want to lose the pictures I just took. I thought I'd just offer them my wallet, and maybe I'd get out of here easy.

"What, you think we're robbing you?" Hispanic Tommy said indignantly, slapping my wallet away. "It's you who are stealing from us!"

I was still holding out my wallet and trying to stuff my phone in my back pocket as I backed away. The two other boys had circled behind to cut off my retreat.

Tommy swiped my hat off my head and examined it.

"Who you s'pose to be, Charlie Chaplin?" He asked, then tossed my hat in the gutter and stepped on it. "You think you can come in here and buy up the whole neighborhood and kick us all out?"

"Uh. What?" I stammered, trying to look the other boys in the eyes. "I don't really know what you're talking about."

"Yeah, that's what they all say. Well, I got a message for you to take back to your boss. It's the same message we're gonna give all his *pinche joto.*"

I was trying to remember my high school Spanish when one of the boys behind me sucker punched me in the kidney. The pain was acute and intense, causing me to drop to one knee. I reached out to catch myself, only to catch a knee to the side of my face. I saw stars from that one. I dropped my wallet and covered my face only to get kicked in the midsection, knocking the wind out of me.

Now I was down on the street. I tried to curl up into a ball, expecting a rain of blows and kicks to shortly descend on me. I still hadn't caught my breath, and the pain was starting to surge. I started panting in quick, shallow breaths. That was all I could manage; my lungs hurt too much. Little Crazy Tommy was saying something, but I couldn't make it out. All my focus was on where it hurt. I was beginning to think they were done and I was going to live when the kicking started again, first in my back, then in the back of my head. I didn't count; I just gritted my teeth and held my breath, waiting to black out. But I didn't.

I lay there for a few minutes, trying, in my mind, to isolate where it hurt. I tried blowing the papers off my face, but I had too little breath. I continued to lie there looking at the tires of the van, at the raised black numbers on the sidewall that made no sense to me. I forced myself to breathe, slower and deeper, even though my ribs ached with every inhale. I finally willed myself up to my hands and knees and
took a few more deep breaths.

As I knelt there, slowly panting, I looked up to see Officer Bowman in his worn-down Buick cruising very slowly past me. He held my stare as he crept by, a bit of a smirk snuck across his face, and then he was gone.

I stared down at the papers that had slid to the pavement. They were a mixture of real estate solicitations and political flyers. Blood from my nose dripped onto one touting a candidate for mayor. I recognized the guy as my General, that tall, good-looking man from lunch the other day. His mouth was smiling, but his eyes were not. I thought my blood spatter enhanced his poster.

I really wanted to lie down and go to sleep, but I managed to force myself to stand up and walk, like Terry Malloy in *On the Waterfront.* But there was no one around, no witnesses, no gawkers, no innocent bystanders to attest to my bravery. Nor was there Mimi or her car, nor the old Asian man who had walked her to the curb, nor the four young toughs who welcomed me to the neighborhood.

I picked up my hat and made a half-hearted attempt to smooth it out. For some reason, I felt compelled to also pick up the various littered flyers at my feet. It hurt every time I bent over, but I persisted. Why, I couldn't tell you. I looked around for a trash can and finding none, slowly and painfully made my way back to my car, tossed the leaflets in the back seat, and slid myself into the front.

That car seat never felt more comfortable. I reached for the glove compartment only to remember that I had left my flask in the office to refill it and never had.

I could sure use that drink right now.

CHAPTER

EIGHT

Jack found me in my office with a handful of ice cubes wrapped in a T-shirt pressed against my black eye and nursing a tall glass of seventeen-year-old Balvenie Scotch.

Jack knew where the Flintstone glasses were kept and helped himself to a healthy pour, then plopped down on the recliner.

"So, one of those husbands finally caught up with you, did he?" He joked. I lowered the T-shirt ice pack and carefully felt the swell on my cheekbone. It really wasn't enough to write home about, though Jack was a bit taken aback by the sight of my face now.

"There were four of them," I muttered weakly.

"Four husbands? Wow!" He made a mock surprised face. "Well, you look like shit, bro."

I had no snappy comeback for that. I took another swig of scotch. It was smooth and warm going down.

"This is where you say, 'You should have seen the other guys." Jack goaded. When that didn't elicit a response, he sensed that I was not in the mood to joke with him tonight.

"Seriously, are you okay?"

"I don't know. This is a new experience for me. Guys of my social status don't get a lot of practice in street fighting. I couldn't even tell you where it hurts except everywhere."

"Maybe you should go to the hospital and get checked out."

"I'll live," I whispered.

"No, seriously, you might have a cracked rib or something. Anyway," he said when I ignored him. "I brought your phones. There on Yana's desk."

He poured himself another drink and topped up mine, emptying the bottle. "So, what the hell happened, if you don't mind me asking?"

I took another big swallow. I was beginning to feel whole again. "This has been a long day."

I started from the beginning.

"I got a new client the other day, my usual stuff, a wife with hubby troubles, nothing different from what walks through my door on a regular basis. Except this time, she's the one having the affair, or so she says, or at least hints at." I'm sipping my drink now, savoring the smell, a hint of lemon and spice, and the taste in my mouth, like sherry but drier, with a nutty, more peppery flavor and smooth, not too much of an alcohol bite to it.

The pain and memory of the afternoon drift a little further into the past.

"Anyway, I'm helping her ditch some shamus who her husband has had tailing her, when suddenly I get busted. Turns out the guy on her six is a cop, or a retired ex-cop at least. That gets me a ride down to the precinct and a couple of hours answering questions on a hard chair in a cold room with bad lighting. Now I'm thinking, 'What do I really know about this dame?' That's when I pinged her on one of your burn phones and tracked her to this little neighborhood in a canyon north of Chinatown."

"So, you're spying on your own clients now?"

"Lately, I've tried to make it my practice to always check out my client first. Rule number one - know who you're getting in bed with, literally and figuratively. I don't want to get set up for a double cross again."

"Okay, so what did you find when you checked her out?"

"Well, that's the problem, I hadn't yet. That's what I was doing, following her to Solano Canyon."

The ice was melting, and water was running down my face, getting my shirt wet and making a puddle on my desk. I wrung my shirt out in the wastebasket and made a poor attempt at mopping up the mess on the desk.

"You should put a steak on that, not an ice pack."

"See that in the movies, did you, or did you read that on the internet?"

"Hey. W.W.M.D. What would Marlowe do?" was Jack's retort, calling out an old game we played back in the day when we traded out old detective paperbacks the way kids did comics. Jack grew out of that phase. I guess I never did.

"You're right, except he never put a slab of raw meat on a black eye."

"You sure? *Long Good Bye*, Elliot Gould? I can picture it in my head."

"Nope. You're having a Mandela moment. Marlowe would slough it off with a drink and a smoke."

"Well, you don't smoke."

"So, another drink then." I said as I reached into my desk drawer for a new bottle of scotch.

Jack stuck his empty glass out.

"Maybe I'm thinking of Charlie Chaplin."

"Yeah, people get those two mixed up all the time. I'm pretty sure the Tramp never had steak; he was eating shoe leather most of the time."

"So, tell me some more of your adventures in Chinatown, Jake. Did you even lay a finger on these guys?"

"I think I may have bloodied their shoes a bit with my nose."

"You're not making a very good showing for the Private Eyes of this world."

"I'm no Marlowe, that's for sure." I sighed.

"Not even close. Marlowe doesn't have a secretary, he drinks bourbon and rye, not scotch, and he has no friends. But in your favor, he does get beat up a lot."

"Sure, he does."

"The dude plays chess by himself."

"True."

Jack and I drank late into the night. I don't know if I looked any better, but I felt better. Good ol' Marlowe magic.

CHAPTER

NINE

The next morning my head was pounding. I ached all over, and the liquor hadn't helped at all.

I opened my eyes into a shaft of light sneaking through the blinds and shut them just as quickly. I was still dressed, stretched out on the couch. I squinted and glanced around the office. No Jack, but the evidence was on the desk, two empty bottles. Good scotch wasn't supposed to hurt this much. My head started pounding again, then I realized it was not just my head, but the door as well. Where was Yana?

I fell off the couch to the floor, struggled to stand, all the while I looked around for my shoes, then gave up and shuffled in my socks over to the front door. I fumbled at the lock and swung the door open to two young boys in blue, and by young, I mean much younger than myself.

"James Gardiner?" the closer one asked.

"I gave at the office," I said as I started to close the door.

I was in no mood to be hit up for donations to the Police Charity Ball. The closer cop put his hand against the door, stopping me. That's when I noticed his partner was holding his unholstered pistol at his thigh.

"I need you to come with me to the station now."

I stared, blinking with a lack of comprehension. "Who, me? Am I under arrest for something?"

"That's up to you, sir."

I was trying hard to think straight. He called me sir. I liked that. Maybe I would go with the nice policeman.

"Can I get my shoes?" I stumbled back into the office away from the door and sat on the edge of Yana's desk. I held up one foot, showing I was shoeless.

"We'll bring them along for you. Where are they?"
I was suddenly very tired. I waved towards my office.

"In there. Somewhere. Look under the desk."

The silent one of the two holstered his weapon and pushed past, going into my office. The talky one grabbed me firmly by the arm, maybe to keep me from running away, but probably to keep me from falling on my face.

"You going to be alright, sir?"
Sir, again. I closed my eyes and nodded in the affirmative, but I wasn't so sure. I am not one to get sick to my stomach from drinking, but this looked like a distinct possibility.

Silent Partner showed in the doorway, holding up a pair of loafers. Senior Partner stood me up and turned me to the door. Yana was standing there, clutching her backpack to her chest, her eyes wide like the proverbial headlighted deer. Then I remembered how bad I must have looked.

"Ma'am. You'll need to step aside."

"Yana." I said, taking a deep breath.

"I think I'm being arrested. But it's alright. These nice officers have been perfect gentlemen, and my face is not of their doing." I stopped talking when I realized I was probably slurring my words. I was still drunk. Yana just closed her eyes and shook her head, disappointed, again. Where did she get off copping an attitude like that?

I've never been arrested before. Yesterday's trip to the station didn't count because they never even booked me.

"My hat. Gotta have my hat if I'm going downtown." I said as I reached past the young policeman to grab my fedora off the coat rack.

Senior Partner snatched it from my hand.

"Leave the hat," he said as he handed it to Yana.

She dutifully stepped back and watched the three of us walk down the hall to the elevators.

The patrol car was parked outside the building on Hollywood Boulevard. Nobody pays the police much attention on this street. They're a regular fixture, making arrests every day. But as I stood at the curb waiting for one of them to open the door, I caught sight of Homeless Jimmy across the street watching me. I have to admit, now I was embarrassed. I could only shrug as the officer gently put his hand on my head and steered me tothe back seat.

It was my first time in the back of a patrol car. Not the old model sedan that I had come to expect, but a new SUV and a hybrid, no less. I tried the door handle and the window button, but they had been disabled as I knew they would be. But I had to try, nonetheless. After being reminded to put on my seat belt, I settled in for the ride to the station, my second trip in two days. I wondered if this was going to be a regular part of my new life as a P.I. I never had any run-ins with the cops before. Would this be good or bad for my street cred?

Back in the interrogation room, I got my first good look at myself in their mirrored viewing window. I was such a mess, not just the clothes that I slept in, or the blood on my shirt, but the enormous shiner where that big guy kneed me in the face. It was black and blue and turning a sickening shade of yellow. I bet I took a hell of a booking picture. I got up and walked over to the two-way mirror to get a closer look.

I still had some dried blood below my nose. I thought I had washed my face, but now I couldn't remember.

That's when Detective Mejia walked in, followed by a uniformed officer. Mejia looked even uglier and angrier than before, if that was possible.

"Sit down." He barked at me.

I didn't have the energy to make any smart remarks, so I did as I was told.

"You look like shit." He added.

I could only nod in agreement. "You're the second person to tell me that."

"Are you still drunk?" He turned to the officer. "Get this kid a cup of that crap from the vending machine."

The officer looked at me with disgust and left to fetch me a coffee.

"I guess I had you pegged right the minute I saw you in here yesterday: rich white boy who thinks the rules are for other people. But maybe it's my fault." He leaned over the table, getting right into my face. "Maybe I wasn't clear enough when I told you to butt out."

"My mistake." He backed away, turning his back to me, then muttered, more to himself than to me, "So, now I've got to live with that for the rest of my life."

He spun around, jabbing his finger at me. "But you, you son of a bitch, you are going to pay."

"What are you talking about?" I protested. I thought his interrogation acting was a bit melodramatic. I didn't think cops nowadays laid it on quite this thick.

"Where'd you get that shiner?"

"I got beat up by a bunch of teenagers who didn't like my face and thought they could improve it."

"Where was this?"

"North of Chinatown, up by Dodger Stadium."

"So, you go to a neighborhood you have no business in to pick a fight with some of the local boys."

"No. I was working a case. They mistook me for a real estate agent."

"What have they got against realtors?"

"I don't know, ask them. Maybe they don't like that people are buying up their neighborhood."

"Where were you last night?"

"I was in my office. I had a couple of drinks to ease the pain and slept there. Your officers woke me up."

"What time did you go to your office?"

"Around supper time, seven or eight."

"Anyone see you there that can verify that?"

"My friend came over and drank with me for a bit."

"Your friend got a name?"

"What's this all about? You drag me down here to file a complaint about getting mugged?" I laughed.

"Play innocent all you want. You are going down for the murder of Detective Miles Bowman." Mejia wasn't yelling or pounding the table. He was giving it his best quiet, menacing, Clint Eastwood style delivery, and it was working. He had my full attention.

"My head is a little fuzzy right now. Maybe you could fill me in on exactly what it is I am supposed to have done."

As if on cue, the officer arrived with a paper cup of the precinct coffee. It was hot, but otherwise undrinkable. I drank it anyway.

"Do I need a lawyer? Maybe I should shut up now."

"Miles was a good detective, but maybe not the best at discreetly tailing someone. Heck, your client spotted him right off. So, she brought you in to help her get rid of him. It wasn't enough to disable his car. A good detective learns from his mistakes; you weren't going to get that chance again. So, you had your client, Mrs. Kim or Lee or Lachlan, whatever her name is, lead Detective Bowman into Solano Canyon, up a dead-end street where you were waiting, and you shot him. We have a witness who places you in Solano Canyon yesterday afternoon."

Now I'm wondering where Mimi is. Is she all right? Did she kill Miles? As soon as I get out, I will have to call her.

Mejia opened a manila evidence envelope and dumped the contents onto the table. It was Detective Bowman's effects – some coins, a pen, a small notebook, an empty shoulder holster, a wallet with a badge pinned on the outside, and a cheap flip phone. Mejia picked up the phone and opened it.

"This your phone? It's got your phone number as the only entry on speed dial. I'm sure we will find it's got your prints on it, too."

Being accused of murder does wonders to sharpen the mind. I don't give any credit to the black stuff I was trying to drink.

"Yeah, that's my M.O. I usually just leave a business card when I shoot somebody, but I was out of them yesterday, so I tossed my phone in the front seat instead."

"Your smart-ass answers aren't going to make it any easier on you. It wasn't on the seat; it was in his pocket. Miles probably took it off your client before you had your chance to plug him."

I'm looking at the small pile of stuff on the table - no service piece, no other phone that might be Miles', only mine.

"Yeah, I was in Solano Canyon; I think I already said that. I was looking up on my client, Mrs. Kim. After you busted me, yesterday, I was trying to reconnect with her, but she wasn't answering her phone. So, I traced her to that location with my locator app keyed to the phone I gave her. That one."

I pointed to the burner on the table.

"I didn't see Detective Bowman, but I had an eye out for him. Maybe he showed up after I got the crap beaten out of me by some local vigilantes, or are those your witnesses? Have you arrested Mrs. Kim, too?"

"We will. That's too bad about your face, but that's not an alibi."

"Well, I would have an alibi if you gave me a time frame. Isn't this where you're supposed to ask me where I was between the hours of this and that?"

Mejia was getting pissed with my back talk, but before he could reply, in walked Mother, channeling Judy Garland, with her white silk men's shirt hanging down over black Capri pants, hair tied up in a scarf, and sunglasses that covered half her face. She had her lawyer with her.

"You've said enough, James." The lawyer counseled me.

"I'll do the talking from here. I've already spoken to the city attorney; no charges are being filed at this time."

He handed a piece of paper to Mejia. Mother took one look at me, and the lioness within her came out.

"Look at your face!" She whirled on Mejia. "This isn't the Forties, Detective."

"It wasn't the cops, Mother." I interjected.

The room was getting crowded when the prosecutor's assistants and a couple of uniformed officers entered.

"Get 'em out of here." Mejia wadded up the paper he had just handed back to Mother's lawyer, then pointed to me. "Don't leave town. Having a fancy lawyer doesn't get you off the hook. I've got you for accessory at a minimum. And I will get to the bottom of this. Believe me. It's personal. In the meantime, I recommend you find a new client or maybe a new profession. You're out of your league here, chico."

Outside, Mother started in on me. "Oh, baby, you look a fright. Did the police..."

"I already told you; they didn't work me over."

"Well, you certainly look as though you got beat up." She wet a handkerchief with her tongue and began wiping my face.

"That's because I did. But it was not what you think. Mistaken identity, they thought I was someone else."

Mother just shook her head in disbelief. "Aren't you ashamed? Now you've got a police record." Her verbal anger was betrayed by the way she fussed over my clothes and hair, trying to make it all better.

"Innocent people get arrested, too. It doesn't mean I have a criminal record." I protested as I pushed her hand away. "And stop that. I'm not a little kid. It's embarrassing."

"I bailed you out, I'm entitled to a little mothering."

"You didn't bail me out, I wasn't arrested!" I argued again, a little louder.

The lawyer chimed in. "Actually, you were. They just didn't press charges yet because once they do, the clock starts. They have to schedule an arraignment, etc., etc. The wheels of justice start to grind. Obviously, they don't have any evidence to make a charge stick, so they will have to get busy and do some police work first. Personally, I don't think Detective Mejia really thinks you did it, he's just pissed that you didn't heed his warning to you yesterday when he pulled you in."

"What?" Mother interjected. "You were arrested before?"

"That wasn't a real arrest; they didn't take a booking picture or print me or anything. They just took me in for questioning." I sighed heavily. This wasn't going well, and I was not going to get away from her easily. She had custody of me now and was going to take full advantage of it.

I think I'd rather have taken a grilling from Mejia. Jail was starting to look pretty damned attractive.

CHAPTER

TEN

Mother dismissed her lawyer, and we both climbed into the back of her Bentley. Her driver, George, a guy who looked too old to still have a valid license, proceeded to drive us back to her house. Mother dug a fancy silver cigarette case out of her purse and extracted a professionally manufactured joint from it. I knew it was marijuana before she even lit up. She had been smoking her 'medicinal pot' for years, claiming it eased the pain from her arthritis. She dug out a matching lighter and sparked her Kief, then took a long draw from it, exhaling a big cloud of pungent smoke before starting in on what was going to be a long lecture. I cracked the window on my side. I never liked the smell of other people's dope.

"Your father would be so disappointed." She held the joint between two fingers and picked a bit of leaf off her tongue with her thumb and ring finger.

"I seem to recall that he was arrested once." I countered.

"Getting busted for demonstrating against the Vietnam War is not the same as being pinched for whatever you were doing - vandalism, obstruction?"

"Interfering with a police officer was yesterday. I think today it was for murder." I said, trying to make light of it all.

Mother was not amused at my attempt at a joke.

"James. You may think this is all very funny, but you can be certain that the police don't."

"I didn't kill anyone, Mother. Jesus!"

"Language, James. I believe you. But why are you throwing away your education? You could have a good-paying paying respectable job, bean investment banker like your father, hang out with people who are making a mark in the world."

"My father hangs out with criminals. They just wear pin-striped suits."

"Your father at least made something of himself, built a career from nothing through good hard work." She replied, though not contradicting me.

"He was staked into the business by Grandfather. Besides, I have a job."

I protested. "I have an office. I have a secretary. I make money. Okay, not a lot, but money isn't everything. And what's wrong with my friends? So, Jack isn't setting the world on fire. Most people who are ass… are asinine anyway."

"Now, you're just rationalizing, James."

We rode for a while in silence.

"We'll talk about this more later. In the meantime, I think you should close that silly detective agency of yours and move back home until you've sorted out what you plan to do with your life. Don't forget you promised to have dinner with me this Saturday night. I've invited Rachel over."

"Who?"

"I told you about her last weekend. Don't pretend you don't remember."

Defeated, I started to tune out, staring out the window at the mansions of Beverly Hills rolling by. Mother's place was a six-bedroom, six bath, six thousand square foot Spanish hacienda in Holmby Hills, nestled between Beverly Hills and Westwood.

It had a wonderful view of the L.A. Country Club, although that was not her club. Her home, our home as she insists, was an all-white stucco palace with red tile roofs, dark wood beams, and ironwork details over the windows and elsewhere. Large mosaics of brightly painted Mexican tile was embedded in strategic places in the walls. Shiny pink Saltillo tile floors flowed from the entry through the house and out to the pool. It was bright and spacious and cold as a museum. It was not the home I grew up in, but I had stayed here often enough.

Her annoying twin Yorkies, Bogie and Bacall, came yapping out to greet us. Mother had always named her pets after old movie stars. She had often said she herself was named Faye after Faye Dunaway, as she was born shortly after the movie "Bonnie and Clyde" was released.

I took her word for it; the dates seemed close enough, though I never really wanted to check to see if it was true. Mother liked that story too much to tear it down. I decided I liked the idea of naming pets after old movie stars. If I ever got a dog, I was going to name him Clooney or Hanks. Mother scooped up her darlings and strode off into the house, leaving me to my own devices. I wandered around the grounds looking to see what was new or different. Mother was constantly either re-landscaping or remodeling. I noticed that she'd recently built a Koi Pond, Koi, the one-percenters of the goldfish world. It seemed fitting.

The rest of the garden looked pretty much the same as always, beds of hydrangea, geraniums, azaleas, and above them an assortment of fruit trees, one of every kind, orange, lemon, fig, peach, apricot, I lost track long ago. I eventually found my way up to my bedroom, or rather the room I used on those rare occasions when I stayed over. She had recently renovated all the baths, bringing them into the twenty-first century. Mine now had a sauna/steam room that smelled of eucalyptus. I was thankful for that as I stripped down to shower.

Glad to get out of those clothes I'd been wearing for two days now. My shirt still had stains from my bloody nose. I let the hot water beat down on my neck and shoulders for a good ten minutes. I was still sore from the beating. After a fifteen-minute sit in the steam room, I took a cold shower. I repeated this a few times until the aches went away.

Wrapped in one of those oversized hotel-style white terry cloth robes, I ventured into my father's old office. He hadn't set foot in this house in over ten years, but Mother still left his stuff here, untouched. Make of that what you will.

The bookcases looked like some interior designer had filled them with books bought by the yard. I scanned the titles, wondering if anyone had ever read even one of these: all the old classic literature: Ulysses, Moby Dick, Beowulf.

There were books on economics, banking, law, and even twenty volumes of a now-useless Encyclopedia Britannica, if you can believe it. The walls were plastered with dozens of old framed pictures of my father with various politicians, bankers, and the occasional Hollywood celebrity. Centered in this display was one of him in his younger days with President Reagan. This was what my mother wanted me to be: a successful businessman rubbing elbows with the who's who of the world. I glanced around – no pictures of me, sis, or mom, though.

A successful businessman he may be, but he wasn't much of a father. No shared Boy Scouts of Little League memories for me as a kid. I rarely saw him growing up. In the mornings, he had his head in the paper and was never home in the evenings unless he was entertaining clients. He was an avid golfer, but we never played a round together. I was never good enough until high school, when I was suddenly

shooting better than him, but by then, he had one foot out the door and couldn't be bothered.

On a side table, next to his desk, was his 'hole-in-one' trophy, a golf ball in a glass box, and besides that, a fancy decanter and a couple of matching cut crystal glasses. I pulled the stopper and took a whiff, scotch. I wondered how old it was. Guess it doesn't go bad. I poured myself a glass and picked up the trophy to read the inscription.

I've never had a hole in one, I thought grumpily. It wasn't fair.

I continued my meandering down the hall, back to my old bedroom, looking for fresh clothes. Finding a pair of swim trunks in a dresser, I decided to take a swim and hit the Jacuzzi after that.

The late afternoon sun airbrushed a soft pink glow behind the row of Italian Cypress that bordered the property. The scent of jasmine filled the air. I listened to the music of the bubbling jets and the tinkling of ice in my glass.

I spotted Anna walking around the pool with a tray. Mother, no doubt, was sending out a sandwich or something. Anna was the only help she kept full-time anymore. She'd let the chef go years ago, and the gardener was replaced by a landscape company. Anna looked like hotel staff in her navy polo shirt and khakis, and sure enough, she brought me a ham and cheese sandwich with the crust cut off and a bowl of grapes.

"Buenos Dias, Anna."

"Buenos Tardes, Senor James." She corrected. "Como estas? Your mother thought you might want something to eat."

"Gracias."

"If you don't like this, I can make you something else."

"No, this will be fine. I appreciate it."

As Anna left, I tried to remember how long she had worked for the family, but I couldn't recall a time that she wasn't around. Life was good here. Anyone could get used to this. But as I thought back over my day, I started getting a little pissed off at the lack of respect by everyone, my client, the cops, even my own mother. I was not a little kid. Alexander the Great had conquered the world at my age.

Intentionally or not, Mimi has made me complicit in the murder of Detective Bowman. I needed to get to the bottom of this, not just to clear my name, but to prove to myself and everyone else that I was more than just a professional peeper and freelance gigolo, that I could be a detective, a gumshoe, a private eye, that I could Philip Marlowe with the best of them. It was time for me to stop playing detective and start being one.

First, I needed to talk to my client. I needed some straight answers. What was she mixed up in that would lead to murder, of a policeman, no less! I wasn't going to play the sap for her, as Sam Spade would say. I called the burner phone I lent her. After a few rings, the phone went to voicemail. I listened to the prerecorded lines instructing me to leave a message at the tone. But at the tone, I was silent, debating whether to say anything or not. In the end, the phone decided for me and turned itself off.

That's when I remembered that the phone was sitting in the evidence box at the police station.

CHAPTER

ELEVEN

I shared breakfast the next morning with my mother – a cuppa tea, half a papaya with a squeeze of lemon and a handful of raspberries and half a joint for her; black coffee, eggs over easy, and buttered rye toast for myself.

I watched as she gave instructions for the day to the housekeeper and the gardening supervisor, like a general to her staff, then she marched off to another charity board meeting or something similar. Despite living alone, my mother was living her best life. Her life was a whirl, always busy. She really needed a personal assistant to keep up. I envisioned her days filled like one of those A-list actresses or celebrities. I imagined she did, too.

She fashioned herself after one iconic woman after another. Today it was Judy, before that it was Kate with her masculine-looking wide-legged trousers, a man's styled button-down shirt, shoes, and hat.

I spent the whole day lounging around the house, alone, in surfer shorts, an old Cardinal tee shirt, and flip flops, trying to figure out a plan. I didn't know what to do first, but I knew I had to do something. A man was murdered, and to clear my name, I had to solve it. I left a message for Yana – I would be in the next morning. We had a new case.

The following morning, I had meant to get up early, call an Uber, and sneak out of the house without saying goodbye, but I overslept.

It didn't matter anyway; mother was long gone, off to some function or another.

I arrived at my office a lot later than most days, but I still talked my Uber driver into making my usual detours for coffee, a Frappuccino, and a goldfish in a bag.

At the office, I noticed that my other goldfish in the bowl was not yet belly up. "Hey, I got a roommate for you, buddy." I said as I poured the new guy into the water.

Yana was not at her desk, only her backpack, so I left her drink there and turned to see my office door half open. Inside was a young girl. I say young girl, but she looked to be Yana's age, maybe 20 or so, but really not all that much younger than myself. She was very pretty, Asian, with a perfect oval face, long black hair, and porcelain skin, accented by dark plum lipstick and matching eye shadow. She was otherwise dressed rather conservatively, knee-length navy skirt with matching cardigan sweater over a plain white blouse, either a sorority girl or office attire of the Young Republicans, I thought. She had a business card clutched tightly in her fingers.

"Can I help you?" I offered as I hung up my hat.

It was then I noticed she had been crying; her eyes were puffy and red. I now recognized her as the girl sitting with Mimi at the Founder's Club last week. Those cheekbones! I could see in her how Mimi must have looked in her younger days.

"Mr. Gardiner?" She began.

"You must be Mimi Kim's daughter."

"Sophie, yes." She quickly dabbed her eyes with a tissue, rose, and offered me my own business card, presumably the same one I had given her mother.

"Please sit down. You can keep that; I have boxes of them. Can I get you anything, some water?"

She just shook her head and sat.

"I thought I recognized you." I went on. "I saw you at the Founder's Club at lunch, a week or so ago, I think."

"You were there? Mom drags me down there on a regular basis."

"I know the feeling," I said with an agreeing nod. "You didn't exactly seem like you were enjoying yourself."

"I'm sorry, I don't remember meeting you."

"Well, we actually didn't meet. I was dropping something off for your mom and saw you from across the room. Never mind. Anyway, what can I do for you?"

"Mother is missing. She didn't come home Monday night. Then yesterday, the police came to the house looking for her and wouldn't say why. They interrogated me, they interrogated father. They even questioned our housekeeper. Then they searched the house!" She grabbed a tissue from her sweater pocket and dabbed her eyes. "She's missing and they searched our house!" she cried out, her hands fluttering about in erratic gestures as she did.

"I'm not surprised. They don't think she's missing; they suspect she's hiding." I explained.

"Hiding? Where? Under the bed?! She's not hiding! Why would she be hiding? Now, they have a patrol car parked in front of our place. I'm afraid something terrible has happened to her, but the cops won't tell us anything." She stood, starting to tear up again. I offered her a new tissue. I have a drawer full of tissue boxes - occupational necessity. She took them and plopped back into her chair.

"Well," I stammered, "Yeah, I'd like to talk to her myself. She's put me in a bit of a bind with her little games."

"Games? What games?" Sophie looked up with a strange expression on her face.

I looked at her beautiful face for a long minute, deciding how much to tell her before I began.

"Less than two weeks ago, your mother was sitting right where you are now. She came here to hire me to help her out with a 'situation'. As she explained it, someone, your father, she suspected, had hired a man to follow her around and keep tabs on her. She said her husband probably thought she was having an affair."

"My mother would not be having an affair. You must have misunderstood." She said with little emotion.

"Well, whatever, maybe she was just joking. Still, she hired me to help her lose this guy who was tailing her. I did, once, that was easy enough, but the second time didn't really go as planned, and I got nabbed by the cops in the process. Then yesterday I got hauled in again for more questioning. It seems that the guy following your mother around was also a private detective, one who just happens to be a former cop himself and has now turned up dead. And now, because of my involvement with your mother and interfering with this guy's surveillance business, I'm a suspect."

"I wouldn't know anything about that." She mumbled.

"I'm not suggesting that you would. Though you can see now how I might be interested in asking your mother a few questions. But then you're telling me she hasn't come home."

"But you can find her, right? You are a detective, aren't you?"

"Not, really, and I don't do missing persons. I specialize in helping women whose husbands are cheating on them. I tail the men, photograph them with their mistresses, and my clients use those photos as leverage when it comes to the divorce settlements. That kind of thing."

"I see." She shifted in the chair uneasily. Uncrossed then re-crossed her legs, pulling her skirt down over her thighs. I tried not to stare.

"Why are you coming to me to find her?"

"I don't know anyone else who does that sort of thing."

"Plenty of detective agencies in the phone book."

"But they don't know my mother. You do."

"We've met once. I've had a couple of phone conversations with her. That's it. I don't really know her."

I fiddled with my pencil, spinning it from finger to finger.

"Have you filed a missing person's report?" I suggested hopefully.

"The police are already looking for her. Did you not hear me? A police car has been parked in front of our house for two days." She said, distraught, looking at me like I'm some kind of idiot.

"Right, you did say that. My mistake."

She said nothing further, just looked at me with her big, wet eyes.

"Do you happen to have a picture?"

Sophie just stared, confused.

"A picture of your mother."

"You know what she looks like, you've met her, you've seen her, more than once."

"Yes, I know, but if I need to show a picture to someone else while I'm out looking, it would be nice to have one."

"Oh." She opened her purse and started rooting around looking for her phone. Her bag was full of who knows what. She started pulling out fistfuls of paper.

"Stupid drug store receipts." She muttered.

"Who uses these coupons anyway?" She held up an exceptionally long strip of paper. I pushed a waste basket toward her with my foot and she tossed it in along with a couple more handfuls of stuff. Finally, she got out her phone and started scrolling through her photos.

"I don't have a real picture, I mean one on paper, but I might have something on my phone."

"That would do. You can just send me a copy, by e-mail, or to my phone. Number's on the card."

"Well, I have this; it's of her and me."

I waited for the picture to pop up on my phone. It was a bit of a strained selfie of the two of them against what looked like the Founders' Club in the background. Sophie didn't look too comfortable in fancy clothes, but mom looked great. She loved being with her daughter.

"Your mom's very pretty. She could almost be your older sister."

"Yes, she was. Is. Are you sure you can find her?"

"I'll see what I can do. Like I said, it's not really my line of work, but I'm pretty sure I can find her."

"I'll pay, of course." She said as she scrolled through icons on her phone. "Do you take Venmo?"

"No need for that. Your mother already paid me for a job I didn't finish."

With some hesitation, she put the phone back in her purse, then added encouragingly, "It will also help your own situation, you know, with the police, if you find her."

"I'll do my best, Sophie." Trying my best to reassure. "Sophie, what's your Korean name?"

"So Young." She looked at me a bit suspiciously.

"So Young. I like that. It fits you…"

"Don't." She cut me off. "I've heard them all before. And it's not pronounced So Young, it rhymes with so long."

"I was going to say it fits you better than Sophie. May I call you So Young?"

I asked taking pains to pronounce it properly.

"Sure. I guess." She composed herself quickly and rose to leave.

"I'll call you the minute I know anything." I said, holding up my phone, still displaying her picture.

"Thank you." She offered her hand, and I shook it and showed her to the door. Yana was now back at her desk and watching discreetly.

"New client?" She asked after I closed the door. "Kind of young to be having husband trouble, isn't she?"

"That is Mrs. Kim's daughter. It seems mother has disappeared."

"And left you holding the bag. Not good, Sherlock." Yana began packing her backpack for school. "So, what does lovely daughter want?"

"To find her mother, of course."

"Oh. Well, solve this case and you'll have a new client almost your own age to fuck." She mocked as she slung her backpack over her shoulder.

"Yana! I'm surprised. What's gotten into you? I hadn't known you to have such a... sharp tongue."

"Sorry, boss. I guess it gets under my skin seeing you chasing after all those old divorcees getting beat up and arrested in the process. You can do better."

"Ha. My Mother's words out of your mouth."

After Yana left, I grabbed my coffee, now cold, and retreated to my office. I glanced down at the pile of trash in my waste basket, and being the incurable nosey type, fished out a few pieces of paper. The drug store receipt was for a bottle of shampoo. Ten feet of paper for a one-item purchase.

There were also a couple of bank receipts, cash withdrawals of a thousand dollars each. This girl was living large, I thought. I sat down with my laptop and began researching her mother. Rule number one – always check out your client first. I now had two clients. Fortunately, they were related, so that might make for a little time saving. This part of the detective game I was well versed in, having to suss out many a client's husband before. It didn't take long to find that Mimi was married to one Alistair Lachlan of Lachlan Development. It did not seem to be a big firm, but it did have a gilded Beverly Hills address. I made a note of that and kept on looking. Not much to be found.

This family kept a low profile. So, Yong was an undergraduate student at USC. Little chance that Yana might know her, that was a big campus, but it never hurts to check. I made a note to have her follow that up.

I called up Lachlan Development to try to get an appointment to see dear old dad. I had mentally prepared two or three bluffs to get past the gatekeeper, but surprisingly enough, the receptionist gave me an appointment for that very afternoon, no questions asked.

CHAPTER

TWELVE

Lachlan Properties was in a nondescript, medium-sized, steel and glass hi-rise on Wilshire Boulevard, one of many such buildings built in the 60's, each one not very distinguishable from the next. The lobby, all polished stone floors and walls, housed a little flower shop and an even smaller convenience store and news stand. I took the elevator to the top floor, then down a short, carpeted corridor to the end suite. Lachlan's wasn't a big outfit, as evidenced by the small reception area that fronted just two inner offices. But it was smartly decorated. A pair of large Asian-styled watercolors dominated the walls left and right above a matching pair of bonsai trees on carved wooden tables.

These flanked a large gnomish-like head carved out of porous black lava rock. A series of framed architectural renderings were arrayed along the wall in front of me, prized projects no doubt. Below them, a middle-aged, slightly graying woman watched me silently from behind her desk, waiting for me to present myself and state my business. I gave her my card. She picked up the phone and announced me to the inner office.

"Mr. Lachlan will see you now." She said as she gestured to the door to her left without getting up. I let myself in. His room was quite spacious, clean, and relatively unadorned with a bare minimum of dated 20th-century Scandinavian Modern furniture to make the place appear even larger. Lachlan sat with his back to a floor-to-ceiling window with a nice view of Cedars-Sinai Hospital and the colorful Pacific Design Center. Not a very big man, he was not much taller than his wife and daughter. He had a large forehead and hair cut so short that he appeared bald at first glance.

He wore a pleasant enough face, framed by big ears on which he hung some steel-rimmed glasses on. He was coatless with his blue and white striped shirt sleeves very neatly rolled up, accountant style, and he wore a yellow bow tie. He rose and offered me his hand to shake. It was cold and dry but his grip was strong.

I set my hat on the corner of his desk, then leaned back, making myself as comfortable as I could in an uncomfortable chair. As I pulled out a pen and opened my notebook, I surveyed the desk top: classic OCD, pens and sharpened pencils lined up in a row by length beside an open notebook at his right hand, a couple of folders and a closed laptop at his left, neatly stacked and perfectly aligned with the edges of the desk, a framed photograph at one corner. If you had a protractor, I am sure you would find it to be exactly at a forty-five-degree angle.

"What can I do for you, Mr. Gardiner?" Lachlan's soft voice pulled me back into the meeting. He looked at my hat on his desk with the half-lidded scorn you would give a stripper at a choir boy convention.

"Yes," I said, recovering. "I have been approached by your daughter, Sophie, who has retained me to look into the disappearance of her mother, your wife."

Lachlan snorted a laugh. "My wife is not missing. She is out of town. She has gone back to visit her parents. I am surprised Sophie didn't remember that. But then again, she's been so caught up in her schoolwork lately that we don't see or talk to her as much as we'd like. I will have to give her a call later to let her know all is well. I am terribly sorry if she has troubled you with this."

Was he lying? I couldn't tell. I had assumed the older man I saw Mimi arguing with might have been her father, but maybe I was wrong. I was new to this whole interrogation thing. I was going to have to get better at it; I really wanted to do this.

"No trouble at all," I replied. "That's the business I'm in. So, that is the same story you told the police last night?"

Lachlan stared at me for a moment over his metal rims. "Of course. Why would I say otherwise? And I don't see how that is any business of yours."

"You say she's not missing, yet there's a patrol car parked in front of your house."

Lachlan's eyes narrowed.

"She occasionally disappears for a few days, but she always comes back. I don't make a big deal out of it. If she needs time alone now and then for her mental health, then she should have it."

"I don't know if you were aware of this, but I had previously been retained by your wife as well."

"Yes, I am very much aware that she hired you and why." Lachlan interrupted. "I don't know what all she may have told you."

He paused, carefully took off his glasses, folded them, and laid them in the center of the desk. He leaned forward as if to say something in confidence.

"You should know that Mimi has quite an active imagination. At times, she lives in a world of her own making. It is all rather harmless, I assure you, but it can be confusing if you don't know her. I think it is her way of coping with the stress of life here in the U.S."

"She has only recently moved here, then? I was under a different impression."

Lachlan sighed as if about to retell a story told too often. He clasped his hands together, fingers interlaced, and glanced at a picture of them as a much younger couple on his desk. Before he began, he impatiently leaned back in his chair, hands to the armrests.

"Mimi and I met some twenty-two years ago while I was living and working in Seoul. I was an accounting manager for an American developer there." He began. "We started seeing each other, fell in love, and got married. Shortly thereafter, So Young was born, and I brought them both to Los Angeles. I was already in my forties by then and, unfortunately, a little too much consumed with work. I suppose I should have done more to help her cope with the transition to life in America. But I thought she managed quite well despite my inattention. I am proud of her, proud of both my girls."

He began to idly fidget with his pencils, straightening them even though they were already perfectly aligned.

"Mimi may have told you some story that she was having an affair, but that was only in her imagination, in her fantasy life, as I said. Her mother was the same way, kept calling me President Truman even though I look nothing like him. Well, you know what they say. Crazy runs in the family."

"And the part about being followed?" I queried.

"Also, part of her fantasy, I'm afraid."

"I understand. I have no problem waiting until she returns, and then we can settle matters then."

"Oh, I don't think that will be necessary. If Mimi owes you money, I can settle that right now." He sat forward, picked up his glasses and put them on, then took out a checkbook from his desk drawer. "With a little bonus for your trouble?" he added with a wry smile.

"No, I didn't mean she owed me anything. Except maybe some answers. Fantasy or not, did you know that she actually was being followed? Or was that your guy, the retired cop, you hired to keep an eye on her?"

"I don't think so." He snapped indignantly,

"I would never hire someone to follow my wife around."

"Then I take it the police didn't tell you last night that this particular detective is now dead, shot, murdered. And your wife is probably a suspect, as am I, because of my dealings with her."

If Lachlan was disturbed by this news, he hid it well.

"They did not mention it, and I certainly did not hire this police detective, but I may know who might have." He offered. "You see, I have a number of very aggressive competitors in my business. They have been known to hire men to follow me and my employees from time to time in the hope of getting the jump on some property I might be looking at."

"Property like those in Solano Canyon, perhaps?" I queried.

Lachlan again looked at me coldly over his glasses. "I have properties all over this city."

"I followed your wife over to Solano last week. She was arguing with an older Korean man, whom I mistakenly assumed might have been her father. Does Mimi help you with your Korean clientele?"

"She sometimes presses me to offer submarket rates to them as a favor, yes. It always costs me extra in cleaning fees to get rid of the smell of kimchi when they leave. Why didn't you approach her and ask her yourself?"

"I was planning to, but I got jumped by some locals and beaten up. By the time I picked myself up, she was gone."

"I'm surprised to hear that. Solano Canyon is a pretty nice neighborhood. Rarely any trouble there. That's why I like it for investing."

"Yeah, I think they mistook me for a real estate developer. Seems to be a pretty hot market these days, judging by all the flyers around. But the locals don't seem to like the idea of being forced out by gentrification."

"Gentrification is just a fancy word for change, and change is life. I think our interview is over. I have other business to attend. Good day, Mr. Gardiner."

So that was that. I was being given the brush-off. I pushed my chair back at an odd angle and swept my hat off the desk, unintentionally disturbing his neat pile of folders. I was sure all would be put back in order before I even made the elevator. He did look a little like Truman, I thought.

The middle-aged receptionist eyed me without a word as I exited. While waiting for the elevator, I stared down at the traffic on Wilshire. I still hadn't formed an impression of Lachlan. It was odd that he was almost expecting my visit. Was he a good guy or a baddie? He was certainly an odd guy. How much was he lying or only telling me partial truths, and why? Maybe he was being forthright, and she was taking some PTO and would be back when she felt better. I decided I needed to know the answers to the questions before I asked. Then I would know who I was dealing with. I glanced at the first page of my new leather-bound notebook that I had bought just for this interview. Having never really investigated anything before, I wasn't sure what I should be noting down. But certainly, something more than the word 'kimchi' and the amateurish doodle of Lachlan I drew. Why would a man who didn't like kimchi marry a Korean girl?

Down in the garage I fished all the flyers off the floor in the back of my car. Flipping through, I found that most were political leaflets, candidates, propositions, and bond measures, none of which I had paid a lick of attention before now, but not as many real estate ads as I had remembered. I decided to drive back to Solano Canyon.

I didn't think Mimi was the killer, so she must have been involved in something bigger and more sinister, unwittingly, of course.
An appropriate word. I thought back to our first meeting and how she had giggled when she confessed to having an affair. How could I have missed it? I mean, who does that?

The Welcome Wagon I had run into there had kind of alluded to some unwelcome gentrification happening in the canyon. I knew I had to go back and see if I could figure out who Lachlan's competition might be. Just don't get out of the car, I told myself.

My return visit to the neighborhood didn't turn out to be too scary. It was late in the afternoon, most people were coming back from work, and the streets were busy, but no sign of the boys. I again drove by the house where I last saw Mimi. I wasn't expecting to see the blue Beemer out front, and I didn't.

I circled the block a few times and grabbed all the flyers I could find of any kind, snapped pics of all the "For Sale" signs, and anything else that had a name or a phone number in the neighborhood until it was too dark to continue.

I dragged it all back to the office and spread it out. It was a daunting mess of information. It was definitely a job for Yana. I left her a detailed note of what I was looking for. I knew she could make sense of it. I was more of an intuition, gut feeling, fly by the seat of my pants kind of guy. Yana was a dot your i's, cross your t's, and check every box kind of girl. That, and I must confess, I could be rather lazy sometimes.

So, I called it a night. I was feeling pretty good about my first day's accomplishments as a serious detective.

When I got home, I noticed the house next door and the light spilling out of that one window, where they didn't do such a good job of papering over the glass. My newfound detective nose felt the need to be nosey, so I wandered over and tried to peek in. Unfortunately, there was nothing to see from that angle but a blank white wall. Undeterred, I wandered around to the back of the house. It was all buttoned up pretty tight. On a hunch, I checked out the trash cans. I was expecting maybe some incriminating documents, something juicy, I don't know. What I found was juicy, alright, note the past tense. Inside were a bunch of Chinese take-out boxes with the remains of half a dozen of everyone's favorite dishes, cashew chicken, sweet and sour pork, fried rice, the usual, all crawling with ants now. Oh, well.

The next morning, Yana had me organized before I could finish my first cup of coffee. While I fed my ever-growing menagerie of goldfish, she whipped up a call sheet we could work through to unmask the various companies behind the leaflets.

None of them were associated with Lachlan, which I thought was curious. Alternately posing as buyers or sellers, or renters, we called the different agencies seeking out information. Some companies had the same phone numbers, others, different numbers, but the same people answered the phone. While I kept calling, Yana got on the internet and started looking up addresses and incorporation records until we narrowed our search down to a few prime candidates. One that I spoke to was Lee Properties, a development company on Wilshire in Koreatown.

I made several attempts to get the Mr. Lee of Lee Development on the phone, bluffing and bullying, as I had learned to do from years of trying to get dirt on philandering husbands.

I was about to strike out and get hung up for the last time when, in desperation, I dropped the name of Detective Miles Bowman.
That got me silence, then a "Just a moment, please." And after at least ten minutes of nothing, "If you can come in this afternoon, Mr. Lee will be able to meet with you then."

Thinking Mimi might be mixed up in some sort of real estate scheme was really a shot in the dark. But they're reaction to Bowman's name was the first break in the case for me.

CHAPTER

THIRTEEN

The Chinese were the first significant Asian immigrant group to settle in Los Angeles in the nineteenth century. They established a community north of downtown, which is, of course, now known as Chinatown. These days, though, most Chinese Americans live much further east in communities like Alhambra and South Pasadena or south in Orange County. Chinatown had become mostly a tourist destination; souvenir shops painted in red lacquer selling pretty colored fans and fake ivory chopsticks. The Japanese followed shortly thereafter, settling south of Chinatown and east of downtown in a neighborhood called Boyle Heights, plus a small enclave in the shadow of City Hall, which they called Little Tokyo.

But the Japanese immigrants also didn't stay downtown for very long, after the war, migrating to other nearby communities like Palos Verdes and Monterey Park. and, Little Tokyo, too, is mostly a tourist site today.

The largest and most recent Asian immigration has been the Koreans. Koreatown, or K-town to the locals, is pretty big, about three square miles, and lies west of downtown and east of Hancock Park. It is the most vibrant community, with several hundred thousand Koreans living in and around the city. Fancy new skyscrapers filled with swank offices and luxury apartments line Wilshire Boulevard, but you will still find a few low-rent souvenir shops on the side streets pushing dollar tchotchkes.

The restaurants, coffee shops, spas, and nightclubs have become the hip destination for young Angelinos.

Lee Development was in one of these new hi-rises, coincidentally, only a few miles down the street from Lachlan's office. But then I imagine there are a lot of real estate developers on Wilshire. I parked in the garage and rode the elevator to the lobby which was in sharp contrast to Lachlan's building, very modern, sleek, and shiny in a way that shouted 'money'.

Lee was on the 19th floor. The black glass door with a fancy 'LD' in script etched in gold with the company name in Hangul underneath was the first thing you saw when you stepped out of the elevator. A very demure young Korean girl in a black skirt suit greeted me with a bow as I entered. I offered my card, which she pocketed, and showed me into an inner office. She offered me tea. I opted for water. Lee's office was expansive, with a terrific view of the downtown skyline. On the opposite wall hung a series of large ink wash paintings of rural scenes from Korea, each with a small solitary accent of color. The room was dominated by a massive desk with nothing but a computer tablet on it. Taking up the other half of the room was a set of eight overstuffed black leather chairs arranged around a large but low-standing coffee table. I sat in one of these chairs, and the girl brought me a glass, not a plastic bottle, of cold water, on a coaster. She placed a covered teacup at the head of the table.

Lee wasn't there yet, so I sat and drank my water and examined the large and intricately carved jade cigarette lighter, ashtray, and cigarette box in the center of the table. Faint strains of Chinese or Korean music drifted through the air. It was more than relaxing; it almost put me to sleep.

Lee finally entered from an inner office. He looked to be forty-ish, maybe younger, quite a bit shorter than me, trim and movie-star handsome. He reminded me of Tom Cruise with his hundred-dollar haircut, thousand-dollar chalk striped suit, and million-dollar smile. Following him was his entourage. I offered my hand with a slight bow. Lee ignored it and seated himself at the head of the table.

The others stood behind him in the background, trying to look menacing. They were about as unobtrusive as a rugby team at a little girl's tea party. After a seemingly long, awkward moment, I let my hand fall to my side and sat down.

"So, Mr. Gardiner," he read off my name card in his hand. "To what do I owe this pleasure? You are investigating something today that requires you to interview me?"

"Thank you for seeing me, Mr. Lee." I began.

"I have been retained by Mrs. Mimi Kim Lachlan. Perhaps you might know her husband, Alistair. He's also in the real estate business."

Lee nodded slightly.

I continued. "Mrs. Lachlan told me she was being followed by a man she believed to be hired by her husband. She wanted my help in being able to shake this guy when necessary. I was able to determine that she was being followed by a private investigator named Miles Bowman, a retired detective from the LAPD. Mr. Lachlan adamantly denied having hired anyone to follow his wife, but he intimated that one of his business competitors likely did. In calling to set up this meeting, mentioning Detective Bowman's name seemed to open the door for me. That made me think it was you who had employed the man. I am just following up to find out why."

Before Lee could answer, his girl Friday brought in a fancy teapot and proceeded to pour tea into the cup on the table.

Lee breathed in a little of the aroma and recovered the mug, holding it in both hands.

"I see. And now it appears that Detective Bowman is dead, and Mrs. Lachlan has disappeared. Is that right?" He said, looking up to catch my reaction. "The police have already been here." He added.

Of course, they had. I was one step behind still, playing catch-up and no clue about what I was doing.

"What gives you the idea that I am the one who employed this Mr. Bowman?" Lee continued.

"I have already spoken with Mr. Lachlan. He tells me that you regularly have him and his employees followed."

"He said that?" He said with bemused surprise.

"Well, he did not mention you by name. He said his competitor."

"There are so many in the development business here in L.A., Mr. Gardiner. I won't deny that Mr. Bowman has a contract to provide security for Lee Development. But he has quite wide leeway to determine whatever course of action he sees fit. If he was following Mrs. Lachlan, it was not at my direction. Perhaps some action of hers warranted such surveillance. She is a rather strange person."

"So, you know her, then."

"Mostly by reputation. She is a woman who lives in her own world. *Doh-rai halmoni,* we call them."

"Yeah, crazy cat ladies."

"How is that?"

"We call them crazy cat ladies. Old women who are a few cards short of a full deck and live alone with a bunch of cats. That was my first impression, too, when she came in claiming she was being followed. But then lo and behold, she was being followed. So, I don't really buy into that explanation anymore."

"Nevertheless, her behavior was disturbing. Perhaps her husband said something at the dinner table, and she goes off and does something foolish, interfering with my business or my employees. I do not blame Alistair; he cannot control her. Therefore, I must take preemptive measures."

"Like using Detective Bowman's connections to the Police to have her arrested?"

"I have the utmost trust in Mr. Bowman to use discretion and follow proper procedure."

"Sounds like you know the Lachlans well, then."

"He did not tell you?"

"Must have slipped his mind."

"Alistair was my first boss. He taught me everything about this business, made me a partner. I owe him a debt that cannot be repaid."

"You know him from Korea, then?"

"Yes, I worked for him there. Those were the boom times for smaller firms like Alistair's. Now the chaebols have moved in and control the industry."

"So, what happened between you two? Why the falling out?"

"Nothing happened. I wanted to have my own firm. Alistair even encouraged me. We are friendly competitors, not rivals."

If Lee gave a signal, I didn't see it, but one of his men had slipped out and now reentered carrying a framed photograph. Lee handed it to me. It was of him and Alistair some twenty-five years ago. Lee looked like a recent college grad in a too-small suit. Alistair was already middle-aged. They were smiling with arms around each other's shoulders and standing in front of a Korean palace.

"Did you also know Mimi during that time in Korea?" I asked.

"I can't say that I knew her well. I met her once or twice while in Korea. She worked in a bar in Itaewon. That's a part of town that is popular with the G.I.s and the foreigners, businessmen and tourists mostly. I went there once for a drink with Alistair and he introduced me to her. Later, I believe he said, what's the American slang for it? Oh, yes, he got her knocked up."

"Oh, I know that play, fishing for husbands."

"It can happen to anyone."

"But usually young G.I.s fresh off the farm, not businessmen."

"Nevertheless, he did the honorable thing in marrying her and bringing her and their child to the States. It would have been very hard on Mimi and her daughter to remain in Seoul. Being an unwed mother is considered shameful, and Koreans can be very cruel to mixed-race children. They prize purity of race in a way that Americans disparage."

"Yeah, well, you could say we still have issues with that."

"I may have met her once or twice since I came to L.A., but most of my knowledge of her behavior was from Allister's complaints to me at work. I can't say that I've seen her in many years. I do hope I have been helpful, Mr. Gardiner, but as I have other pressing business, I am going to have to ask you to excuse me."

"Kamsahabnida," I said, showing off my twenty-word vocabulary again, and bowed.

Since I was in the neighborhood, I thought I'd grab an early supper. I knew a little noodle place on Wilshire that served the best chicken noodle soup. *Kal guksu* they called it.

The soup would come out of the kitchen still bubbling. The locals would dive right in, finishing before it had a chance to cool. I usually had to wait five or ten minutes, or I would scald my mouth trying to eat. But it was delicious.

I drove back to my office. I was going to check out Lee's story, the best I could, newspaper coverage, and incorporation records. It's not that I didn't believe him. I couldn't help but try to imagine Alistair back then.

In the picture, he wore a short-sleeved white shirt with a pocket protector, classic nerd. He was short, nothing to look at, but American and had money. Mimi was probably poor and from the countryside, but obviously quite beautiful. A lot better looking than any girl stateside would give Alistair the time of day.

Of course, he was hooked. But what's the harm? They both got what they wanted, didn't they? And why were both Lee and Lachlan so eager to paint Mimi as a good candidate for the funny farm? They were both too eager to volunteer that information by half. She was quirky, not cuckoo.

I liked her. I smelled a cover-up.

It was late by the time I parked my car and walked to the building. Standing on the corner waiting for the light to turn, I couldn't help but notice a car, a big beige barge, parked in front of the entrance. Nothing unusual about that in most cases, but that was a red curb, buses, and emergency vehicles only. The guy leaning against his hood, smoking a cigarette, must have had a lot of balls.

Or, he could have been a cop. I recognized Detective Mejia's ugly mug before I had finished crossing the street.

"If you're working vice tonight, the hookers are on Fountain," I said as I approached him.

"If I'm going to bust anyone tonight, it's going to be you." He replied angrily, lighting a fresh cigarette from the old one and dropping the butt in the gutter. "I thought I was pretty clear about you keeping your nose clean. I told you to leave it alone."

That's when the light went off in my head.

"So, you're working for Lee, too, huh?"

"Miles was my friend, my ex-partner. Of course, Mr. Lee is going to give me a courtesy call when someone uses his name to get in the door and then starts asking a lot of nosy questions that are none of his business."

"Hey! Cut a guy some slack, Okay? My client went A.W.O.L. on me, disappeared. Her daughter came into my office yesterday and said her mother was missing. So, I'm doing what any Good Samaritan would do, I'm helping look for her."

"Then, file a missing person's report."

"That's exactly what I told the daughter. But then she explained to me about the patrol car parked in front of her house. You're looking for her, too. You think she killed your old partner. So, I tell you what, if I find her, you'll be the first to know."

"Listen, you, rich punk," Mejia snarled. "Just stick to taking your dirty pictures and leave the homicide stuff to detectives who know what they're doing. If I bring you in again, your mother's lawyer will not be getting you out anytime soon."

Mejia flipped the half-finished coffin nail towards the building wall, slid into his old Crown Vic, slammed the door, then peeled away, running a red light and almost hitting another car.

I wondered how much stock I should put into Mejia's threat as I rode the elevator up to my floor. The other offices were all dark now, along the corridor to the office. I unlocked the door and looked for messages on Yana's desk. There were none.

The last red rays of sunset slotted through the blinds onto my desk in perfect noirish fashion, inspiring me to roll up my sleeves and start digging. Work in the office turned out to be pretty unproductive. Don't let anyone tell you that you can find anything and everything on the internet. It may be there, but that doesn't mean you can find it. My bigger problem was focus. Conflicting images of Mimi kept swirling around in my head.

I needed to talk to So Young again. Putting a call on her cell phone only got me her voicemail. What college girl doesn't answer her phone? She certainly can't have already turned in for the night; it's only eleven thirty. Nobody in college goes to bed that early on a Friday night, at least not alone. Maybe she's on a date.

Myself, being an old geezer pushing thirty, was ready to call it a night.

CHAPTER

FOURTEEN

The next morning, I was sitting at the kitchen table letting my morning coffee steep for a few minutes and looking through the window at the house next door. I didn't know why I was getting obsessed with it, but I was. As I was watching, two young guys exited out the back door. They were both wearing those Timberland work boots, short cut-off blue jeans, tool belts, and no shirts. The guys were both good looking Asian guys in their twenties and even for being day laborers, they were pretty buff, and granted it was unusually hot for this time of year, so the shorts and shirtlessness I'd buy, and the glistening sweat on their backs and chests, but damn if they didn't look like a couple of porn actors out for a cigarette break. I watched them smoke for a minute or two, then one of the gals I had seen earlier, the real estate agent, or so I thought, came out. She was wearing Capri pants, a man's shirt, and too much makeup for this hour of the day.

Now I was guessing maybe she was the actress, and was this some internet amateur porn shoot? They talked for a few minutes, very animated with a lot of gestures that could have meant anything, then all three went inside.

I was left to drink my coffee and wonder what they might be filming inside there, "Debbie Does the Department of Building and Safety?"

I tried calling So Young again. This time I got lucky. I could tell there was a guy in her room by her hushed tone and evasive answers. Guess someone else got lucky, too. Ah, to be young and in school again. I was getting so nostalgic. I sarcastically asked her if she was up late last night studying for exams.

Maybe she was too sleepy to get my joke, for she reminded me that it was still only September. School had only been in session for a few weeks; it was a little early even for pop quizzes. I let it drop. Bad joke anyway. I told her I needed to see her again. I had questions. We agreed to meet later that afternoon on campus.

USC is a pretty nice school. Never mind that I'm a Stanford grad, I would even go so far as to say it's the second-best university in the state. It has its reputation for sports and academics, and tuition costs. People like to call it the University of Spoiled Children.

I'm sure the Trojans have similar dismissive put-downs of us Cardinals, but I wouldn't know what those would be. USC is a beautiful campus, too, with lots of stately brick and stone buildings, just two miles down Vermont from Koreatown.

We had agreed to meet on the Quad in front of the library, someplace easy for us non-students to find. Even though it was a Saturday and no classes, I figured I would never find her, so I would just have to make myself easy to spot. So, I stood by the fountain, looking lost, smiling at all the cute co-eds who proceeded to ignore me, with or without giggling accompaniment.

Soon enough, So Young came hurrying up the walkway.

I wouldn't have recognized her if she hadn't called out my name. Now she was dressed like a college girl with money, tight jeans, and a brightly colored off-shoulder top, knee-high leather boots, and a matching Hermes bag. Her face was much different, too. Maybe it was the makeup or the hair, but she looked nothing like the girl who sat in my office a few days ago.

She looked much prettier, but part of that was on account of that she wasn't crying and her eyes were not puffy and red.

We walked over to a nearby coffee kiosk. I found us a table while she placed the order at the counter. I asked for a coffee, black, no sugar. Soon, So Young joined me, plopping down a heavy stack of books.

"Library day? Wow, O'Neil, heavy stuff," I commented, noting her copy of 'Mourning becomes Electra' on top.

"American lit." She answered. "I don't see how any of this stuff is relevant anymore."

"Yeah, Gen Ed requirements are a drag. It's not like we didn't get enough of that in high school."

We sat awkwardly for a moment in silence.

"I went by your father's office, Tuesday." I said, getting down to business.

"He denies that your mother is missing. He says she has gone to Korea for a few weeks to visit with her parents."

"Kind of funny, that she would go without a word to me, don't you think?" She snapped.

"Well, have you talked to your father about this? I mean the police visit and all?"

"Yeah, of course. He just rolls his eyes and says, 'You know your mother. She'll come home in a few days and act like nothing unusual has happened."

"So, this isn't the first time?"

"She does stuff on her own. I don't know if she leaves without telling him. They don't do anything together anymore. It's like they live on separate planets. I mean, is that what happens to old married couples? They just lead their own lives under one roof?"

"Does your mother ever work for the business, office stuff, or whatever?"

"No, never." She sniffed. "She didn't have a head for that kind of stuff. But I help out with the bookkeeping from time to time."

"Really? I wouldn't have pegged you for a number cruncher."

"My father thinks having work experience is more valuable than textbook learning." She added.

"So, what are you majoring in?" I asked. "I take it's not English Lit."

"City Planning. Equally as boring." She rolled her eyes and gave me a little conspiratorial smile.

"Daddy wants you to take over the business, is that it?"

She nodded and shrugged with a sheepish smile. "What was your major?"

"I have a BS in Finance. Stanford's GSB."

"Hmmm. I guess that's not as sexy as being a private eye, huh?"

"Sherlock, your order's ready." The barista called out.

I could only close my eyes and shake my head at that. So Young giggled, just like her mother.

I retrieved my coffee and her green tea, stuffing a five-spot in the tip jar, and returned to the table.

"I already tipped the girl when I placed the order."

"Oh, well, she got an extra tip then."

"You still use cash?" She said in mock surprise.

"Not really, but for valets and tips, I do. They like cash tipsso they don't have to report it to the IRS."

"Ah, the black market."

"Yeah, pretty much. Anyone who uses cash these days is probably hiding something."

"Seriously. I don't even carry a credit card. I pay everything with my phone." She waved her phone as evidence.

"Anyway, your father told me that he suspected one of his business rivals might have been tailing your mother." I continued, picking up where I left off.

"He says that happens from time to time. You ever sense that you were being followed?"

She shook her head, no, serious again.

"I was able to track that down. It turns out that Mr. John Lee of Lee Development hired Detective Bowman to keep an eye on your mom. Mr. Lee claims she was causing problems with some of his employees."

"Seriously?" She said, suddenly intrigued. "I thought that whole 'I'm being followed' thing was just in her imagination."

"So, you knew about it?"

"Only after she had hired you, I guess." She said a bit defensively, then added, "She came to tell me about you. She was so excited, like it was some big, mysterious adventure. I figured it was another one of her fantasy trips."

"Did she tell you she was having an affair?"

"You didn't seriously believe that, did you? That was definitely a fantasy. My mother would never cheat."

"Cheating on your spouse is second in popularity only to cheating on your taxes in my experience."

"I think I would know if she was seeing someone. Guys can never tell, but you can't hide it from another woman."

"Oh, really?" I take a long sip of coffee, trying to figure out this chameleon in front of me. "Do you know this, Mr. Lee?"

"I think he used to work for my dad, but now he's one of his competitors, I guess. I don't go out into the field. I just do office work, bookkeeping after school."

"Does your mother have any close friends?" I asked. "Someone she might go to with a problem?"

"I guess she has her friends. We all do, don't we? I don't know any of them well enough to say whether she would turn to one or another for help, though."

"Does she keep an address book? I could try contacting them and see if they've heard from her recently."

So Young gave me a look. "Address book? All her numbers are on her phone. Who keeps phone books anymore? She's not that old." She laughed.

"Yeah, I guess you're right. Times have changed."

"I wish I could help, but mother's few friends are a rather eclectic bunch, not especially Korean nor American."

"Anyone besides the ladies who lunch at the Founder's Club? Is there anyone whom you might also have a phone number for?"

She had to think for a minute. "No, I don't know anyone. Our lives don't cross paths much. She drags me to the club at least once a month. It's our mother-daughter thing. Sometimes we'll have lunch with other mother-daughter pairs, but they're not friends. They're white and patronizing. Mom can't see it, but I can tell. It makes me sad sometimes to see Mom try so hard to fit in. Sometimes we've gotten our hair done together. You could try mom's hairdresser. She's pretty friendly, Miss Jo. I'll send you her contact number."

"Things good at home between your parents?"

"As near as I can tell. I'm not there much, I have a room on campus. They get along. He treats her like a child, but then she acts like a child. It doesn't help that he's ten years older and looks old enough to be her father."

"Lots of people make it work with age differences bigger than that."

"I suppose. But Korean girls, at least from my mom's generation, mature later, emotionally, not physically. They don't have sex; they don't even date until they graduate from college. Then they get married, handed off from father to husband, one man to another."

"Your mother doesn't fit that stereotype."

She snorted sarcastically. "Ask me how many dates I had in high school." She asked, holding up her thumb and forefinger in the shape of a zero. "High school is too young to be dating. She'd say." So Young said, mocking her mother's voice.

"Well, you're in college now. You can make up for lost time."

"Yeah, right. As long as mother doesn't find out. I just hang out with my usual gang of friends. We group date. That's the Korean way."

"I've met your mom. She seems very Americanized."

"Maybe that's how she appears, but it's deeply cultural. Koreans treat their women like children. My dad has become the same way. When mom disappears for a day or two, he scolds her when she comes home."

"Well, since, according to your father, she is not really missing, I need something to track her down as soon as possible. What with Detective Bowman's murder and all ..."

"My father is in denial, or he's just lying." She cut me off. "I would know if she went back to Korea. She didn't."

"I guess I'll need you to talk with your father again. Or you'll somehow need to prove to me that she is really missing."

"Then, I will." She stood up suddenly, grabbed her books, and stormed away across the Quad without even saying goodbye.

Later that day, I was at this aquarium store in Hollywood, buying an aquarium tank and all the good stuff that goes with it: bubbler, multi-colored gravel, plastic kelp, the works.

My goldfish had suddenly stopped dying on me, and since I couldn't say no to Jimmy on the corner, I was up to four goldfish now, way too many for that one-gallon fish bowl. I drug it all up to the office and got it all set up, even found a place for Yoda in the kelp, his own private Dagobah.

When I poured the fish in, they seemed so happy. Feeding the fish, now I wondered: how did I look for a missing person if that person was not really missing? Either Alistair or So Young was lying, but who? Who had an angle here, and what was it? I could sort of understand Alistair covering up an embarrassing domestic situation, but what would motivate So Young to lie that her mother was missing if she wasn't? That didn't make any sense at all.

I contemplated getting Yana or Jack to tail So Young. Maybe she was meeting up with Mom in secret. I put that thought on the shelf to examine again later.

I decided to follow up on the only good avenue I had left and investigate Detective Miles Bowman retired. I picked up the paper. News of the officer's death was front page. Reading the articles didn't tell me anything I didn't already know. But a little research on the Internet and I learned that he had been fired from the force for assault.

Naturally, it didn't say he was fired. But the journalistic euphemisms translated into 'fired'.
And rumors of more than an assault popped up. Seemed he was also suspected of shaking down some local businessmen for off-duty security work. After leaving the force, he set himself up in private practice in Culver City.

Beautiful! I loved Culver City, such as 40s noir town, more of a James Ellroy kind of town than Raymond Chandler: oil fields, movie studios, speakeasies, a hot spot for murder, corruption, union battles, and Zoot Suit Riots.

CHAPTER

FIFTEEN

I decided Sunday morning would be a good time for a little black op. I laid out my kit: camera, check; gloves, check; lock picking kit, check. I was actually surprised how readily available lock-picking kits were for sale, even at Walmart. I bought the deluxe set from a site on the Internet. As I played with my toys, my phone buzzed. A quick glance showed my mother texting me yet another reminder of my blind dinner date with Rachel tonight.

I had seen this movie before. Mother's arranged dates were more like job interviews than social occasions.
The girls would all show up in high heels with clutch purses and pearls and conversations that ranged from name-dropping celebrities to dissing five-star vacation spots. I tried to run through in my mind some of the disastrous dinners she had conned me into before,
but the images were too fleeting. I must have repressed these memories into the deepest reaches of my mind.

At least it was a nice evening for a drive thru town in Lola with her top down. The So-Cal sun was too brutal to enjoy driving around topless. Summer nights were the best time to enjoy the perks of a convertible. I turned onto Sunset on my way to Mother's. Driving past the Marmont reminded me of the kind of date I'd rather be on. It didn't look like this case was going to end up in the penthouse, though, especially since I had somehow misplaced my client. Careless me.

The brightly lit animated billboards turned the night into day. The colored neon sights played across my windshield like a hippie's acid dream as I inched on down the strip.

Traffic was always worse on a Saturday night, but the people watching made up for it. As long as you weren't in a hurry, it was a nice enough drive, even at five miles an hour. The sidewalks were as packed as the street, not only with pedestrians, but with countless little Bistro tables, candlelight, bottles of wine, and happy, laughing diners.

As I never allowed enough time for traffic, I was fashionably late for dinner. Mother and Rachel were strolling the grounds, glasses of Merlot in hand, Mother pointing out her latest remodeling project. As long as she was working on the house, she wasn't working on me, so I was all for her little hobby.

"There you are." Mother called out as I climbed out of the car. "I thought you might have forgotten again."

"Evening, Mother." I gave her the obligatory peck on the cheek. "And you must be Rachel. Mother has told me so much about you." I said, feeling like an actor reciting his lines. She gave me her hand, and I swear the tiniest hint of a reflexive curtsey. She must have been a debutante — couldn't help herself.

I tried sizing her up without being too obvious about it, but women always know. Rachel was tall, maybe five-eight, and with heels almost as tall as me. She wore a sleeveless dress tonight, so I could see she was pretty slender, but not toned, probably not into sports. She had a pretty face set on a longish neck, sans pearls, but I'd be hard-pressed to describe it tomorrow. Her long brunette hair was brushed back from her face in a way that reminded me of Katherine Ross from the Graduate. I suddenly felt like Ben, being fixed up by my mother. You would think she would know by now that I'm more the Mrs. Robinson type.

"Would you like some wine, James?" Mother inquired.

"I'll get myself a scotch, thank you. Refills anyone?"

"I'll join you in a scotch, James," Rachel said as she separated herself from her mother and closed in on me. "You don't mind if I save the merlot for dinner, do you, Mrs. Gardinier?"

"No, of course not, Rachel, let me take your glass."

Good old mom, stepping back to let the young lioness stalk her prey. Rachel followed me to the sideboard, where I uncorked a decanter and poured us each a neat glass.

"Your mother tells me you're thinking of getting into banking." Rachel opened, then paused to slip her nose into the glass and take a deep sniff. She swirled the amber liquid once and took another smell. She took a good sip and let the whiskey sit in her mouth for a minute before swallowing. She knew how to drink scotch.

"Good stuff." She said, the offhand compliment of a connoisseur. "Now I'm going to smell like a campfire all night. So, banking?"

I laughed. "Ha, I passed on that offer. I already did my time in the financial world, two years at my dad's old firm after I graduated. I'm not cut out to be a paper shuffler. No, I'm sticking with my detective agency for now."

"Your what?"

"I have my own detective agency. Well, really just myself and some temporary help for now, but it's a start, and I'm enjoying myself. So, why the hell not?"

"So, a detective agency, huh. That's interesting." She said unconvincingly. "What inspired you to go in that direction?"

"Oh, I don't know. Maybe because I've always been enamored by the stories of Chandler and Ellroy, and Hammet. You know, the hard-boiled private eye who has the heart of gold and is never afraid to get a little dirty to do the right thing."

"You realize, of course, that those characters are all just fictional. In real life, you have your police detectives and then you have the guys who sneak around shooting photos through bedroom windows."

"And how do you come to know so much about detectives?"

"My father hired one a few years back to do some legwork for a case he had. It didn't go well. After that fiasco, I decided to do some research into the profession on my own, just to satisfy my own curiosity. I tend to be a bit of an internet junkie."

"So, you're dad's a lawyer?" I said as I started to lead her out to the rear patio.

"John Warren, of Warren, Marshall and Holmes."

"Doesn't ring a bell."

"They're like the top firm in town."

"Oh, right. Mother said you're a lawyer, also. You work at your dad's firm as an attorney, now?"

"I do, only for a few months so far."

"Where did you go to law school? Let me guess, Harvard?"

"Seriously? Stanford. Cardinals all the way!"

"No way. Me too!"

"Oh, really?"

For some reason, being a fellow alum did not seem to impress Rachel. Maybe I take a little of the shine off a Stanford degree.

"Are you working on a case now?" She asked, changing the subject.

"Yeah, sort of. It's not going as planned, though."

I didn't really want to explain it all to her, but she just sat there in the patio chair, swirling her drink in the glass and smiling, waiting for me to continue.

"I have a client; she's got a problem with this guy who has been following her around…"

"Like a stalker?"

"Not really. Another detective, a professional, who had been hired to follow her."

I continued, choosing my words carefully.

"My client thought her husband was behind it. Anyway, she wanted me to get him off her tail, so to speak. So, I intervened a couple of times, and then a few days ago, my client goes missing, and this other detective, who now turns out to be a retired cop, is found murdered. So then, of course, I get hauled in as a suspect."

"Well, that certainly sounds a lot more exciting than what I'm doing." She leaned forward, elbows on her knees as if truly interested. "So, what's your next step?"

"I can't really interfere with a police investigation, but I need to locate my client, so I guess I'll try to do that without crossing paths with the cops." I paused to down the rest of my drink. "Of course, that won't be easy since the cops are looking for her as well."

Just then, George silently appeared.

"Dinner is served." He intoned.

"To be continued." Rachel said with a mischievous smile, and we followed George to the dining room.

CHAPTER

SIXTEEN

At seven O'clock on Sunday morning, I was driving down Jefferson Boulevard. It was not so early as to invite suspicion, but early enough that there was no one else around. I drove by Detective Bowman's business address; it was in a small mini-mall, definitely low rent.

I drove slowly past and then circled back. Leaving my car a block away, I walked to the site. It had the usual mix of businesses: nail salon, dry cleaners, sandwich shop, and beauty supply. On the second floor was an insurance office, a cut-rate dentist, and Miles–Bowman's Security Services, it said on the door. The parking lot was empty. There was no elevator, so I took the stairs. From the second-floor walkway, I got a good look across the street at a series of oil pumpers, big black iron birds dipping their beaks in the hills, steady, hypnotically, endlessly. These hills had been pumping out oil for a hundred years and probably would continue for a hundred more.

It was late by the time I parked my car and walked to the building. Standing on the corner waiting for the light to turn, I couldn't help but it occurred to me that this wasn't the crime scene. Mejia had said Miles was killed somewhere in Solano Canyon. So why the tape? And how long had it been up? It had been almost a week since they hauled me in. I gloved up and pulled out my hand lock-picking tools and got to work. I could see traces of fingerprint powder on the door handle. I had practiced this at home and at the office; it was not so hard, but it was no snap, either. After about five minutes of fumbling around, I heard the telltale click, and I was in.

It was immediately obvious that maybe more than just the police had been here before. The place looked tossed in a way that only people who didn't care would go through it. They must have decided just to take everything and sort through it all later. Drawers were empty, file cabinets, too.

They had even unscrewed the air vent covers, looking for hiding places. All the electrical outlet covers had been removed and left lying on the floor. The leather chair behind the desk, apparently Miles' chair, had the back and seat coverings cut and peeled back. Well, somebody was looking pretty hard for something. There was a small toilet room in the back. The toilet tank cover was askew, kind of too obvious. They didn't have much respect for Miles's hiding prowess.

I stood in the middle of the room, slowly looking around. I wasn't going to find anything here. The place had been picked as clean as a dead cow at a buzzard convention. Except for a few pieces of junk mail on the floor next to an overturned waste basket, there wasn't a trace of Miles in this office.

I picked up scattered envelopes and flipped through them, credit card offers, Medicare supplement offers, vacation time share ads, the usual junk. They were all addressed to a house in Inglewood. That must be his home. He probably picked this all up from the mailbox on his way into work. Well, that saved me the trouble of looking up his home address. I quickly googled it on my phone. It was in an old neighborhood, backed up against the 405 Freeway. The street view just showed a typical 50s track home.

I circled back to La Cienega and drove through the Baldwin Hills to Inglewood, about a mile or two down the road, just south of Manchester. It's pretty much the next town south.

A nice little suburb, except that it lay directly under the flight path of the airlines coming into LAX. I circled the block slowly, checking for nosy neighbors, but it was still early. I parked a couple of houses away and walked back. A young Hispanic woman in bicycle shorts and a Laker jersey was walking her yellow lab down the sidewalk, nose buried in her cell phone; she didn't even look up.

Across the street, a man was tinkering with a lawnmower in his garage. He glanced up as I walked by, then returned to his repair work. Otherwise, the street was empty. I walked slowly past Miles' home.

It was a small California cottage with no police tape in sight.
It needed paint, a burnt lawn in front was edged with diseased and spider-webbed juniper hedges, and the Christmas lights still hung from the gutters, which sagged forlornly. A row of oil stains spotted the driveway like so many Rorschach tests. Behind the garage twelve-foot-tall tan cinder block sound wall separated the backyard from the freeway.

I stopped and glanced around once more. The Laker girl was blocks away, and the man in the garage must have gone inside.

I quickly walked back to the rear of the house and jimmied open the sliding glass door into a rear family room. I locked it behind me and pulled the curtains shut. The house looked searched as well, but this time they didn't take everything. Did they find what they were looking for? I wandered around, snapping pictures with my phone as I worked my way through the house. The house was fairly clean, but ancient; 1970's décor, ugly gold shag carpeting, worn thin and discolored, Naugahyde-covered sofa and recliner, TV trays in attendance, a stack of "outdoor" magazines listed against the ottoman. The only newish item was the flat screen mounted on the wall.

The air was stale and smelled of medicine. In the bedroom, I found a wedding picture. There were no other pictures of the wife anywhere in the house, so I assumed he was either widowed or divorced. No pictures of kids, either. The force must have been his life. Pictures of the Academy graduation and a commendation picture with the Chief adorned the wall of another bedroom. Apparently, he used this as a home office for his detective business. Here, the file cabinets and desk drawers had been emptied.

The living room looked unoccupied, like a room for guests who never visited. Multiple pictures of Miles, fly fishing on some scenic trout stream, some with Sam, hung askew on peeling wallpaper. One particularly old picture showed Miles and Sam in their younger days as bicycle cops at the beach, shorts, sunglasses, the works. I guess he and Mejia were good friends after all. A couple of prize fly rods hung above the pictures. I took a closer look, being sort of a fan. I was not very good at casting, but I liked to get my waders wet now and then. I noticed on one of the reels that the line was unraveling. The leader has been cut off.

Not very professional of him was my first reaction. The line wouldn't be usable again in that condition, not that Miles would care anymore, but it seemed unlike an avid fisherman to not take better care of his equipment. Then again, maybe he didn't. Maybe he didn't cut the line. Did the cops find something interesting on the hook? Just then, I heard the front door rattling. I froze, then moved quietly against the wall. The front door was locked and deadbolted. I waited.

A moment later, I saw the face of an older black man pressed against the window. It looked like the lawnmower repairman from across the street. He hooded his eyes with his hands as he peered into the living room. He must have seen me go around back, either that, or he was suspicious that I had suddenly disappeared.

"I know you're in there." He shouted.

"I'm calling the police!"

He crossed the street to his garage, looking back several times, then started up his mower and began cutting his grass, continuing to watch the house. I worked my way through the remaining rooms, then headed to the garage. Half the garage was full of junk, boxes and old tires, and more stacks of fishing magazines. Half of the room had been kept clear. Miles had a workbench there with a couple of tackle boxes and a fly-tying stand. I also found a file cabinet with his tax returns and still more back issues of Field and Stream.

I flipped through the most recent returns and found the 1099s. Miles had been working for Lee for some time. Even from before he was fired. I wondered if Sam worked or works, present tense, for Lee? That would be interesting.

It threw Sam's interest in the case into a whole new light.

I looked around some more. In the back bedroom he used as a storage room, I found empty packaging for SD cards for a digital camera. Digging around in the junk, I also found the foam cutout for a camera case. The shape of the cutout was for a telephoto lens.

Being the ace detective that I am, I quickly deduced that Miles had been taking pictures, and probably not of his fishing trophies. Were they pictures of Mimi or someone else, entirely unconnected? Further searching didn't turn up a camera or those memory cards. If they were here, Sam may have gotten them, but I was betting not.

I let myself out the back door and walked carefully around to the front, keeping an eye out for the nosy neighbor. The middle-aged black dude across the street, mowing his lawn, stopped and gave me a long look. This was the kind of neighborhood where you knew your neighbors even if you didn't talk to them.

Did he know Miles was dead? Did he see or hear about the police searching the house? Maybe it didn't mean anything, them being here. After all, Miles was a cop himself. I glanced towards him, neither wanting to make eye contact nor wanting to look guilty. Was he going to confront me? After a moment, he turned off his mower and went inside, probably to call the police. I kept walking to my car, trying not to look like I was fleeing.

I headed back to the office again, scouring the internet, this time for any pictures or stories about Miles, Sam Mejia, or Mr. Lee, hopefully together. I tried the LAPD official site, the police protective league, various police social groups, real estate sites, LA's city council news page, but struck out. A deep web search can be an adventure into itself.

Time passed unnoticed, you follow one link to another, wandering in the dark like a digital spelunker. You find a random picture here, a mention in an article there, but nothing substantive.

Finally, something, I ran across a picture of Mr. Lee was with a bunch of city officials, the mayor, councilmen, all the usual camera hogs. They were at a ribbon-cutting of some sort. Behind them was a small crowd of onlookers.

It was in the crowd, off to one side but pressed to the front, that I spied Mimi, not looking at the camera. I scanned the other faces for her husband, but Alistair was not there. So why was Mimi? Who was she looking at? I guessed Mr. Lee, although it could be any of the politicians beside him. Was Mimi on another make-believe adventure?

I kicked my shoes off, poured myself a drink, and dove in again, looking for more pictures, articles, anything on anyone connected to the case. I tried Facebook, Instagram, and Pinterest. It was a futile effort; this group just didn't use social media. One website blurred into the next as I tried all the browsers, even the really obscure ones that I had never heard of before I started this search. It was hard not to get distracted. So much information, so much useless trivia.

I didn't know my goldfish has a memory span of three seconds and that there are 336 dimples on a golf ball.

Fascinating.

CHAPTER

SEVENTEEN

I woke up with a start. I was on the couch again in my clothes. I should get a shower installed here, I thought, right after I start to keep a change of clothes in the closet. Falling asleep in the office was becoming a thing with me.

Yana stuck her head in the door.

"Pulling another all-nighter? I thought you would have had enough of that in school." She teased.

"Good morning to you, too, Yana."

"You know, you should keep a change of clothes here at the office."

"Why didn't I think of that? That's why I keep you around, I guess."

"I see you've been redecorating."

"Huh?"

"Aquarium?"

"Oh, yeah. Business is so good; Gardiner Investigations is expanding."

"You want me to get you a coffee while you freshen up?"

"I'd love a cup, Espresso with an extra shot."

"Um, yeah. I think your choices are, 'do you want fries with that?'"

Fifteen minutes later, Yana was back with a cup of something from the fast-food burger joint on the corner. But it was hot, and it was black and had caffeine. A couple of swallows and I was feeling awake, finally.

"So, how was your weekend?" Yana asked. "I see you didn't get beat up or arrested this time, so I'm guessing not all that exciting, huh?"

"Well, let's see. Saturday, I interviewed young Miss Kim again. She was very upset and insistent that her mother is indeed missing."

"Daughters can be like that when mom is suddenly not around anymore."

I decided not to mention my blind date with Rachel, not that it was all bad, it wasn't, but who wants to admit that their mother, who is obsessed with finding you a wife, might actually have hooked you up with someone you found interesting?

"Then yesterday I went by Detective Bowman's office in Culver City." I continued. "The police had already been there, of course, and they'd pretty much stripped it bare."

"I'm sure they had it taped off. Don't tell me you went in."

"Would I do that?" I asked. "They didn't leave me much to sift through anyway."

"Not even a discarded matchbook from some exotic nightclub with a mysterious phone number written inside?"

"You know, ever since people stopped smoking, the detective business has gotten much harder. I was able to glean his home address from some junk mail in the waste basket, so I drove down to Inglewood and checked it out."

"What kind of time are you looking at for two counts of breaking and entering?"

"You're the law student, you tell me."

"I only study contract law, not criminal. I'm not up on the latest sentencing guidelines."

"The cops had been to his house as well, but they left most of his stuff there. Maybe there was just too much junk to carry off. It's amazing how much crap you accumulate over the years. You know?"

"Well, did you find out anything there?"

"Yeah. Miles was quite the fly fisherman. Tied his own flies and everything."

"Boy, Marlowe is on the case!" she teased.

"But," I said, holding up a finger for effect. "Last night I found this."

I ran back into my office and printed out the picture I found on the internet. Yana followed me. As we both watched it print out, I continued. "I don't think Lee was being entirely truthful when he said he didn't know Mimi."

I pointed them out to Yana. "That's Lee, and over here is Mimi." Yana pulled it out of the printer. "Well, this doesn't prove anything. They're in the same photo, but it's not like they're standing together. It doesn't look like he even knows she's there."

She handed me the picture. "So, what is it that you are looking for?"

"I don't know. Who killed Miles, for starters?"

At that moment, the front office door opened. So Young stood there, again, on the verge of tears. She marched into my office, opened her backpack, and threw something from it onto my desk.

"There! There's your proof!" she shouted.

"What's this?" I said as I picked it up. It was Mimi's American passport.

"She didn't go to Korea without her passport." She plopped down in the chair.

I flipped through the booklet. Mimi was forty, a mere twenty years older than her daughter. The pages showed she was a regular traveler to Korea. The last stamp was from six months ago.

I looked up to see Yana had discreetly slipped back to the outer office and closed the door.

"You're right. This proves she hasn't left the country. It also proves your father lied to me. Why do you think he did that?"

"I don't know." She slumped down into her seat, letting her backpack drop to the floor with a soft thud. "He's always covering for her when she goes off on some delusional misadventure."

"Maybe that's what's going on again, now."

"No, it's different this time. It's been almost a week she's gone. Something's wrong. I know it."

"What does your father say?"

"He won't talk about it."

"Where would she go? Would she stay with a friend?"

"Mom doesn't have any friends like that, not really."

"She must have some friends, maybe not BFFs. Who does she chat with?"

"I don't know, her hairdresser, maybe. Did you talk to her? I sent you her number." She began to cry.

"Actually, you didn't," I muttered and went out to the little refrigerator in Yana's office to grab a bottle of water.

The fridge was empty, so I had to crack open a new case from the closet for a warm bottle. When I returned, So Young was standing by the window, dabbing at her eyes with a handkerchief. I gave her the water and grabbed the picture I had just printed off my desk.

"Do you know this guy?" I pointed to Lee. She shook her head. "Do you know any of these men?"

So Young gave it a good, long look but shook her head 'no' again and then noticed her mother.

"That's mother!"

"I think your mother was stalking Mr. Lee. He claimed she was following someone else at his company and that he didn't know her, but I don't believe him. I think Lee knew her from Korea."

"I wouldn't know. Mom doesn't ever talk about her life in Korea."

"Did your parents ever tell you the story about how they met?"

"What do you mean, story?"

"Every married couple has that one cute story they tell when asked how they met."

"Oh. Yeah, I guess they have their story. They met in a bar in Seoul. Mom was working there as a cocktail waitress. It was a country western bar that catered to Americans. Mom said she had to wear cowboy boots, denim short shorts, and a red and white plaid shirt with the shirt tails tied in a knot in front to show off her belly. She said they were told that was the style in Texas."

"No cowboy hats? Sounds like the Hooters' dress code. I didn't know Koreans were into America's Wild West heritage." I added.

"They aren't. Those bars are aimed at the GIs. Koreans never go there; in fact, they are discouraged from going in."

"Why is that?"

"Just to keep trouble away. A bunch of drunk Korean guys seeing American boys hitting on their women, you can guess what usually follows."

"Yeah, makes sense, I suppose."

"Anyway, the story goes that one time Mom asked him which beer he liked best, and father answered that he really didn't like beer at all, was more of a gin and tonic drinker. Mom thought that was pretty funny."

"Why was that?"

"The bar only had a license to serve beer."

"Oh. So, I guess he wasn't coming there for the drinks."

"Yeah, seems not. That must have been what sold Mom on him." She took a drink from her little bottle, and we let the silence linger for a while.

"Does your father have any property in Solano Canyon?" I asked, pretending to change the subject.

"I don't know. I suppose I could find out for you."

"Do you know if there has been a history of vandalism or any physical violence associated with any of your father's properties?"

"Just the usual graffiti, some neighborhood protests about gentrification, but nothing that father was ever worried about. Why do you ask?"

"I think your mother might have gotten mixed up in some rivalry between your father and this Mr. Lee."

"But she was never involved in father's business in any way. I think my father didn't think she was smart enough to be of any help."

I found myself staring at her as she dabbed her tears with a tissue. She was dressed differently today, scruffy jeans and brightly colored Vans, a coordinated flannel shirt, and a sock cap – very hipster-ish. This girl had a lot of different looks.

"Are you hungry? You want to get a bite to eat?" I asked. "I know a place nearby."

She looked up at me and blew her nose. "I could eat. Sure, why not?"

I took her to a little falafel shop down the street. There were not a lot of good Asian choices in Hollywood, but I didn't figure her for one of those who had to have kimchi and rice with every meal.
We both had a couple of shawarmas and tabbouleh salads and ate in silence. I could see that her mood was lightening.

"Rude question, just where did you grow up? You don't have any accent." I ask, breaking the ice.

"Yes, but I guess I speak Korean with an American accent. Or so they tell me."

"Do you go back often?"

"I used to when I was little. Not so much anymore. It's been more than a few years since I've been back."

"You and your parents don't go back to visit friends and relatives, your grandparents?"

"Only, to see my grandparents. Mother doesn't really have many connections there other than them."

"They live in Seoul?"

"No, they lived in the country, near Taegu. Do you know where that is?"

I shook my head no.

"But they live here now. My mother finally got them visas to move to America to be near us. What about you?" she asked. "I hear everyone in L.A. is from someplace else."

"No, not me, I'm a native, born and raised in Beverly Hills."

She laughed. "You must have had a charmed childhood."

"I can't complain. My parents are divorced, but half the kids in

America can say that."

"Still, that always hurts."

"I was grown, already away at college. I guess my dad never really wanted to be the family man. He was always about his career, so he stuck it out till I was grown, then packed up and moved to Manhattan."

"But you didn't hate him for that."

"Oddly, no. He was never there for me growing up. I guess I got used to it, just me and mother and the help."

"No brothers or sisters?"

"I have a stepsister, from my dad's first wife. But she was eight or nine years older, so I didn't really know her. She was off to college before I hit middle school. When my dad left, Muggs - Margaret never came by again. I haven't heard from her in over ten years."

"You're even more deprived than me."

"Yes, we're a pair all right, a pair of poor little rich kids feeling sorry for themselves."

"Pathetic, aren't we?" she chimed in. "So, what are you doing in this part of town, slumming?"

"No, I like it here. I have this nostalgic thing for old Hollywood, that 30s and 40s scene from the old movies. You know, Humphrey Bogart, Robert Mitchum."

"I don't know who they are, but you see yourself as someone like them?"

"Oh, no, I'm not a tough guy. I just like the romance of it all."

"So, you're a romantic guy then."

"I wouldn't go there, either, not with my track record."

"Maybe your luck will change." So Young looked me in the eyes and gave me more mixed signals than a navy flagman with Tourette's syndrome.

I walked So Young back to her car and had her text me the name and address of the hairdresser. Then, I returned to my office and dove once again into the bowels of the internet. I was still staring at the photo of Lee and the councilmen with Mimi in the background looking on. I recognized one of the politicians, the tall hard hard-looking Clint Eastwood type. He was the guy on the flyer, the military dude at the Club where I dropped off Mimi's burner phone. Messer, Arnold Messer was the name. Now, where had I seen that name before? I grabbed the folder where I saved all the leaflets from Solano Canyon and flipped through them. Yes, there he was, running for mayor. Damn, you would think I would know that. But then again, I never paid much attention to politics. Could this be Lee's inside man? Was Lee funding his mayoral run- in exchange for some payback with grease on his development projects? What did any of that have to do with Mimi or Miles?

I sat down at my computer and dug into Messer's life story. There was plenty on that, what with his bid for higher office – distinguished military service, Army Ranger, two tours of duty in South Korea, among other places. I'll bet that's where he met Lee. Coincidence? Could be, but always better to assume not. He was still in his first term as a city councilman and already running for mayor. This guy didn't believe in paying his dues, just jumped the queue.

Playing a hunch, I tried looking up Miles' biography. Maybe he was in the army at the same time as Messer. No luck finding anything on Miles. Not surprised, not everyone on the planet has their life on display on the internet. Hardly any mention of Miles at all. Even his death was just a few lines – retired LAPD, now in private practice, found dead, shot, in his car on Bouett Street.

I looked that up. Surprise, surprise, it was in Solano Canyon.

I ran home for a quick shower and a change of clothes and switched cars. The Mercury just draws too much attention.
It was time to be more incognito. I also ditched the fedora for a golf cap. No more playing –doing, I told myself.

At the top of the canyon, the road took you into the park and eventually to one of the Dodger Stadium gates, but a left at Bouett Street took you to a service road, a dead end that stops above the canyon and below a reservoir. Of course, there were Water and Power signs everywhere warning about not trespassing, and the entrance was chained off, but easy enough to step over and a short walk to the end of the road. The road ended at a steep cliff face overlooking the old Pasadena Freeway, the first freeway in Los Angeles. Above and to my right was the reservoir, below and left was Solano Canyon. Straight ahead, beyond the freeway, was Chinatown, and beyond that the skyscrapers of downtown. It was plenty hot again today, now two weeks straight of hundred-degree days, and I was already sweating through my fresh clothes. I took off my hat and wiped my brow with a handkerchief.

For a moment, I felt like I was channeling Jake Gittes. There was nothing to see here, a blacktop road, scrubby hillsides. A little fragment of yellow police tape, still tied to the chain across the road, was the only evidence that nothing at all had transpired here. I stared down into the canyon. It was a sleepy little neighborhood: no thru traffic shortcutting to the city to clog up the streets, no big apartment complexes, no retail. There was not even a good view of the Lachlan's rental house from here. Not likely that he was sitting here on a stakeout, maybe a meet-up? What was

it about this corner of Los Angeles that drew Miles to his death?
What had Mimi gotten herself mixed up in?

As I drove out of the canyon through the neighborhood, I snapped
a few pictures of graffiti and what looked like gang tags.
They were mostly in Spanish and what looked like a mixture of Korean
and English. As I was driving and snapping, I got the evil eye from those
four youths who so kindly greeted me on my first visit. I just lowered the
brim of my cap and kept driving.

Koreatown wasn't too far out of the way, so I decided to see
if I could find Mimi's hair stylist. The salon was on Western,
the main drag. It was a big place – dozens of chairs, each sectioned off
with curtains for a little privacy. I asked the receptionist for Miss Jo. She
pointed me toward a middle-aged woman sweeping up her area.

Feeling more than a little out of place, I walked over to her station.
"Excuse me, Miss Jo, I was wondering if I could ask you a few questions
about a client of yours, Mrs. Lachlan. Maybe you know her as Mimi Kim?"
She looked up from her sweeping with narrowed eyes but said nothing.
Ms. Jo was a very thin woman. I guessed about Mimi's age, but with a
darker complexion and more lines in her face. She wore her hair in a very
curly perm – a little walking advert, I guessed.

"I'm a private detective." I showed her my badge and ID. "One of
your customers, Mrs. Lachlan, has been reported missing. I was wondering
when you saw her last."

She made me wait a bit before she decided to answer.

"A week ago." Was her terse reply.

"A week ago, like last Monday, or Tuesday? Do you know exactly?"

She walked over to her appointment book. "Monday, Two
O'clock, with daughter."

Funny, So Young didn't mention that part. Still, Mimi couldn't have been concerned about Bowman following her to the hairdresser. She must have met her mysterious someone before that.

"How long was their appointment?"

"Daughter was first, half hour, just for trim. Mimi was one hour, cut and color."

"So Young waited for her mother?"

"Of course."

I must have seen Mimi at the house with her parents shortly after she'd had her hair done. I guess So Young went back to school.

"How long have you known Mimi?"
The hairdresser had been very suspicious at first, but I figured if I could just get her talking, she might open up a bit with something useful.

"About ten years, I guess. She comes about once a month."

"So, you are good friends?"

"We don't see each other outside of the salon, but we are friendly."

"I see. Do you know any of her other friends or family? I'm trying to find someone who might be able to help me find her."

"Husband, daughter, cousin, not too many friends, at least she doesn't come with a friend to get her hair cut. Only sometimes her daughter comes."

"A cousin? Do you know his or her name?"

"Mr. Lee, but they are not friends, she wouldn't go to him. They don't talk to each other, not for a long time."

"Family squabble?"

"Yeah, she says he cheated her husband's business. Stole his best client and started his own company. They never talked after that."

"Wait, you mean Mr. Lee, who worked for Mr. Lachlan in Korea?"

"Yeah, he's the one."

"Oh, really? They never mentioned that he was family. I suppose that Mimi prevailed on her boyfriend at the time to give her cousin a job."

"Oh, he knew Mr. Lachlan first, introduced him to Mimi. She was pregnant with no husband. That's very bad in Korea. But Mr. Lachlan was a good man. He agreed to marry her and take care of her and the baby. Of course, didn't hurt that Mimi was the prettiest girl in all Korea."

She said with a knowing smile.

"No, that would seal the deal for a lot of guys. I suppose then, Mimi sponsored her cousin to come to the States later." I said more to myself. My mind was racing with all this new information. So many secrets with this family. I wondered if So Young knew about Lee. Everyone seemed to have their own version of this story, a real Rashomon. I owed some people a second visit.

"So, you said not too many friends. Did she have any friends, even one, who she talked with?"

"Maybe Mrs. Jun. She's the only friend, I guess. They sometimes have coffee after hair if they're here the same day."

"How do I get a hold of this, Mrs. Jun? Do you have a phone number?"

"No, I have no phone numbers of clients. They call me."

"Well, is she due for a trim any time soon?"

Miss Jo consulted her appointment book again. "Wednesday, three o'clock."

"Thanks. When you saw Mimi on Monday, did she seem upset or act differently than usual?"

"No, she seemed happy, laugh and chat with daughter. She told a funny story about some man following her, getting arrested at the park that morning."

"Oh, really. She thought that was a funny story."

I left her my card and asked her to call me if she heard from Mimi again, then walked out onto the avenue.

It dawned on me that I hadn't eaten since that shawarma this morning, so I thought about some place to get food as I drove home. Hollywood Boulevard, east of the freeway, used to be the 'down and out' side of town, the 'other side of the tracks' if you will, that never got any respect. West of the freeway, where all the tourist attractions were - the Walk of Fame, the theaters, and faux museums. If some poor rube drove too far east, he'd think he wandered onto skid row. It was mostly pawn shops, tattoo parlors, and dive bars, but I liked the east side better. It still had an air of old Hollywood, a lot of the old buildings hadn't yet been torn down, and the streetlights were still the same as fifty years ago. I had a favorite dive there, the Brasher Doubloon. The food was nothing to write home about, but they have a great scotch selection and a generous pour.

On the weekends, they had a mixologist behind the bar and more of a hipster clientele. Yeah, they were moving in and taking over, but it was early and a Monday to boot, Mitch was pouring the drinks today. Mitch was eighty, at least; the whiskers on his chin were whiter and more plentiful than those on the top of his head, and if you asked for soda with your scotch, he would probably throw you out. 'Neat, with a water back.' That's what he liked to hear, and that's what I always ordered.

Sometimes I thought my friend Jack had put a GPS tracker on my phone. I'd looked for it on occasion but never found one. He always seemed to know where I was at. Before I'd even finished half my drink,

Jack plopped down beside me. To be fair, Jack comes here more than I do. In fact, it was he who first introduced me to the place. Mitch doesn't even have to ask, just slid a double Jack in front of him. Yes, Jack drinks Jack. It gets old fast.

Jack was a great guy to talk to; he was a good listener. You could air things out with him, bounce ideas around, question yourself, voice all your doubts and fears, if you asked a rhetorical question, he didn't answer. We talked about the Dodgers instead.

"I hear the Giants are in town for a four-game series. Wanna go?"

Everyone in L.A. hates the Giants, even if you never went to the ball games and could not name a single player, you could find it in your heart to hate the Giants.

Jack shrugged. "Nah, it'll be too crowded. I prefer going to games nobody else wants to see."

"Well, I think they've got a good team this year," I noted. "I don't imagine you will find many games empty enough for your liking. Everybody loves a winner, especially in L.A."

"Who's pitching?"

"You're asking me? I don't follow baseball. I just go for the hot dogs."

Jack ordered another round for the two of us. "I hear from Yana that you got busted again."

Yana was not one to gossip, but then Jack was almost an employee, so I guess I couldn't fault her for telling him.

"Not really, 'again'. That first time didn't count."

I gave Jack the rundown of my past week, everything since my getting beaten up, which was the last time I'd seen him.

"And now I find out everyone I've been talking to has either been lying or hiding stuff from me."

I downed my drink and banged the empty glass on the bar in a show of righteous frustration.

"You expected something different?" Jack replied with mock surprise.

"I also think there's some kind of funny business going on in that neighborhood below the ballpark. Those kids who attacked me, they thought I was some sort of developer or a real estate agent. I think they feel like someone's buying up the neighborhood, forcing out the people who used to live there. I mean, I'm not an expert or anything, but that place doesn't strike me as particularly ripe for gentrification."

"You never know these days," Jack replied. "It's not that far from downtown, short commute. It might have that kind of appeal."

"I don't know. Neighborhoods usually change slowly. This seems more like a concerted effort. I grabbed a bunch of flyers looking for houses for sale when I was there."

"Maybe it's up for rezoning."

"You mean for apartments?"

"Or the casino."

"What casino?"

"The casino bond proposition., Jimbo. It's on the November ballot. It's in all the papers like every week. You read the papers. Everybody in town knows about it. Everybody except you, I guess."

As we were talking, I got a text from Rachel. *"You were going to call."* I texted back, *"Sorry, been busy. What are you doing tomorrow night?"* I hadn't meant to blow her off. I really had been busy. I returned to the conversation at hand.

"So, they're thinking about building a casino in Solano Canyon?"

"Nobody knows where just yet," Jack informed me. "There are lots of places being floated around, though I don't recall Solano being one of them."

"How are they going to get a casino approved anywhere? Aren't there laws against that sort of thing?"

As Professor Jack filled me in, beginning at the beginning, about a group of Native Americans claiming to represent the Tongva tribe who wanted to build a casino in downtown L.A. I half listened while keeping a text conversation with Rachel going on my phone.

"What did you have in mind?" – Rachel texted.

"Now, the Tongva Indians were the original settlers of the Los Angeles basin and have records showing their being here when the Spanish arrived." Jack droned on.

"This group said they had the land and demanded the same rights as other tribes in the state."

"Dinner? Any good movies playing?" – Me.

"Of course, there were multiple sides to the issue now." Jack went on with me only half listening.

"Nothing I'm dying to see." – Rachel.

"Tribes that owned big casinos in Palm Springs and Santa Barbara, currently the two nearest to L.A., were against it. Not to mention the card palaces that I play at. Even some members of the Tongvas said this group didn't speak for the tribe." Jack explained. "Both sides were bitterly entrenched, and secret money was flowing into each side."

"Isn't there a casino in Commerce? Where is this land?" I asked, suddenly looking up.

I motioned to Jack, asking if he wanted another round. Jack asked for a menu and continued with his history lesson.

"They're getting closer all the time. Apparently, their land is just a single city block, apartments, or a parking lot or something, totally inadequate, and everybody involved knows it. But it's downtown!" He said before finishing his drink and motioning for another.

"There's a Bogart festival at the Beverly." I texted.

"It's just a bluff, or you can call it blackmail." Jack continued. "They are trying to force the city to accept the casino in principle, and the site will be worked out later in some back-room dealings. The latest speculation is that they're looking across the 5 at Aliso Village or Boyle Heights. Now those residents have gotten wind of it and are up in arms as well."

"When did you suddenly become the expert on this?" I asked.
"I've got a buddy who is a stringer for the paper. He covers City Hall for them and writes a blog about local politics. It's all he ever talks about."

Mitch slid another double Jack down the bar. It coasted to a stop like it had eyes.

"Twist my arm and I'll go." – Rachel.

"I can put you in touch with him if you want. His name's Ted Carmady. He could use some dough, if you know what I mean. Newspaper biz doesn't pay like it used to. Everybody's on consignment. Paid by the word. Either that or their blogging on Substack. I think I have his card somewhere."

Jack pulled out a thick wallet, bulging with cards, both credit and business, scraps of paper, and a few odd dollars. It was held together by a fat rubber band. He unwound it and fumbled through the contents before finally fishing out a dog-eared card, handing it to me. It was a plain card, no pictures, but the basics set in a typewriter font – cute.

"Thanks. Maybe I will. Wow. People still have cards?" I mused aloud as I stuck it in my pocket with my own. "What's this bond measure about?" I asked. "I've got to start paying more attention to the news."

"Money to fund the land purchase," Jack replied. "Investors will fund the construction, but the city is going to have to buy the land and swap it for whatever the Tongvas are pushing."

"It's a date. I'll pick you up at seven." I texted back to her.

"How much are we talking about?" I asked.

"Two hundred million is what's on the ballot."

I choked a little on my drink. "Wow! If Lee or Lachlan or someone was a front for running the real estate action, they could clean up."

"You mean if they had inside info on where the casino would land, they could buy up the land cheap and hold out for top price with the city."

"It's a scam as old as they come."

Jack's sandwich came, and he dug in. I played with my drink, thinking. "I've got a job for you, Jack," I said.

"I need you to go downtown to the assessor's office and see what kind of trends you can find in recent real estate transactions. The ones we are looking for will probably be corporations on title, shell companies to hide the real owners. But if there's a run on land in Boyle Heights or nearby, it should show up."

Jack nodded, chewing and saying nothing. I gave Mitch the high sign for the check.

"On me this time, buddy." Jack says, not looking up.

I give him a side-eye glance. He gives me a smile back.

"My fortunes have turned. Lady Luck is back on my shoulder."

"Do tell." I said with a smile.

"I cleared five grand last night. Nothing helps you reel 'em in better than having a sudden change in the cards after a long, cold spell. They sensed desperation, like sharks, they smelled blood in the water, but they didn't know I was chumming them, luring them in for the hook."

"Well, good for you, Jack, and thanks for the drinks."

CHAPTER

EIGHTEEN

Tuesday morning, I drove around Boyle Heights checking out the neighborhood. The Heights has always been one of the poorer neighborhoods on the East side of the LA River, this town's version of the wrong side of the tracks, if you will. It's been home to one ethnic minority after another: the Japanese, the Jews, the Russians. Now it was a Hispanic community

. Before, there was never much gentrification pressure on this neighborhood. L.A. went in for sprawl rather than denser growth downtown. But everything is cyclical, and now downtown is booming again, and the fringe neighborhoods, including Boyle Heights, are facing pressure from developers catering to the young and the hip. I didn't know my way around this part of town and got lost more than once.

When I got back to my office, a package from So Young was waiting for me. She had brought some records from her father's office of all his real estate transactions. I checked my watch. I could spare about an hour looking over this stuff before I needed to head home to clean up for my date. I started to spread the files out on my desk, separating the Solano Canyon properties into one pile apart from the rest. I didn't know what I was expecting to find, a clue somewhere, a pattern maybe.

I wasn't familiar with the streets. I started to look them up on my Google maps app when it occurred to me that I had an actual paper map in the office. I dug through the bottom drawer of my file cabinet, under piles of old take-out menus, and fished out an even older Thomas Map Book. Funny how something once so ubiquitous could so quickly become obsolete.

I began diligently circling the addresses of the Lachlan properties. Just then, I heard the front door loudly bang open. Detective Mejia barged in with two other officers in tow.

"I'm sorry, I didn't hear you knock" I said as I turned around. Mejia waves a couple of pieces of paper around before dropping them on Yana's desk. He stood for a minute in the doorway, expressionless, dead eyes, perhaps thinking of some witty retort to mine.

"I guess I wasn't clear enough when I told you to lay off." He said, like a teacher to his failing student. "You're not a detective. You're just some kid, running around, breaking into other people's offices and homes, trespassing on crime scenes and other restricted city property, and generally sticking your nose where it doesn't belong."

I shook my head with disbelief and looked to Mejia with a "you've got to be kidding me" expression.

"Have you been following me?" I asked. I walked over to the desk to look at what he had tossed there. He'd gotten one warrant to search my office, and another one for my arrest.

"I gave you too much credit. Thought you might actually uncover something we missed." He laughed.

"Did you know Lee is Mrs. Lachlan's cousin?" I pronounced proudly, thinking I'd throw him.

"It's on his visa paperwork; she sponsored him." Mejia did not have time or patience for my amateur sleuthing.

"Well." I stalled, scrambling for anything to re-establish some credibility. "Did you find Bowman's cell phone?"

"What makes you think we don't have it?"

"It wasn't in the evidence bag when you emptied it onto the interrogation table and pulled out my burner. Obviously, someone left mine there as a plant and took his."

"Cuff him." Mejia directed one of the officers.

"Then again, you probably already knew he was snooping, taking pictures." I continued as they roughly handcuffed my wrists behind my back. "He kept them on separate SD cards, you know. I assume he might still have had some on his phone as well. I'd wager some people might want to see those. Don't you?"

Mejia said nothing, just jerked his head slightly, and the officers pushed me out the door.

Hours later, at the station, I was sitting again in the interrogation room. Mejia was flipping through papers in a file, ignoring me.

"How long have you been carrying water for Mr. Lee?" I asked.

"I'll ask the questions, and you'll answer them." He replied tersely.

He continued to ignore me until another officer entered and dropped an evidence envelope onto the table. Mejia already knew what was inside, but he pretended to be surprised for my sake. He shook out a 22-caliber pistol with a floral-engraved slide and a dark wood grip.

"Recognize this?"

"Nope." I said, though it did look like the automatic Mimi had in her purse that first day.

"Found it in your office, tucked in the back of a file drawer. Think we will find your prints on it?"

"I'm gonna say... no."

"Yeah, you're at least smart enough to wipe it down. Same

caliber as the gun that plugged Miles, though. Think ballistics will make a match?"

"Seeing as you've already had several hours to run a test, I'm guessing you already know the answer to that."

"Yeah. It's a match. Pretty stupid of you not to hide it in a better place."

"Yeah," I fumbled for a reply, "that was pretty careless of me, wasn't it? What was I thinking?" My mind was racing now. I couldn't believe Mejia would plant that on me. I knew I was rubbing him the wrong way, but this was pretty extreme.

"I'm going to have to book you." He looked at his watch. "Your mommy and her lawyer must be caught in traffic. I would have expected them to be here by now. Or maybe they're just as fed up with their little make-believe private eye as I am."

He got up and left, and I mentally shouted at him, 'well, maybe if someone were to let me make another phone call, I could let her know that I'm down here!'

But I just smiled at the one-way mirror and figured patience would win out. I was really working on the patience thing, now. I was in lock-up, didn't have a watch, and they took my phone, so I had no idea how long I had been sitting here cooling my heels. I was guessing it had been a few hours. Maybe Mejia was right, maybe my mother was going to let me stew for a while to teach me a lesson, although that's not like her. Her style is more - bail out my baby as soon as possible, and then spend the next however many hours laying on the guilt trip.

In anticipation of this tongue-lashing, I prepared my defense. Anyone who might have a chance to look into my cell could easily have mistaken me for Norman Bates as I played both roles in this fantasy conversation with my mother. When at last the jailer came to announce that bail had been posted and I was free to go. I collected my things at the window, including my phone. There was half a dozen missed calls from Rachel. It was ten o'clock already.

"Oh, shit." I thought. "I've stood her up. I'll never hear the end of this."

I steeled myself for the face-to-face with my mother. When I opened the door to the lobby, it was So Young who stood there waiting for me. I quickly searched the shadows just in case mother was lying in wait to pounce on me unexpectedly.

"You posted bail?" I asked her.

"Yes, it wasn't all that much. I have a savings account for my tuition. I used that." She added in a loud whisper, "I knew that no judge would buy that you did anything, a privileged, rich white boy like yourself. The cops are just jerking your chain."

"What do you mean? How did you know I had been arrested anyway?"

"I came back to your office with another box of files, and your secretary told me. I was so worried that I came right down. They didn't beat you up again or anything, did they?" She grabbed my chin, turning my face this way and that, playfully searching for bruises.

"They didn't beat me up the first time."

Then, she drove me home. Being polite, I invited her in.

"You didn't have to bail me out? I could have handled it myself. I mean, I have people who can do that for me."

"Who, that girl in your office?"

"Yana? No, I haven't set her up with access to my account. I should probably do that if I'm going to keep getting arrested like nobody's business. No, I have a lawyer. Yana was supposed to call my lawyer."

"Anyway, I don't expect you will ditch bail on me, will you?" She teased as she wandered around my living room, picking up and examining things like she was in some gift shop. "Got anything to drink?"

"Sure, in the kitchen. What would you like?"

I headed for the kitchen and stuck my head in the cupboard, pulling out bottles. "Tequila, vodka, gin?"

"Make me a gin and tonic." She called out from the living room.

"I don't think I have any limes." I hollered back.

"That's okay. You live here alone?"

"Yeah, no roommates."

"I mean, no lady in your life? Things at work keep you too busy, do they?"

"What is that supposed to mean?" I said defensively. "If you've been hearing things about me, it's a lot of exaggeration. And before you even ask, I did not sleep with your mother."

"Whoa, whoa, James, why would you say such a thing? I was not even going there. But since you brought it up, maybe I should be asking around a little more. You may be more of a bad ass than I took you for."

I brought her the drink. "Sorry, I guess that was a little outrageous. In my business, people say a lot of things that aren't true. I guess it comes with the territory."

"You not drinking?"

"I will, I just want to change out of these clothes first."

"Ha! That's supposed to be my line."

"Now, who's going there? Oh, since you're here, maybe you could translate some Korean graffiti I spotted. I took some pictures."

I scrolled through the pictures on my phone for her to see. "I'm thinking John Lee may have hired a Korean gang to intimidate the residents, and these are their gang signs."

"It says 'Korean Boys', Korean in Hangul and Boys in English, but it's totally bogus."

"What do you mean?"

"This character, the Riul, it's the Korean 'R', it's backwards."

"You mean like the 'R' in Toys-R-Us."

"Well, that's intentional, to make it look childish. We don't do that in Korean. Whoever spray-painted this tag wasn't Korean."

"It could just be a slip-up," I argued.

"No Korean would ever make that mistake. It's just not possible. Some ignorant fool is trying to make it look like there's a Korean gang presence there."

I thought about that for a moment and then made a quick exit to my bedroom to change, leaving So Young to poke around freely. My place was pretty spare; I didn't go in for nesting, but the few things I did have laying around would probably seem interesting to the casual observer or baffling to someone trying to size me up based on my possessions.

"Where did you take those pictures of the graffiti?" She called out.

"This neighborhood is called Solano Canyon. That was where I followed your mom. I think she may have accidentally gotten herself caught up in some shady dealings." I shouted, trying to continue the conversation from across the house. "I don't know what it is yet, maybe some sort of real estate scam, but it is big enough that someone's willing to kill a retired cop to keep it quiet."

It was all quiet on her side.

"Still, I'm pretty sure your father's former partner and now competitor, Mr. Lee, is involved somehow. He seemed pretty gangster when I met him in his office." I grabbed whatever was on top in my dresser drawer and dressed quickly.

"Speaking of Mr. Lee, you never mentioned he was your mother's cousin, or maybe you didn't know. I remember you telling me that your mom didn't like to talk about her life in Korea. But, still, he is family. That's a pretty important detail to leave out."

I walked back into the living room in some long surf shorts and a Stanford Cardinals Tee.

"I take it you haven't heard from your mother yet."

So Young was sitting on the window seat, staring out into the darkness. It was very quiet up here in the hills. My street doesn't have many streetlights, and the nearest one is blocked by trees, so it was also very dark outside.

I could see her face in the reflection in the window. I could also see she'd been crying again. I walked up behind her and put my hands on her shoulders. She caught sight of my face in the glass and quickly dabbed her eyes dry, then turned around and gave me a hug, burying her face in my chest. I hugged her back.

We stood there at the window for a minute or two, just holding each other. She looked up, her eyes wet and mascara starting to run, and I gave her a brotherly little kiss on her forehead. She tilted her face up, and I kissed her again on the lips. Suddenly, she grabbed me like a drowning swimmer and kissed me fiercely, harder than I had ever been kissed before.

CHAPTER

NINETEEN

It had been more than a few years since I had slept with a girl as young as So Young. I had forgotten how awkward it was back in my college days, when I was so much less experienced. I was a virgin all through high school. I didn't get lucky until a wild summer after I graduated. I can't for the life of me even remember my first time, though I'm sure it was embarrassing. Now, I almost felt like a teenager again.

She seemed a bit shy and awkward herself, making sure all the lights were out before crawling under the sheets, still in her bra and panties. But she was naked soon enough.

Her hair was thick and smelled slightly of coconut. I had noticed how silky soft her skin was when I helped her out of her clothes. We didn't say a word, no screaming or moaning, we didn't make any sound at all. It wasn't wild and passionate sex like I was becoming used to with women trying to prove they were still attractive to a much younger man. This was tentative and virginal. I felt like I was having sex in a church, trying not to be discovered by the pews full of nuns. Maybe the owls in the trees were watching the show. Theirs were the only sounds that night.

Was it pity sex? No. Opportunistic sex? Certainly. I lay in the bed, staring at the ceiling long after I thought she had closed her eyes. I listened to her soft breathing and watched the gentle rise and fall of her chest. Here was another girl I would never have a relationship with. Her case would come to an end somehow, good or bad, and we would go our separate ways. She still had college to finish.

And me - I really needed to make some changes in my life.

I left her there the next morning, slipping out of the house as quietly as possible. A quick coffee with Jack and I could be back in an hour. Hopefully, she would still be here. I left a note on the bedroom door – Eggs and English muffins in the fridge. *Back soon.*

There was a new text on my phone, from Rachel, from last night.

"Waiting to hear your excuse. Hope it's at least entertaining."

Jail's a good excuse. I thought. It was too early to call. I thought it better to wait a few hours.

There was one of those private security patrol cars parked outside the house next door. The guard in the car was asleep at the wheel, head tilted back at a painful angle, mouth open, and a little drool on his chin. I looked back at the house and noted that they'd also added security cameras out front. Must have had some unwanted visitors, I thought. I strolled quietly past the sleeping guard and walked down the hill to the 101 Coffee Shop, where I was to meet Jack.

"That's a new look for you. Let me guess, Travolta in Pulp Fiction." Jack teased, seeing me approach in my surfer shorts and sandals. "Don't tell me you've taken up surfing, now."

"Just this morning, I thought a few sets might clear my head." I laughed. "Don't worry; this isn't going to be a regular thing. You know how much I hate driving to the West Side."

"Yeah, about as much as you hate drinking."

I plopped down in the booth, and Norma slid a cup of coffee in front of me seconds later and stood there with her order pad and that Ma

Kettle look on her face.

"You eating?" Jack asked from behind the menu.

"Of course. For some reason, I'm hungrier than usual this morning. I think I'll have the green smoothie, a side of scrambled egg whites, and a bowl of oatmeal. How about you, Jack? It's on me, business brunch."

Like Jack needed any encouragement, I was just helping him rationalize away his dependent habits. I would be buying breakfast, business or not, just like every other morning.

"I'll have the steak and eggs, short stack, and a large orange juice." Jack ordered.

After Norma left, I leaned over to Jack, and in a half-whisper said, "I gotta tell you there is some weird shit going on next door."

"Next door, here?"

"No, at my house. The house next door was for sale, but now it's not. I'm guessing it's been sold. But the new owners are being very secretive."

"How so?"

"Well, they've papered over all the windows so you can't see inside, for one, and the lights are on all night long like they're working or doing something in there, but when I look through the crack in the paper, the house looks empty."

"Maybe they were informed that they have a professional Peeping Tom living next door."

"Ha, ha, very funny. So, I never see anyone come or go, but there is always a pile of Chinese takeout cartons and other food stuff in the trash."

"Oh, so you are going through their trash now? You're like that nosey neighbor from 'I Dream of Jeannie'. What was her name?"

"I think you mean Gladys Kravits and the show was 'Bewitched' not 'I Dream of Jeannie' and anyway it was only once or twice. I was curious. Anyway, the other day I saw a couple of young guys hanging outside the back door that looked like a couple of porn actors, and then this hot-looking woman joined them for a smoke and they all went back inside."

"And you think they're porn actors because they were naked?"

"No, of course not. They just had that look about them. You know, shirtless and sweaty with tool belts and short pants."

"Oh, you mean like the bored housewife who does the repair guy?"

"Exactly. And then this morning, there's a security guard outside."

"Probably to keep you out of their trash. You know it is not against the law to shoot porn movies in this town if you have a permit. But it is against the law to dig through someone's trash unless it's out on the curb."

"You think it might be a clandestine porn shoot?" I said, ignoring the rest of his statement.

"Why would they risk it? A permit doesn't cost that much money. Course you might get your blue haired neighbors up in arms. That's probably why they have the windows covered. Things like that are probably specified in the permit. Can't have kids watching from the sidewalk now. But no, I think it's probably a meth lab." Jack added nonchalantly.

"Really? Don't those things catch fire easily?"

"They've been known to. Then again, they could be growing pot. That would explain all the lights at night. That would be safer than a Meth house. Those things have been known to even blow up when you least expect it. Little pieces of siding fluttering down all over the neighborhood lawns. Plus, they smell to high heaven."

"Is that really true, or did you just watch that on TV somewhere?"

"I can't say from personal experience, but I'm pretty sure."

"So, what did you find out about the other thing?" I asked.

"Nothing. Zip. Nada. There's nothing out of the ordinary going down in Boyle Heights as far as the real estate biz goes that I could find. Stuff is for sale but not moving. What few sales I could run down are all owner-occupied and sold for the market average or higher. If someone is buying up property on the cheap, it isn't there. Not in Aliso Village, either."

I stared into my coffee, only half listening, thinking still about last night with So Young. And then remembering the mess I was in with Rachel. I had to think about how I was going to repair that.

"What's the best way to apologize to a girl after you've stood her up, if it wasn't your fault that is." I asked Jack as nonchalantly as I could muster.

"I would start with an apology. So, what? Are you dating now?"

"Sort of. Not really. Mother set me up with this girl. We were supposed to meet last night for a movie, but then the cops dragged me downtown again for another grilling."

I was not telling Jack the whole truth for some reason. I didn't know why. He'd eventually hear about it from Yana, but I didn't feel like talking about it this morning.

"Tell her that. And make another date right away so she knows you're still into her. The longer you wait to deal with it, the less she's going to believe you."

"You're right. I'll send her a text right now."

"Sorry." I texted. "Spent the night in jail. If you are still interested, we could meet. I'll tell you all the juicy details."

"Well, either she's interested or not, the ball's in her court." I said, staring blankly at the phone screen.

"Texting is kind of chicken shit. You need to call her. Let her yell at you if she wants to."

"It's kind of early." I rationalized.

"I'll call her later this morning after I'm sure she's up."

Jack gave me some serious side eye as I started to put my phone away. Just then, a random thought popped into my head.

"Jack, I'm going to send you the number of the phone I gave Mimi. Get me the call history, would you? I'm curious if she made any calls except to me."

"Sure, buddy. It may take a few days. These smaller outfits don't respond like AT&T."

"You know, Boyle Heights is a bluff." I said to Jack, changing the subject.

"What do you mean, bluff?"

"To keep out the competition. Those in on the deal know the real location, they're just saying Boyle Heights to keep attention focused elsewhere."

"So, who do you think is in on the deal?"

"Lee, Lachlan, those two for sure. Probably a few city councilmen are being paid off, too, I'll bet. You need insiders to grease the bureaucracy in City Hall. Maybe this guy, Messer, who's running for mayor. Lee is probably funding his campaign on the sly. There could certainly be others we aren't aware of."

"So, what's next?"

Our breakfast feasts arrived, and Jack started eating like he'd been stranded on that desert island with Wilson.

"Solano Canyon. I don't know why, but things keep pointing back to there. Mimi, her parents, the flyers, the welcoming committee, and not the least of reasons, that's where Detective Bowman bought it."

Jack ate, occasionally nodding his head so that I knew he was still listening.

"After breakfast, why don't you give Solano the same once-over you did for Boyle Heights. Look for a pattern of sales and blind holding companies. I'm certain you are going to find something." I took one last big swallow of coffee and got up to pay the bill on my way out.

"You know it is still pretty damn hot outside." He noted, mouth full of pancakes.

"What's that supposed to mean?"

"Well, that would explain the shirtless, sweaty boys in shorts next door. That's all."

I hustled back to the house, silently cursing that I had worn flip-flops and couldn't run. Of course, So Young was gone when I returned. I wandered around the house just to be sure.

In the bathroom, I had a large round mirror over the sink. So Young had drawn a little heart to one side and initialed it, S.O. She'd left the lipstick open on the sink. I picked it up. It smelled like vanilla.

I stared for a while at her little heart on the mirror, thinking. Was So Young aware of any of this, except for what I've told her? She did work for her father, she said. I wrote "Mimi" in lipstick just above So Young's heart, and then higher up, "Lachlan".

I started writing names, going clockwise around the perimeter of the mirror: Lee, Miles, Mejia, Messer. Was I forgetting anyone?

Then I started connecting names with lines. Of course, So Young knew her mother and father. Lachlan knew Lee, Lee knew Miles, Mimi knew Miles, right? Or did she, had they ever met? Mimi and Lee are family, but are they really on the outs? Certainly, Sam knew Miles; they were partners, but did Sam know Lee? Could I really connect Lee with Messer? How about with Sam or Miles? Where did Messer fit in? That was the next question. I stared at the mirror, now a spider web of interconnecting lipstick lines.

I drove to the office. It was a mess. Yana was there, cleaning up. The cops had not only tossed my private office, but her space as well. On quick inspection, nothing seemed broken, just a lot of papers littered on the floor.

"Wow, they really did a number here." I observed.

"It's not as bad as it looks, just needs some straightening up. But I think our boys look a little stressed." She was peering intently at the goldfish in the aquarium. "I'm especially worried about Groucho."

"You named my fish after the Marx Brothers?"

"Why not? I love the Marx Brothers, and it seemed fitting, four fish and all. Although I don't know what I'm going to do if you bring home another."

"There were five."

"Five what?"

"Five brothers, nobody remembers Gummo because he wasn't in any of the films, only the vaudeville act."

"Oh." Yana stood there, nodding her head, mouth open like I'd just told her the meaning of life.

"So," I said, changing the subject.

"Did they grill you, too?"

"Yeah," Yana's head was still bobbing in acknowledgement, but her eyes had that far-off stare, still coming to grips with the knowledge that she didn't really know her loves as well as she thought.

"Yeah," she continued, snapping out of it. "They were jerks. Not the Marx Brothers, the cops. They seemed very pissed at you for some reason."

"So, what did they ask you?"

"Oh, how many times Mrs. Lachlan was here, how many times she called, and when. Stuff like that. They asked if I could vouch for you for the Monday afternoon and evening before last. I told them I only work mornings on Mondays because of school."

"Yeah, that would probably be around when Detective Bowman was killed."

"I called your mother and let her know you'd been arrested. It's funny; the way she talked, I was sure she wasn't going to bail you out this time. And your client called, that girl, So Young. I told her you'd been taken to the police station. I hope that was all right to say."

For some reason, I decided not to tell Yana that my mother actually didn't come to get me, that it was So Young.

Usually, I don't keep anything from Yana, but I was feeling a little uncertain about what was happening in my head as far as my relationship with So Young was concerned. I hadn't been exactly forthcoming with Jack this morning either, come to think of it.

I was not being a very good team leader, I told myself. And why was I suddenly being so secretive, anyway?

Yana handed me some phone message slips. "Looks like business is picking up again. More lonely, neglected wives looking for a savior. Your reputation must be spreading."

"I'll pass. I'm on a case." I said, but I stuck them in my pocket anyway.

"I guess there are no fringe benefits on a murder case, or are there?" She gave me the eye.

I ignored her. "Can I borrow your laptop while you're here?"

I pulled it out of her backpack before she could answer and opened it on her desk.

"Do we have a printer cable for this?"

"It's Bluetooth." She replied and then headed into my office to start putting all the files back in the file cabinet. I looked at the mess on the floor and vowed to stop using paper. Long past time to go fully digital. I sat down at Yana's desk and opened up a blank word document. I played around with various fonts and font sizes, trying to create something for the best effect.

Finally, I was ready to type out my ransom note. I had been thinking about this gambit all morning, since making my little diagram with the lipstick on the mirror. Mejia wasn't going to scare me away. I was a licensed detective and had every right to investigate for my clients. For sure, he knew a lot more than I did about what was going on. It was time for him to give back, knowingly or not.

After a few false starts and word substitutions, I was finally satisfied with my note. It read: 'I have the photos you are looking for. Instructions to follow.'

I printed it out and then hit don't save and closed the computer. Using a tissue to prevent fingerprints, I grabbed the note from the printer, fished through Yana's drawers for an envelope and stamp, and scrawled Detective Mejia's name and precinct address on the outside.

"I'll be back in a bit," I shouted to Yana as I headed out the door. It's a short walk to the post office.

I checked the mail pickup time on the mailbox. I was just on time. Mejia should get this tomorrow. I decided to take the scenic route back. I've found walking helps me think through things. I strolled through the Hollywood neighborhoods, past drab pastel apartment buildings with neglected lawns and peeling pink or yellow stucco, past ageing elementary schools that doubled as flea markets on the weekends and drug markets at night. This was what Hollywood looked like for the locals, not what the tourists came to see. My meanderings ended up on the corner of the old Hollywood

Roosevelt Hotel, across the street was the Chinese Theater. Now, here was the epicenter of the tourists' Hollywood, the old and the new. The hotel and the theater are the grand old dames of Tinsel Town, each almost a hundred years old and still going, but surrounded by new Hollywood, all bright and shiny.

I stood there, watching the sea of tourists ebb and flow. It was a city of make-believe, all right, a place to live out your fantasies. Was that what Mimi was doing? It seemed like everyone couldn't help but point out her active imagination. Almost as if to say she'd lost touch with reality. Where was that line? How different was she from me? I knew I took my fixation on dime store detectives a bit to the extreme, but where was the harm in that? Couldn't the same benefit of the doubt be extended to Mimi? Maybe it had, for a long time. But now something had changed, a switch had been flipped, and now it had become a vulnerability to be exploited. What price would she pay?

I took the phone messages out of my pocket and threw them away. I needed to call Rachel.

I called So Young instead. "Hey." I said.

"You ghosted on me. Was I that bad?"

"I didn't. I had an early meeting and thought I could take it and still get back before you woke up, but I guess not."

"Chasing down another hot clue, were you?"

"Something like that. You left pretty early yourself. Did you really think I wasn't coming back?"

"I had a class."

"Yeah. Life fills up with lots of little obligations, and before you know it, you're too busy to really live."

"Well, aren't you the philosopher?"

"Can I see you later tonight?"

"I'm kind of busy tonight, study group. You know, one of my little obligations."

"What's a good night for you, then?"

"Don't you have rules about client relationships, Mister Detective?"

"Of course, but in my business, it's all about knowing when to break the rules."

"Let's find Oh-ma first, shall we?"

"You're right. Business before pleasure."

I hung up, then, for reasons that escaped me, I texted Rachel again instead of calling. Chickenshit was me, alright.

"If you haven't given up on me already, I have a good story to tell. Coffee sometime?"

She didn't call or text back all morning. Probably still mad. Man, who did I think I was, chasing two girls at the same time?

I headed back to the hair salon, hoping to time it so that I could catch Miss Jo's client and Mimi's friend Mrs. Jun as she finished her hair appointment. I was a little early, but not by much. Miss Jo came over and relayed to me that she had already given the lady a heads-up and that I might be coming in to talk to her. She asked that I take our conversation outside. I agreed and proceeded to sit and flip through the many magazines piled on the coffee table while Mrs. Jun got her blowout.

Most of the magazines were in Korean. I found one titled Korea-Boo, which was in English and seemed to be all things K-Pop and celebrity-based. I didn't know who's who in the K-pop scene, and couldn't name a single Korean actor, but it was in English. What else was I going to read? One pictorial section was about the K-Town scene in L.A. with various celebrities photographed entering and exiting the local night spots, restaurants, and Nohrebangs. One picture in particular caught my eye.

"Mayoral candidate and city councilman Mr. Arnold Messer likes the local nightlife!" the headline read. It captioned a picture of Messer surrounded by a bevy of young Korean girls outside a local nohrebang. "And he can sing!" quoted a word balloon from one of the girls. How times have changed. Used to be a political candidate wouldn't be caught dead clubbing. It was soup kitchens or kissing babies.
I checked the publication date on the cover. It was only two months old. That was pretty current by my barber's standards.

About that time, I noticed that Mrs. Jun had finished and had moved to the cashier. I put down the magazine and stood up, waiting politely for her to finish her transaction.

"Mrs. Jun," I said as I approached. "I understand you arefriends with Mimi Lachlan." I quickly showed her my PI badge. If she mistook me for a police detective, that was okay. "I'm looking into the disappearance of Ms. Lachlan. I wonder if you wouldn't mind speaking with me for a moment." I held the door, and we stepped outside.

"May I buy you a cup of coffee?" I asked. There was a coffee shop next door. We went there. It wasn't your typical Starbucks type of coffee shop, but rather a homey, boutique kind of place with a variety of mismatched living room furniture that reminded me of my grandmother's house – doilies on the tables with shaded lamps; landscape paintings in overwrought frames decorated the walls.

We sat down and the owner brought us a menu book of laminated photos of teas, coffees, and desserts. Mrs. Jun ordered a cappuccino and a cake. I just had a black coffee.

"I suppose you've heard by now that Mrs. Lachlan has gone missing." I began after we had placed our order.

"I only heard a short while ago from Miss Jo. Mimi and I are not all that close." She replied. "We usually only see each other when we meet here."

"What did you usually talk about, family, husbands, children?"

"No, not so much. We mostly talked about the old days in Korea. I think she missed Korea, didn't like living here in America."

"Why do you think she moved here, then?"

"Because she got pregnant. She told me it was an accident, but when they found out she was going to have a baby, they decided to get married."

"So, you don't think she got pregnant on purpose to catch an American husband."

Mrs. Jun laughed. "That was not her plan. She wanted to be a model or an actress. That's why she came to Seoul in the first place. She is very, very beautiful. But she's from the countryside and not very well educated. Being good-looking is sometimes not enough."

"Why did you come to the U.S.?"

"My husband came here for his work. He is an engineer for L.G."

"He's Korean?"

"Yes." She laughed. "But just barely. He was schooled at MIT and has been working in the States now for almost 30 years. Longer than he lived in Korea."

"Wow, MIT. That's impressive."

"That was his fallback when he didn't get into Seoul University."

"Ha. First time I've ever heard MIT called their fallback option."

"It's true. Elite schools are all about connections. If he had gone to Seoul, we never would have moved here. But MIT education made him a good fit for a US office."

"Getting back to Mimi." I was interrupted by the waitress bringing our coffee. We sat in silence as she set down the cappuccino and cake and then poured mine into a delicate china cup and left a little pot on the table for seconds.

The coffee was very good. We drank a bit before resuming our conversation. I was hopeful to learn something. Mrs. Jun was certainly open to talking.

"Actually, it is a little unusual that we are friends." She continued.

"How's that?"

"We are of different social classes. If we were back in Korea, we would never know each other."

"You never know. Her husband makes a fair living, they have money. You might have met at the spa or someplace." I postured.

"That's not how it works in Korea. You can't easily earn your way out of your social class like here in America. Don't misunderstand. I like Mimi. But even though she has learned to dress nicely, the minute she speaks, she betrays her upbringing."

"I see. Then she's done well by coming to the States. I would think she would be happy."

"One would think so. Certainly, her cousin is happy."

"Yes, I understand that she sponsored him to immigrate here."

"Oh, I think that was always the plan. Mimi didn't come right out and say it, but from our conversations, it was clear he had been manipulating her the whole time to get himself out of the country. I think he's smart and very ambitious, but like Mimi, with no college education, he would never achieve his dreams in Korea. He brought her to Seoul with dreams of being a celebrity. When that didn't work out, he got her a job as a room salon hostess."

"What's that?"

"It's a bar for businessmen. The girls wear hanboks, traditional outfits, they pour drinks and chat up the customers. It's not a good place to catch a husband, though. Those men are looking for mistresses. I think Lee steered her away from that and succeeded in getting her a job as a barmaid in an expat bar in Itaewon with an eye for landing an American husband. He managed to hook her up with Mr. Lachlan. I wouldn't put it past him to be behind her getting pregnant. As you might guess, I do not think highly of Mr. Lee."

"I spoke to Mr. Lee. He never mentioned that he was related to Mimi."

"Why would he? He doesn't need her anymore. He's well established. No doubt he tells a different story about his background and journey to the States."

"So, besides yourself, does Mimi have any other friends that you know of? Someone she might stay with if she was in trouble?

"No, well, none that I know. As I said, we are just friends through our hairdresser's connection. I think she plays Mahjong with a couple of other women, but I don't know them very well. She invited me one time to join them. Well, her friend did, but…" Mrs. Jun looked out the window for a moment. "I guess I'm still too Korean. Too hung up on class distinction. You might think me a snob."

"No, not at all. It's only natural to want to be around people who make you feel at ease. It's not easy getting out of your comfort zone."

"I still have the number of one of the ladies, Mrs. Shin. Let me ask her first. If she's agreeable, I can give you her number and you can call her."

I gave Mrs. Jun my cell number, then we sat back and sipped our coffee for a moment, not speaking.

"How about their marriage? Do you think Mimi was happy?"

"No, I don't think either was really happy. Resigned and making the best of it would be a better description."

"Why is that?"

"She was too pretty for him. I'm sure you've read about people who win the lottery, and it ruins their lives. I think it was a little like that for Mr. Lachlan. In Mimi, he caught a girl more beautiful than he could ever dream of having, but it didn't make him happy. And while he provided well for her, Mimi wanted the storybook romance, the commoner who marries the prince. She was a little immature in that way."

We sat for a little while longer, finishing our coffee. I listened as she told me about her husband and LG's new flexible screen technology. But my mind was on Mimi. I was learning a lot about my client, my client whom I had only met for less than an hour.

I went back to the office. I figured I could read up on the casino business. There wasn't much online that Jack hadn't already mentioned. It seemed like the whole business was flying under the radar, probably by design. Wouldn't do to have outsiders horning in on a good thing.

There was certainly enough money at stake to tempt people to cross the line, to do what they wouldn't think themselves capable of doing. And where did Mimi fit in all of this, or did she?

I looked up from my laptop and caught sight of my Maltese Falcon statue. Famous clips and quotes flitted through my mind. What about Mimi? I hadn't really considered that she might be more than what first appearances would lead you to believe. Could my client be the killer? After all, it was her gun. Was she missing by design, holed up somewhere?

"I won't play the sap for you." I could hear Bogart saying. I had to get my mind onto something else. I always found that things sorted themselves out quicker if I let my subconscious do the work. I called Rachel.

"Hi. Didn't know if you were going to pick up. How much in the doghouse am I?"

"You say you have a good excuse. Is this an original story or something you cribbed from one of your pulp fiction detective novels?"

"I'm sorry. I really was arrested. You're a lawyer, I'm sure you can make a few calls and check that out."

"Okay, so you were arrested. Isn't this like your second or third time this month? What did they bring you in for this time?"

"Well, I told you about that retired cop who was tailing my client getting killed. They found the murder weapon in my office. Obviously, someone planted it there and dropped a dime on me."

"Dropped a dime?" She laughed. "Listen to yourself. You think you're some modern-day Philip Marlowe? Is that it?"

"No. Maybe." I stammered.

"I used to. Not so much anymore."

"Aren't you a little old to be role-playing?"

"I wouldn't call it that. I'm just emulating my heroes."

"Your heroes are make-believe. They're fictional characters. They're not real, James."

"So. Even your real-life heroes' lives are embellished. It's not so much a stretch to get inspiration from a literary figure. Is it?"

"As long as you can separate your fantasies from reality."

There was a long silence on the phone.

"You want to grab a bite to eat?" I asked finally. "I know a great fusion taco truck. They make their own tortillas from scratch. That's always a good sign. It's in Boyle Heights, not far from you. I can pick you up after work."

"Okay. But if you get arrested again on the way here, I expect you to find a way to call me on your way to the joint."

"Deal."

She's waiting for me on the steps of the US Bank Tower, of course, why would her firm be anywhere else, when I pulled up in Lola, with the top down. It's seven o'clock, the sun is going down, and there's no better time to drive topless than on a summer night. I hopped out to open the door for her.

"You really dress the part, James, classic car, Fedora. I suppose you'll be putting on some lonesome sax music to set the mood."

I could only smile. "I thought we could just talk. But, if you'd rather…"

"No, talking is good."

I circled around the back, past the Club, and onto 6th street, taking that East across the river on the new bridge and into Boyle Heights. The food trucks were lined up alongside Hollenback Park. There must have been a dozen of them, each with their own fusion/flavor hook. We drove slowly by, eyeing each other, then parked and walked back.

The setting sun colored the smoke rising from my fave, a barbecue taco joint that was one of a kind. The park was a handy and popular place to sit and enjoy dinner while we talked. We talked about our days at Stanford, we overlapped by a year, the good old days of college life, Palo Alto, and fun times in the Bay Area, rivalries with other schools. This, for some reason, reminded me of Mrs. Jun's comment about MIT being a fallback school.

"Do you think America has rigid social classes, like England or India, where you can't rise above the social standing you're born into?"

Rachel thought for a moment. "Maybe on the East Coast, like New York, but not out here, I don't think. Why do you ask?"

"Oh, someone was explaining to me how Korea has social class distinctions. They can peg you right away from the way you talk."

"That sounds more to me like a matter of education. You can learn your way to a higher social standing, I would say."

"Maybe. Do the ultra-rich, the old money rich, talk differently than you or I?"

"I wouldn't know, I don't know any super-rich people. And besides, the richest people in America weren't born into it anyway. They came from middle-class backgrounds."

"So, we're sorted by education, but we can rise above our station by getting an education. So, your father went to college, did your grandfather?"

"Yes, after the war on the GI Bill."

"How about his father?"

"I don't know, probably not. I think he was a shopkeeper."

"Same here. My great-grandfather went to University of Michigan, but his father was a railroad man. So, it seems everyone immigrates to America to educate their children to rise up in their social class."

"Maybe not so simple as that. But they come for the opportunity."

"How was your taco?"

"I loved it."

CHAPTER

TWENTY

The next day, I staked out the Central Police station, waiting for Mejia to get my anonymous letter. I got there early. I had no idea when mail was delivered at a police station, or even what hours Mejia kept. But I had nothing but time.

Fifth and Wall was not the ideal place to sit in your car all day. It was in the heart of Skid Row in L.A., the mission district. Getting down there early meant having no problem snagging a good parking spot from which to keep an eye on the place, but it also meant dealing with the tents and sleeping bags and cardboard homes that filled the sidewalks and spilled out over the curbs.

I brought food and coffee with me, so I locked the doors and hunkered down for the long haul, waiting for Mejia to make his move. Not half an hour after I got settled in, the natives started to stir. Like a scene out of an old war movie, they broke camp. Bags and boxes began to disappear, to I don't know where. The sidewalks were suddenly crowded with people going places. One unusually dressed fellow spotted me in my car and slowly stumbled toward it, tapping at the window, trying to get my attention. He wore a black tuxedo jacket over surfer shorts and a Beach Boys tee. I couldn't see his feet. I'm guessing either sandals or patent leather to tie the whole outfit together.

He tapped for a little while, hoping to get a handout. I turned up the radio and avoided eye contact. Eventually, he wandered off, only to be replaced later by another.

The foot patrols started soon after. Police on their beat, charged with clearing the sidewalks, worked their way through, rousting those still asleep, shooing away the rest. The last of the tents came down, as did the cardboard bungalows, and soon the sidewalks were clear. Everyone wandered off to do whatever they did. The city wakes up like a pot put on to boil. It bubbles slowly at first, then it's alive with roiling energy. The sidewalks and streets were alive now.

I saw Mejia pull into the precinct parking lot just before noon. Having already seen his car once was a help. Him being a detective and all, he didn't drive a squad car, but a very innocuous '99 Crown Victoria. It probably used to be a pretty shade of beige, but now it had faded to a smoggy tan – the classic car for an L.A. gumshoe.

Cold coffee and a peanut butter and pickle sandwich was my lunch. Stakeouts can be killer if you're not used to them. It required a strong bladder, among other things. I had a lot of experience in this regard, having sat outside many a love nest hideaway with my trusty camera waiting for the incriminating shots to appear.

This was going to be a piece of cake, comfy car, snacks, radio, now if I could just avoid falling asleep. Mejia finally pulled out around 8:30 that evening. up fast and started the car. He turned right on Seventh Street and headed west. I followed.

Majia drove quickly down Seventh Street; I had to risk being spotted to keep up. Just past MacArthur Park, near the fringes of Koreatown, he pulled into a parking lot of the Dong Seo Nohrehbang, a Korean-style karaoke bar, similar but different from the more well-known

Japanese ones. The parking lot valet seemed to know him as Mejia hopped out and ducked inside without even waiting for a ticket.

I drove slowly by, then circled around the block a couple times, finally risking a red painted curb to park where I could watch the door. Clustered outside was a throng of 'Doumi Girls'. Yeah, I know, sounds like "do me, girls", and that's pretty much what they were. They were supposedly there to join up with single guys getting off work who were looking for a singing companion, or a drinking companion, or just a companion. You get the picture. Buy them a drink, give them a tip. For a little extra, you get a little extra. I hear Korean girls are great singers.

They stood around in their short shorts, or even shorter skirts, with bedazzled bolero jackets and foot-high platform heels. With their Kabuki-like make-up and multi-colored hair, you'd think they looked like clowns, but somehow, they pulled it off and were quite sexy.

I was sitting there, evaluating the lot, trying to decide on my favorite look, when a black town car pulled up and parked in the loading zone. Just then, Messer stormed out, followed quickly by Mejia and a very distressed young girl. Messer climbed into the car, and it took off in a hurry. Mejia stood there looking quite pissed himself. He looked at the girl, pulled out his wallet, and fished out a small wad of bills and shoved them at her, saying something I couldn't hear, but judging from her reaction, it was quite insulting. She stomped off, back into the club. So, it looked like Mejia knew Messer after all and it was more than just a casual acquaintanceship.

The photos meant something to them both. Blackmail? Someone threatening to derail Messer's budding political career? Or was it tied to Lee or Lachlan and the casino real estate scam? Lee was standing next to Messer in that picture with Mimi in the background. How did she figure in? I kept wandering away from my client on this case, and she kept finding her way back in.

Mejia stopped fuming long enough to signal the valet for his car. I needed to wait for him to drive off before giving up my illegal parking spot. I also needed to access the internet. I had no computers at the office right now, thank you very much, Detective Sam. Yana was either at home or at school with her laptop, and while USC was nearby, that would be too much of an imposition. I could always buy one. I checked my phone for the time. It was going on ten.

The stores were going to be closed. But there was Jack, good old Jack.

"Jack. I need you to look something up for me. Look up the Dong Seo Nohrehbang on Seventh Street." I said a little too loudly on the phone. "See if you can find out who owns the building it's in. If it's an LLC or some other kind of shell company, compare that to any of those listed on title to properties in Solano Canyon."

"Sounds like you're making progress, Sherlock."

"I'm taking some shots in the dark, but I'm feeling lucky. Get back to me as soon as you can with whatever you find. Thanks, Jack."

With the detective now gone, I pulled out and headed up Western toward home. The computer stores may be closed, but the liquor stores weren't. I stopped by my favorite on the way. I liked to think of myself as a bit of a Scotch aficionado, preferring Highland or Speyside over others, something with a nice caramel color, port or sherry cask, maybe 18 years or better.

"Hey, Jules. How's it going tonight?" I greeted the owner. "Got anything special for me this week?"

"Evening, James," Jules called out to me from where he was

cleaning his cabinet windows. There he keeps the expensive stuff.

"Yeah, I do. We got a case of Glendronach last week. I saved you a bottle, but the rest has already sold out."

"Yeah? I heard about that. I'd love to give it a try. But I'm going to be mad at you if I love it and there's no more to be had."

"You will love it, and don't worry; I've already ordered more." He put the boxed bottle in a bag. "Anything else for you tonight?"

"No, just put it on my card. Have a good one." I said as I pushed through the door, again ringing the little bell overhead.

When I got home, there was a fat manila envelope waiting for me. It was half stuffed in the mailbox, but it was too thick to fit inside. I pulled it out, no name, no address, of course, no postage.

First things first, I poured myself a nice glass of the new scotch. Good scotch, you're supposed to drink at room temperature, neat with just a few drops of water to open it up. Diluting it with anything, especially soda water, would be criminal. The first taste certainly lived up to my expectations.

Then I dumped the contents of the envelope onto the kitchen counter – copies of real estate titles, dozens of them. I quickly flipped through them; all located in Solano Canyon.
I surveyed the owners of record, they were all different, and all Korean, or at least Asian, could be Chinese. Then I noticed that stapled to each title report was a Quit Claim form, deeding the property to Lachlan and company. All the quit claims were dated in the last three years.

Well, So Young had certainly come through. Strange that she seems so eager to fink out her father like this. More family issues, I wondered.

I took a big swallow of my drink, draining it. I let the amber nectar linger in my mouth, savoring the taste, then felt its warmth slide down my throat. I stared at the pile of papers, hoping that by that simple action I would achieve some epiphany, but no.

I poured myself another glass and headed to the bathroom mirror. I picked up the lipstick and drew a line connecting Messer to Mejia. How is Mimi mixed up in all this? Was she having an affair with Messer? Did her husband pack her off to some secluded spa in the desert to get her out of the way? How exactly was she causing trouble for him? What's the story with cousin Lee? Did he use Mimi's marriage to get a visa to the States? Maybe Lee was using her now to get inside info. Or maybe Mimi was trying to do that to Lee for her husband. Who was in those photos? I stood there and stared at my spider web in lipstick, thinking there were too many questions and too few answers.

Wait a minute. If Miles took the photos, was he double-crossing Lee? Was Mejia in on it, or had he been blindsided by his old partner, who maybe was out looking for some extra pocket money? I could just imagine the scene where Lee told Sam that his best friend was screwing him. But Sam would have taken care of it quietly. He would not have shot his old friend. Maybe Lee hired a hit man to take out Bowman. What would Mejia do if he found out?

I went to my bedroom closet and pulled an overnight bag from the top shelf.

Inside was a Luger 38 special revolver and a shoulder holster. I checked the gun. It was not loaded, but there were a couple of boxes of ammo in the bottom of the bag. I put on the holster and fastened all the straps, then holstered the pistol. It had been about three years since I purchased it. After a nasty run-in with an errant husband, I thought better safe than sorry next time. I dutifully went to the range for a few months to learn how to handle it. But this is the first time I had gotten it out since then. Still was debating with myself whether it was a good move or not.

I recalled the advice I had given Mimi about carrying a gun, which increases your chances of getting shot. I looked at myself in the mirror. I didn't look any different, but at least I didn't look stupid. I unholstered the gun and started loading the bullets. It was heavier now, more than it should be, or so it seemed. I picked up my glass and took another swig.

As I did, I caught sight of myself in the mirror, drink in one hand, gun in the other, holster strapped on over my shirt, bags under my eyes. Was this my vision of the detective me? Was I just role-playing, fooling myself? Or does anyone who puts on a uniform have these same thoughts?

I stood there all night, finished that bottle, but made no progress on the tangle that stared back at me from the mirror.

CHAPTER

TWENTY-ONE

The next morning, I did a short half-hour jog through the neighborhood to burn off all the alcohol from last night. Afterwards, I met Jack again for breakfast. Rather, I had breakfast and Jack had breakfast, lunch, and supper.

"What's with the suit?" Jack asked.

I was wearing an ugly old brown hound's-tooth to conceal my shoulder holster today. It was the only thing left in my closet as two of my regular suits were still at the cleaners, and another still at my mother's. "Nothing, just thought I should occasionally try to look more professional," I answered, watching him shovel in a mountain of food. "Where do you put it all?" I asked.

Jack mumbled something, but his mouth was full of pancakes.

"Do you even weigh a hundred sixty?" I queried.

"One fifty-five, sorry, I can't help it, I can't put on the pounds. I have a high metabolism."

"You can tell me." I pressed. "You're really a tri-athlete, aren't you? You know, that Iron Man thing."

"I wish." He protested between bites of toast and eggs. "I don't have time for exercise."

"What do you do?"

"You know it's a fact - your brain uses the most calories of any organ in your body. I spent all night doing research for you. Least you can do is buy me breakfast."

He reached down to his seat and tossed a folder towards me.

"Like I don't always." I half complained.

As I read through the contents, Jack continued. "The same company, Han-Mi Properties, which owns the Dong Seo, also owns dozens of properties in Solano Canyon."

"That's got to be Lee." I muttered to myself.

Jack continued, "There are one hundred and two residential properties between the freeway and Academy Road. Average market value today, according to real estate dot com, is just under seven hundred fifty thousand. About half of them are small apartment complexes or duplexes, and the rest are single-family homes. About sixty have changed hands in the last five years. Average transaction was about five hundred thousand. So, the whole canyon has appreciated from fifty mil to seventy-five in just the last five years, but if it can all be bought up and sold to the city for two hundred mil, well, I think even you can do that math."

Nice profit, I thought. Lachlan had about twenty-five properties, Lee maybe another forty, and they were both scrambling to lock up the rest. Those thugs who beat me up were probably right to be angry.

"You're quite the detective yourself, Doctor Watson." I told him.

While Jack ate, I decided to bring him up to date on my latest gambit. "I'm pretty certain that Detective Bowman took some pictures that he was using for blackmail. I was guessing they may or may not have been of Mimi and somebody else." I started.

"You think she was seeing some guy?"

"Maybe, maybe not. She kind of teased that she was playing around when she first came to see me, but I thought she was joking."

I wondered aloud. "I sent an anonymous note to Detective Mejia saying I had the pictures, and what do you know, he immediately ran to Councilman Messer. So now I'm guessing Messer is the one in the pictures, probably with my client. But then again, she seems a little old for his taste. I could be totally off base, and it could be something else entirely."

"And what has that got to do with cornering the market on property in the canyon?"

"I don't know that it does. It's just a hunch so far, but that is the last place I saw Mrs. Lachlan, and that's where Detective Bowman was killed. There's got to be a connection there somewhere. Maybe Lee is using Mimi to blackmail Messer. He's been using Mimi his whole life. Why stop now?"

"Seems like Lee has more money than Messer, though."

"Not for money, he's keeping Messer under his thumb for this casino deal!"

"I think your deductive skills need some work, bro."

"Yeah, I know. I've got to really find those pictures. Obviously, the police don't have them; that explains Sam's reaction when he got my note. Plus, he tore apart his old partner's office and home looking for them. He must want them pretty badly."

I sipped my coffee and thought for a minute.

"Okay. So, Jack, imagine your Miles Bowman, an old man, maybe not all that comfortable with digital technology. You use a digital camera because what choice do you have? They don't sell film anymore down at the Seven-Eleven. You have these pictures that you're blackmailing someone with, and you want to stash a copy for insurance."

"What do you do?"

"What would Marlowe do?" Jack answered after washing down his food with a big gulp of coffee. "He'd put a flash drive in an envelope, stick it in a locker at the bus station, and mail the locker key to himself. Or to his post office box." He added with a grin.

"Nah, the cops would have uncovered a post office box soon enough. What if he emailed it to himself?"

"Pictures are pretty big file sizes. Kinda stands out like a sore thumb."

"Code name the files and bury them in some folder within a folder on his drive?"

"Kid stuff. He'd need an encrypted secret partition on his hard drive, and you said he wasn't that smart. But he could have a secret e-mail address, like a cloud account, one that he doesn't access from his personal computer or his phone."

"Okay. Do you think you might be able to hack into his Gmail account and see if he left any crumbs that might lead you to this secret account?"

"You've been watching too many TV shows. But I'll see what I can find. You wearing a gun?" He said suddenly.

"What?" I replied, a bit taken aback. "You can see it?"

"Yeah, you're jacket's open, dude. Don't you need a concealed carry to do that?"

"I have one. I'm a licensed detective. Remember?"

"Shit's getting real." He mumbled. Breakfast finished; Jack started in on a pair of Danish for dessert.

I arrived back at the office with my usual Frappuccino for Yana and another goldfish for the aquarium. I poured it in and watched as it swam around with the others.

"Gummo." I announced to Yana's inquiring glance. I dropped a pinch of fish food into the water and watched as they gobbled it up.

"The other day, when I got arrested, So Young called up and you told her I'd been pinched."

"Yes, she called around the middle of the afternoon looking for you. Was I not supposed to say anything? Usually, a run-in with the law is a badge of honor in this business. At least it is in all the movies I've ever seen."

"No, I was just wondering why she didn't try my cell first," I said as I continued to watch the fish.

"Maybe she did, but you didn't pick up because the cops were working you over with a rubber hose at the time."

I chuckled. My strange sense of humor was rubbing off on my friends.

"No, I checked, no missed calls. You wouldn't happen to know So Young from school by any chance?" I asked.

Yana rolled her eyes. "You're kidding. Do you have any idea how many students are enrolled there?"

"Well, do you know any Korean students?"

"I don't think so. I know a few Asian students, but they're all Chinese. Anyway, my friends are all in grad school. It's unlikely they'd know any undergrads unless they were TA's. And why are you asking? Are you thinking she's a suspect, or are you checking her out for a date?"

"Why would she be a suspect?"

"So, is the leopard finally changing his spots? Are you seriously thinking of dating a woman not old enough to be your mother?" Yana laughed.

"Well, I am thinking about getting out of the divorce business." I replied.

"Should I be looking for a new job?"

"Maybe fraud or white-collar crime is more my line."

"I dunno, James. You start messing around with real criminals, and there's likely to be gunplay involved."

"Believe me, when you get between warring spouses, there's ample opportunity to get plugged there, too."

"Are you wearing a gun?" Yana suddenly asked in surprise.

"Is it that obvious?"

"Duh!" Yana just shook her head. "So, what's your next move? Did you speak to her father, Mrs. Kim's husband?"

"I did that first of all. He's too cagey. I've got to find some leverage to pry him open with before I can go back."

During this conversation, I had wandered back into my office and plopped down in my overstuffed leather swivel chair, and put my feet on the desk. Yana stood leaning against the doorway, drinking her Frappuccino and looking at me like a disapproving older sister.

"So, I'm confused." Yana begins.

"Are you still working to find your client, or are you just trying to save your own skin from a murder rap?"

"Whoa, that's harsh," I reply. "The truth? Fifty-fifty. I am still working for Mrs. Kim and now for her daughter, I guess, and if I can get to the bottom of it all, I should get myself out of this mess I'm in."

"Okay." She drawled too slowly, not entirely believing anything I said at this point.

"In the meantime," I added, "I suppose I should buy a new laptop. No telling how long the cops are going to keep our stuff."

"Well, they didn't take your trash."

She leaned over and grabbed my wastebasket to empty it. Our building has a trash chute in every corridor to save you a trip to the basement. "Is this all trash?" She asked, pawing through the paper. "I see bank receipts in here." She fished out a handful and gave them back to me.

"That must be So Young's junk. She was cleaning out her purse that first day."

I glanced through the teller receipts. Each was for a thousand dollars, once a week, according to the dates. Why would So Young need so much cash, I wondered. She, who pays for everything with her phone, no less. Unless she was secretly giving the money to someone. But who?

"I'm off to school then. By the way, nice suit!" Yana called out as she slung her backpack over one shoulder and walked out the door.

I really wanted to talk with Alistair once more, and the Mahjong lady and I also needed to talk to Mr. Lee again. His connection to this whole mess seemed to be more than happenstance. He probably wasn't going to take another meeting with me, but I had to try. I called his office.

"Chairman Lee is busy all morning." The cheerful voice on the phone informed me.

"Perhaps he would be free for lunch?"

"I'm afraid he already has a lunch appointment and he will be out of the office for the rest of the day. Would you care to leave a message?"

I declined. So, I would have to catch him out in public somewhere. I checked my phone for the time and saw a text from Mrs. Jun with Mrs. Shin's phone number. That would have to wait. If traffic were only half as terrible, I might be able to ambush him as he was leaving for lunch. I grabbed my hat and keys and dashed.

Lee was not the kind of businessman who drove himself anywhere. When he went to lunch, his driver would bring the car around and pick him up either on the street outside the lobby or, more likely, in the parking garage. That's where I was staked out.

I didn't have to wait long. Lee's car, a big, black Hyundai Town Car, pulled up to the curb, and the driver hopped out and ran around to open the rear passenger door. Lee exited the elevator alone and spied on me advancing toward him. He didn't try to avoid me, but waited, motioning away his driver/bodyguard who had started to move to intercept me.

"Mr. Lee, I don't mean to bother you. I just had a quick question. It won't keep you from your lunch appointment."

"Yes, Mr." He opened his hands, gesturing that he had forgotten my name. The bodyguard caught his eye and gave him a silent signal.

"Gardiner. James Gardiner." I said.

"My driver says you're wearing a gun in a shoulder holster. You may keep it, but I would warn you against any sudden movements."

"I'm sorry, it's only for self-protection. I didn't know it was that obvious."

"He's a professional. Now, what can I help you with, son?"

"Son?" I thought. Lee couldn't have been any more than ten years my senior.

"You mentioned before that you had originally met Mimi at a bar where she worked as a waitress."

"Yes, that is correct."

"I heard you two were cousins, though."

Lee didn't flinch. He chuckled, though.

"Did Mimi tell you that?"

"No, I think I heard it from her hairdresser."

"Maybe you misunderstood. In Korea, we avoid calling each other by our given names. Everyone is either Auntie or Uncle, Big Brother, Big Sister, or Cousin, you see."

"So, you're not related?"

"Actually, it seems we are. Distant cousins, I think. I recognized her accent. We are both from Taegu. We talked and compared notes, and one thing led to another. Although there are many Kim families, we decided we might be related." Lee lied so easily that I reconsidered challenging him as I knew differently. Better to keep it under my hat for now.

"Quite a coincidence, though, running into her working at a Country Western bar, one that catered to American soldiers. Not some place that you would have normally been welcome in, I would think."

"Yes. If I remember correctly, it was called Willie's Joint or something like that. You are right, not a bar that I would have gone into on my own, but Alistair brought me. He wanted me to meet his girlfriend, Mimi."

"And that's when you two met?"

"Actually, not then. She was with some G.I. that night. Alistair pointed her out, but she never came over to our table."

"She was quite attractive, wasn't she?"

"Yes, very beautiful. So?"

"Didn't it bother you to see a girl like her flirting with the Americans?"

Lee laughed. "She was just a bar girl, from a poor family, uneducated, not someone I would ever be remotely interested in. It's a class thing. You're American, you probably wouldn't understand. It bothered Alistair, though."

"Did he make a scene?"

"Oh, no, that would be the last thing he would do. Alistair's not the type. He tried to get her to come over for a minute, but she didn't. Her Army boyfriend came over, though. I think to rub it in and make Alistair realize that he had no chance with her."

"That Army boyfriend was Councilman Arnold Messer."

Lee didn't answer right away; he looked at me for a long time, measuring his reply.

"Yes. How did you know that?"

"I didn't. Just a lucky guess."

After Lee left, I walked back to my car to call Mrs. Shin. That bit of information about Messer, Lee, and Lachlan was key. It tied them all together and tied them all to Mimi. But what did it mean? It could not be a coincidence, not after more than twenty years.

Mrs. Shin cheerfully answered the phone. Apparently, Mrs. Jun had filled her in on my intent. We agreed to meet at the little coffee shop by the hairdresser's.

I had time to kill. At first, I drove aimlessly, into Los Feliz and past all the old mansions. Before Beverly Hills, this was where the movie stars lived –Tom Mix, W.C. Fields, Charlie Chaplin. I kept driving, turning south into Silverlake, a nice hillside community now a mecca for the urban hipster.

Then I wandered through Elysian Park, circling around Dodger Stadium. Eventually, I found myself back at Solano Canyon, coming in from the north side this time. Solano – I had looked up the name. It comes from the name of a hot, oppressive east wind in Spain. It was certainly living up to its name this week. The name also had roots in the Latin solus, meaning alone or lonely. That felt pretty well to I felt.

I stopped to take a picture of some more Korean graffiti with my phone. Now I was beginning to think of this place as Seoul Canyon, not Solano. I would get So Young or someone to translate it later.

I drove down the street to the house where I last saw Mimi. I parked in front and sat in my car, staring at the house, contemplating the details of the exterior. On impulse, I hopped out and walked up and knocked on the door. After a few minutes, someone parted the curtains that covered the glass in the front door.

I held up my detective license. Conveniently, it includes a badge so to the casual observer could be mistaken for a police badge. The door slowly opened, revealing an elderly Korean man. He wore loose-fitting dress pants held up by suspenders over a sleeveless t-shirt, white socks, and house slippers.

He blinked at me through thick glasses.

"I am looking for Mrs. Kim. Mimi Kim," I said, too loudly. I didn't know why. It wasn't as if I thought he must be hard of hearing. But when you suspect someone doesn't speak your language, yelling makes it easier for them to understand.

"*Obseyo!*" He shouted back.

"Mimi Lachlan? I was told I could find her here."

"*Obso, obso!*" He shouted angrily, shaking his head and waving his hands, trying to shoo me away.

"I'm sorry. *Mi an hab nida.*" I tried my limited vocabulary.

The old man was momentarily taken aback by hearing a bit of Korean from me.

"*An yang haseo.*" I bowed politely to him.

He nodded slightly in return, but with a very suspicious look in his eye. In the darkness behind him, an old woman appeared in the hall. She said something in a flurry of Korean, none of which I could make out except the word Mimi-ya. The old man turned and shouted at her, and she disappeared back into the house.

Meanwhile, I had pulled out my phone and pulled up the translation app. I set it for English to Korean and spoke into it.

"Are you Mimi's father?" I said, then turned the phone to him so that he could hear better.

"*Dangsineun mimiui abeoji ibnikka?*" the phone translated.

The old man blinked in surprise. "*Nay.*" He said suspiciously.

Slowly, I proceeded to interview the old man. He tolerated my questions because he was fascinated by the translation technology.

I learned he had no idea where his daughter might be. They hadn't seen her in almost two weeks, and they were worried. I asked if their granddaughter had been by.

"No So Yeong!" He shouted.

I couldn't tell if he was mad that she hadn't been by or that he was disavowing her because she hadn't.

He asked if someone would be bringing some food by. They had run out of anything to eat and were hungry. He pulled out his wallet and tried to hand me a wad of hundred-dollar bills, which I refused. Why was everyone trying to overpay me, I wondered. I promised him I would send someone over with some food right away.

It briefly crossed my mind that they had been getting their cash from So Yeong. He turned and walked quickly back into the house, slamming the door behind him.

As I walked back to my car, I took a little detour by the garage and peeked in the side door. The blue convertible was parked inside.

Dad could be covering for her, or she could have ditched the car here and grabbed another set of wheels. The door was unlocked, so I snuck in. The little bit of dust on the windshield told me that the car had been herefor a while, maybe for the two weeks since I'd last seen it. The car doors were locked, and as there wasn't anything visible on the seats or the floor, I opted not to try to break in. I snapped pics of the license and VIN number just in case, but I really didn't doubt that this was her car.

I pondered this all as I headed back to my own ride only to find it surrounded by the same four Latino toughs who accosted me the last time. I squeezed my left arm against the side of my chest but found little comfort in the feel of my gun there.

"Oye! Pinche Gavacho!" The short one shouted at me. "I thought we made it clear you aren't welcome around here."

"I think you misunderstand." I started to reply.

"I'm not a real estate agent, I'm a detective. I'm looking for a missing person."

As they started to close in around me, I talked faster. "Look. I don't know anything about whatever turf war is going on here between these developers."

"Sounds to me like you know plenty."

"Hey, I see the flyers on all the door handles and in the mailboxes. I can figure that much out without being in on the game. But listen, I think I can help you out with your situation here."

It didn't look like I was going to be able to talk myself out of another beating when there was a squeal of tires up the street and the roar of a gunning engine. Everybody looked up.

Barreling down the street was a black Lexus. The four boys scattered, diving behind parked cars. I just stood there like an idiot watching the car race toward me. I mean, it was not like I was standing in the middle of the street or anything.

The sight of the nine-millimeter poking out of the back window slowed it all down for me.

"Oh, I get it now, it's a drive by" I thought stupidly, not that this realization made my legs move. I still stood there as I watched three muzzle flashes erupt from the barrel in quick succession. My body frozen, I just calmly turned my head as I watched the car whiz on by.

Did I get hit? I didn't feel anything yet except the rush of hot air in the car's wake. It continued further down the street, squealing tires once again as it took the corner too fast and was gone. I realized I was slightly trembling and then was startled to find the Luger in my hand.

As the four toughs reconvened around me, they, too, noticed that I was now armed. I don't know if I felt safer, but they didn't crowd me now. They acted nonchalant, pretending to not seem particularly phased by the sight of my gun. One of the boys examined the bullet holes in the door panels of my car, poking his finger in the jagged punctures, two to my right and one to my left.

"Looks like we aren't the only ones who don't like your face." The short one said as he pointed his finger like a gun at my chest and pretended to shoot.

"That was a warning, amigo. Those gooks could have wasted you if they wanted." He said, walking backwards away from me.

"Hey, wait!" I yelled, unthinkingly gesturing with my gun hand. That sent them running.

"No, wait," I yelled after them. "I want to ask you about the flyers." They were too far away now to hear even if hearing would have stopped them. I watched as they cut up a driveway and disappeared into a backyard. Probably one of their homes, I thought. I looked stupidly at the gun in my hand, shoved it into its holster, and climbed into my car.

I started her up and pulled slowly out of my parking spot, being careful to look that I didn't bump into any of the boys in the Lexus. I headed south, out of 'Sol' Canyon, into Chinatown.

I continued south through Chinatown over the 101 Freeway and into downtown, through the skyscrapers that kept pushing up, that kept marching south, that kept crying for attention, trying to say, 'Yes, this is a really big city like all the rest'. Turning west on Wilshire took me back toward Koreatown.

I was back in that same quaint little cottage turned coffeeshop where I had sat not two days earlier. Being early, I chose a table in the front room by a window and ordered a plain black coffee. Mrs. Shin, as she turned out to be, bustled in not a few minutes later.

She was as opposite in manner from Mrs. Jun as one could imagine — effusive and bubbly with a wide grin and a sparkle in her eyes, she hurried toward me with her hand outstretched and shook mine vigorously.

Being the only single, young white man in the place, she must have taken a wild guess that I was her guy.She settled in noisily and quickly ordered a chai tea latte and cake from the waitress who magically appeared behind her at that moment. Mrs. Shin had a wide, tanned, and friendly face, framed by a very curly perm. She wore a loud, colored floral print dress and carried an extra-large purse, more of a carpet bag, which she set on the empty chair beside her.

"And how are you, Mr. Garner is it?"

She asked in a reasonably unaccented voice.

"Gar-di-ner. But call me James. I'm doing well. How about yourself?"

"Oh, wonderful. I've never met a real detective before. That must be a very exciting business to be in."

"Not as much as you would think, but it has its moments," I replied, thinking back to the drive-by attempted assassination I survived less than an hour earlier. "But it has its moments." I repeated. "What about you? What do you do?"

"I'm busy enough raising a family, I don't have time to do anything else. I have three kids at home, two in high school. I drive them around to their activities, and they drive me crazy." She laughed aloud, drawing stares from the other patrons.

The waitress came with the tea and cake, and while Mrs. Shin stopped to take a sip, I decided to skip the pleasantries and get to business.

"I suppose Mrs. Jun already told you why I wanted to talk with you. Were you close friends with Mimi Kim?"

"We were friends, but I wouldn't say we were close friends. She never invited me to her house or anything."

"Were you aware that she was missing?"

"Well, she did miss our monthly mahjong game last Wednesday. She usually will call if she can't make it, so we can find a third to take her place."

"Don't you usually play with four players?"

"Not Korean style, that's Chinese style. We play with three hands."

"So, you, Mrs. Jun, and Mrs. Kim, meet once a month to play?"

"Yes, and I know a couple of other ladies who are always happy to fill in if one of us can't make it."

"I suppose you talk about the usual things, gossip, husbands, and children while you play."

"Oh, yes. Girl talk. You know, complaints about life in

America, missing back home. Those things."

"Did Mimi ever tell stories about how she met her husband?"

"Ha, ha, ha, yes. She's told that story more than once. It changes every time, too."

"So, what was her story?"

"She worked at a bar in Itaewon, that is a street where all the tourists and GIs go. It's all souvenir shops, bars, and restaurants. She had two suitors, one was an army officer, tall, muscular, and good-looking, the other was a businessman, not so tall, not so muscular, and not as good-looking, but he was kind and generous, so she picked him. She said it was hard dumping the soldier, but she thought it best for her future."

"But you didn't believe her."

"Oh, God, no. If you knew Mimi, you would know she would always go for the flashier man. That was the way she was. He probably dumped her."

"Why would he do that. She's certainly pretty enough."

"Any experienced bar girl would tell you that you never get involved with officers. They often have a wife and kids back home."

"If she were that type of girl, why do you think she settled for the businessman?"

Mrs. Shin leaned in close and whispered loudly. "Turns out she was pregnant. Said she didn't know who the father was. The businessman said he loved her just the same."

"Have you ever met her husband or seen a picture of the soldier?"

"No, I've seen a picture of the daughter, though." She leaned back with a laugh. "Even prettier than her mom."

"So, Mimi moved to the States and lived happily ever after. Is that it?"

"Until recently. She told us a couple months ago that she happened to see her old soldier boyfriend on the street. She was tempted to go up and talk to him, but was afraid to. She was asking our advice on whether that was a wise thing to do."

"Do you think she listened?"

"I hope so. But she missed our last get-together a week ago, so we haven't heard any news." She chewed her cake thoughtfully.

I also wondered what Mimi was up to now.

"I'm looking for someone whom she would know well enough that she might stay with if she was in trouble and afraid."

Mrs. Shin thought for a moment. There's another lady who fills in from time to time. Park Ji-An, she goes by Jean to Americans. She and Mimi get along pretty well. I'd have to call you back with her number.

"That would be great."

After my meeting with Mrs. Shin, I stopped at a popular spot for tofu soup, Soon Dubu, they call it in Korean. I ordered a bowl of the hot stuff, and by hot, I mean both spicy, like really, really spicy. Maybe it was not so spicy as to take the paint of your car, but close, and hot, like still boiling when they set it down in front of you, a black stone cauldron of bright red lava, bubbling and spurting like something hell borne, but safely resting on a wooden trivet to keep the table from catching fire. The 'dolsot' bowl will keep your soup bubbling away for the duration of time it takes to eat it. It's sort of like eating right off the stove. Before long, I was sweating, and my nose was running, and the used napkins were piling up on my table as I tried unsuccessfully to put Solano Canyon in my rear-view mirror.

Mimi's parents didn't fit in the puzzle. What were they doing there, and why did Lachlan lie about it? They did reinforce the notion that she was missing. Then I remembered that I had promised to send someone with food.

Should I call So Young? They reacted rather strangely at the mention of her. Maybe I should let Lachlan know. Or, did he already know that they are there? How could he not? He seemed to be pretty well plugged into what was happening around him. But why put these old folks in the middle of a war zone?

While I was thinking about all of this, the waitress came by to fill up my water glass.

"Do you deliver?" I asked suddenly.

"You want something to go?" She asked.

"No, not to go. Do you deliver? Can I order food and have it delivered to my house?"

"Yes, but not far." She said, looking at me suspiciously.

"Downtown?" I ask.

"Downtown, no problem." She replied, still giving me the narrow stare, not convinced I lived near enough. She probably thinks I live in the Hollywood Hills or someplace equally white and far away.

I ordered half a dozen entrees to be delivered to Mimi's house in the canyon. That should buy me some time until I sort this out. I gave the waitress a nice big tip, even though she showed no faith in me. While working my way through lunch, I kept checking my phone for a message from Mrs. Jun with a number for the Mahjong players. Finally, I put in a call to Yana. No leads on So Young from her end, but she did find out that she goes by a different name at school, Sophia.

"That's her American name," I informed her.

"A lot of Asian kids adopt English names because theirs are too difficult for Americans to pronounce."

"What's so hard to pronounce about So Young?" she asked.

"Maybe it's what it sounds like in English that she doesn't care for." I mused.

She sends me a copy of her school photo. Sophia could easily pass for white with her makeup done just right. It's tough being bi-racial, I think. The Asians are even more prejudicial than the Americans on that front. Maybe she's trying to hide her Korean roots.

I fill Yana in on my most recent encounter with the natives.

"You've got to stop going there." She admonishes me. "You've been beaten up and shot at, and your predecessor is dead. Get the message, will you?"

"Listen, it seems Mimi has her parents stashed in one of her husband's properties, but with her missing, no one is keeping an eye on them, and they don't know how to get food for themselves. I need you to call up "Shop-4-You", you know, that grocery shopping service. My mom uses it occasionally. They are pretty good. Arrange for some groceries to be sent there. Put it on my card. I'll text you the address."

I paid my tab and stepped outside. The sun had already set. It was going down earlier and earlier. I kind of liked that. The days can be uncomfortably hot, but the nights are great. Nothing beats driving thru the city with the top down on a warm night.

Nevertheless, I decided to leave the Merc in the restaurant parking lot and walk over to the Dong Seo, it being only a few blocks away.

CHAPTER

TWENTY-TWO

A lot of Koreans, like a lot of Asians, I guess, still smoked much more than the typical Californian. But city ordinances will always trump culture, so even in the Nohrehbangs, it was strictly no smoking. Knowing this, I figured that if I walked around to the back-alley exit, I would find some employees taking a cigarette break from time to time.

Sure enough, there were three Doumi girls back there, passing around a single cigarette. These girls get harassed all the time by Vice, so their guard was up the instant they saw me in my jacket and hat. I showed them my P.I. ID and tried to reassure them that I was not a cop. That got me about one percent more past their defenses.

"I like your hat." One girl said, fishing.

I pushed it back slightly on my head and gave her my best Robert Mitchum bedroom eyes. That elicited a giggle.

I tried to segue from there to some small talk, what songs they liked to sing best, who were the better singers, Americans or Koreans. I tried to steer wide of any questions about "special requests". Turns out many of these girls were in college and working one or two nights a week to meet expenses. Not all the clientele are lonely businessmen, either; lots of mixed groups and lots of kids on dates, especially on the weekends.

"The lonely guys tend to come around weekdays after work." The first girl opined.

"Business is kinda slow on the weekends, ya know?" the second agreed before taking a big drag on the last of the cigarette.

"Oh, that's right," I remarked. "It is Friday,isn't it? Guess I lost track of the days."

I took out my phone and pulled up the photo of Mimi that So Young sent me. I show it around, asking if any of the girls recognized her, maybe here with a boyfriend. They all politely gave it a careful look, but no, no one recognized her.

"But I know her." One of the girls said, pointing not to Mimi, but to So Young next to her. "That's Ah Na. She works Thursdays, I think."

"Look at how they're dressed." One chimed in. "Her mom totally doesn't know."

"Totally not." The third agreed.

"What can you tell me about her?" I asked.

"Not much. A lot of the girls around here are pretty guarded about their personal lives. You can understand why."

"We don't pry." The one chimed in again.

"She's a favorite of the councilman. He comes here every Thursday just for her."

"What's his name?"

"Messer. You know, like Mack the Knife. Mackie Messer."

"That's a pretty obscure reference."

"I'm in theater, studying to be an actress. I like musical theater. "*Und der Haifisch, der hat Zähne.*" She started singing. "*Und die trägt er im Gesicht.*"

I thanked them and left; strains of Kurt Weill followed me out of the alley.

Wow. Did not see that coming. Was So Young having an affair

with Messer? It sure looked like it. And now I was guessing she might be the one in the photos. Did he know who she was? She was not underage, I thought. I hoped.

So, if Miles took photos, who was he blackmailing here? Maybe it was not a rogue operation after all. John Lee must have known what was going on; it was his club after all. How could he not know? Was he trying to get leverage on Lachlan, force him out?

I walked back to the restaurant parking lot and grabbed my car, pulled out, and headed West, down Wilshire.

I still couldn't get my head wrapped around it.

I thought I had it all figured out, but now all my theories were blown to hell. Pictures of people having sex were pretty small potatoes these days. I should know. That was my specialty. They were certainly not warranting a murder. How was Mimi involved? And why was Miles tailing her if he was taking pictures of So Young? Maybe he was double-dealing, working two clients at the same time. And how did Detective Mejia fit into this whole thing? And what about Lachlan? Maybe Miles was shaking down Lachlan with photos of his only daughter, and it had nothing to do with Lee or Mimi. So then why was Mejia spooked enough to go running to Messer when he got my note?

Subconsciously, I turned off Wilshire onto Freemont Place, the only gated community in Los Angeles, and home to Mimi and Alistair Lachlan. I pulled up to the guard shack. The guard phoned ahead.

"Sorry. No one is home. Are you sure they were expecting you?"

"No, it wasn't a set appointment, more of a 'if you're in the neighborhood' type of thing."

The guard was not buying it.

"Gimme a sec." I asked.

I phoned So Young from my cell. No answer. For the guard's benefit, I left a message.

"I guess they're not home." I offered politely, then said goodbye to the guard and turned my car around. That's not easy with a big boat like mine, which makes for an embarrassing couple of minutes while I see-sawed back and forth with a couple of impatient residents waiting behind me now. I drove back to my office. It was dark now.

The new digital billboards outshone the old neon of Hollywood. Kids were lining up outside the velvet ropes, waiting for the clubs to open. Many of the newer clubs had moved in this direction from the Strip. It was the new happening place. Or so I was told.

I opened the office and flipped on the lights. Yana was long gone, but she'd put the place back together so you wouldn't have known a wrecking crew of gorillas had ever been through the joint.I opened the door to my inner office and turned on the overhead. There, lounging in the guest chair, making himself at home, feet on my desk, smoking a cigarette and drinking my scotch, was Detective Mejia. He didn't look up as I entered, just nonchalantly blew out a long plume of smoke into the room.

"Good evening, Detective, how did you get in here?"

"The door was open. Or maybe I picked the lock, I don't remember. Cheap locks, you should get better." He flicked a piece of ash into one of my Flintstone glasses. Noticing my look, he added, "Don't you got any ashtrays around this place?"

I had asked around about Mejia. He was a Lieutenant, had been on the force well past thirty years and was probably already counting down the days till retirement. That would explain his overly casual attitude and manner of dress. His brown tweed sports coat was cheap, off the rack, and wrinkled. He wore an ugly brown tie that was loosened at the neck and hung askew across a well-worn white shirt, frayed and sweat-stained around the collar. He wore white socks under his black pants. Well, maybe Michael Jackson could pull that off, but…

"No. I believe smoking is against the law in the workplace in California. Maybe I should call the police."

"Yeah. You do that." He took a sip from his glass, staring at me over the rim with his tiny black eyes. "Why are you packing that cannon?"

"Jeez, does everyone know I've got a gun now?"

"Why don't you put it in the drawer? Lighten your load a bit." He held the scotch up to the light. "Don't you got better than this? I would think a rich kid like you would have some top-drawer shit."

"Yeah. I keep it in the top drawer for my top-drawer clients. I took off my jacket, went to the file cabinet and deposited my holster and gun, and pulled out a bottle. "How about some Yamazaki, twenty-five?"

Mejia downed what was left in his glass and held it out. I poured him three fingers. I grabbed a Barney Rubble glass from the shelf and poured myself the same.

"Now that's what I'm talking about." He held the whiskey up to the light, like he knew what he was looking at; stuck his nose deep into the glass and took a big sniff, then sat back and savored his drink. I waited.

The detective began again. "You sent that note, didn't you? But you don't really have any pictures to back it up. You're pretty slick for a college boy. You embarrassed me, made me screw up like a rookie. So now you think you've got it all figured out, don't you?"

I plopped down in my chair and took a sip. It had been a long day, and I was beginning to think it was about to get even longer. I sensed I was on thin ice with this guy, so I curbed the snark and played it nice and polite.

"I take it you're not here in an official capacity, right?"

Sam said nothing, just took a long drag from his cigarette exhaled another big cloud of smoke and gave me a thin smile.

"Did you figure out who killed your old partner, yet?" I prodded.

The detective didn't look at me, but at the scotch he swirled around in his glass.

"Workin' on it. I'm putting my money on the Lachlan's wife. That Jennings' twenty-two is a lady's piece. Not very accurate from a distance. No stopping power, either. It's something you'd only use up close and personal. Even if it didn't have prints, no self-respecting man would be carrying around a toy gun like that."

"Does that include me?" I asked.

"Maybe. You're just a kid after all."

"I'm no amateur."

"You're no detective, either. What are you, twenty-five?"

"Twenty-eight. I'll bet you've got guys my age making detective."

"You'd lose that bet. Got to be twenty-one to get on the force, and you need five years uniformed to even take the test, and no one gets through on their first few tries."

"Maybe I'm a little smarter than the guys you recruit."
Detective Sam just gave me his best Jack Nicholson grin and didn't answer.

"Mimi had a gun like that, I remember. I saw it in her purse the first dayshe came to my office."

"Yeah, we traced it in a few hours. It's registered to your client. And I haven't ruled you out yet, either, in case you were wondering."

"She asked if I thought she should carry some protection." I lied.

"Of course, I advised her against it."

"Doesn't seem like she took your advice. You realize now, don't you, that as long as Miles was on her tail, she was safe. The minute you interfered, you put her in jeopardy."

"Wait a minute. Who hired Miles to follow her anyway?"

Mejia just drank his drink. He wasn't going to answer that.

"So where is Mimi, then?" I asked.

He frowned at me. "That's what I've been expecting you to turn up. I must say I'm a bit disappointed in you."

"Me?" I laughed. "Last I saw of her was a minute before I got jumped by those neighborhood kids. That's the last I saw of Miles, too. He drove by and sneered at me as I was picking myself up off the pavement. What about the police? You have more resources than I do. You haven't traced her phone? Haven't got a hit on her credit cards? Nothing?"

"Phone's been turned off, and she hasn't touched her money since she withdrew a couple grand from a local branch, teller's window. Not that that's any of your business."

"Yeah, you can't get that much scratch from an ATM. But that won't last a big spender like her very long." I offered.

"If a person wants to lie low, you can make it last a good long while," Mejia said absent-mindedly as his eyes wandered around the décor of my room. "This looks like some movie designer's idea of a detective's office. Where'd you get all this stuff?"

"So, how long have you been tailing me?" I asked.

"All fucking week long," Sam said, suddenly annoyed. "Long enough to figure out, as I've always suspected, that you ain't got a clue."

I smiled and shrugged.

"Oh, I've got clues. I make John Lee for it. Not him personally, mind you, but a hired hit. Oh, did I mention someone took a couple shots at me this afternoon?"

Sam looked up at the news.

"I guess you'd pulled your surveillance on me before that. Maybe I should file a police report. No, I wouldn't put it past Lee to frame this job on his poor cousin, Mimi. You know they're related, right?"

"So, you think your client was set up?"

"Sure, why not. What? You think she was setting up somebody else?"

"Nah, she's not that smart, got a few screws loose, I hear, a little bit loco is what everybody says."

"Yeah, that's what everybody says, all right. If I heard it once, I might believe it or might not. But if everybody is singing the same song, well then, either it's got to be true or it's pretty damn coincidental, don't you think? And when was she supposed to have planted the murder weapon? As I said, I haven't seen her since you first pinched me."

"I think I already showed you how easy it is to get into your office."

"For you maybe, for one of Lee's guys, yeah, but not Mimi. As you said, that's giving her a little too much credit.

Sam snorted and shook his head. "Now why in the hell would Lee send one of his goombah's to do that?"

"Miles was taking dirty pictures. Maybe of Lee, but my money is on his best bud, Messer. He doesn't want his boy, Arnold, to get dirty." I answered. "He and the councilman have plans, big plans. It would not look good for the future mayor to be caught with some girl half his age."

"Try a third of his age," Sam added with derision. "He's old enough to be her grandfather."

"Mimi's daughter, So Young?"

"Yeah, her. Gives Mimi plenty of motive."

"Well, how about Messer? He could have done it, too. He's Special Service, knows how to kill."

"You be careful making unsubstantiated allegations against a sitting councilman, son." He warned.

"Well, I don't like Mimi for it because unless she knows about the pictures, she's got no motive. And then she'd go after Messer first, as any mother would."

As these words were coming out of my mouth, I was thinking, maybe she did know, maybe she was stalking Messer.

"Then again, maybe Alistair." I continued, slowly. "Maybe your ex-partner, Miles, was blackmailing him, and he wasn't going to stand for it. But" I paused for dramatic effect. "You've been having me followed all this time, hoping I'll shake something loose, either unwittingly or accidentally. But the only thing I've figured out is that you yourself are mixed up in all this somehow."

"Are you accusing me of breaking the law, there, buck-o?"

"Maybe. You ran to Messer when you thought the photos were going to resurface. So, now I'm thinking, maybe it was you, Detective. Your ex-partner double-crosses you. Lee gives you the order to take care of it. You broke into my office easily enough tonight, what's to say you didn't break in before and plant that gun?"

"I must say you're pretty relaxed for being alone in the office at night with an armed killer across the desk from you." Mejia dropped his butt into the glass and doused it with a splash of scotch.

"That's because I don't really think it's you. But the only person we both know for sure didn't do it is me."

"You're pretty quick on the uptake, kid. You might make a good detective someday. But this is not that day."

He began shaking out a new cig from a crumpled pack he kept in his shirt pocket.

"I'm here to give you one last friendly warning." He said as he jammed a new cigarette his between his lips.

"Drop the case before you get hurt. You almost got yourself shot once today, prying into that family of mental cases. Yeah, I heard about it. Don't press your luck. I'm done following you around, so I ain't got your back if you get in trouble." He said, lighting up once more. "Thanks for the drink, kid."

With that, Detective Sam Mejia set his empty glass on my desk, paused, and picked up one of my business cards from the cardholder. He gave it a quick perusal, then proceeded to use it as a toothpick. He turned and left without another word.

I lingered over my drink, trying to make sense out of Mejia's visit. Was I really a pest, getting in the way of his investigation, or was I his stalking horse, bumbling along, flushing out the real culprit with my ineptitude?

I decided on the latter. I convinced myself I must have been doing something right, or Sam would have been harder on me. I checked my phone. There was a day-old text from Rachel, snidely wondering if I had gotten myself killed yet. I texted back.

"No, just been busy detectin'. You know how it is. I still owe you a make-up dinner if you're still interested. Tomorrow night?"

I finished my scotch, waiting to see if Rachel texted right back. She didn't. So, I turned out the light and locked up. I wondered as I turned the key why I even bothered. It wasn't like the locks were keeping anyone out of my office. Then I headed home, looking forward to a soft bed and a good night's sleep.

So Young was waiting by the front door, standing just out of the light. She was wearing short denim shorts and a gray boat neck t-shirt pulled down to expose one shoulder. Being the gentleman that I am, I invited her in - again. Before I could even unlock the door and turn on the lights, she was grilling me.

"Well, did you find out anything new?" She asked as she followed me inside.

"I did. Do you know your mother's parents are living in Solano Canyon?" I answered her question with one of my own.

"Well, of course. That's a rental property of ours, I mean of my father's," she explained, following me into the house.

"Mom put them there until she could get them better situated. They only just arrived here a few weeks ago."

"Her car's in the garage."

So Young blinked. "Really? Which one?"

"She has more than one? The blue Beemer."

"That's hers. She sometimes drives the Audi, though." She said, lost in thought now.

"Then you must be aware that with your mom missing, no one is looking out for them." I continued. "They told me they haven't had any food for days."

That brought her back. "You talked to them? Oh, my god, really?! Of course, you're right."

So Young was suddenly very upset, pacing back and forth and trying to figure out a plan on the fly. "I've got to go over there. They are probably freaking out."

"Relax. I sent over some food, enough to last a couple of days. It's late. They are probably asleep. If you go over in the morning, that will be soon enough. But I think you or someone needs to take overlooking after them. I got the sense they know absolutely no one else in this city."

"Of course, you're right." She said, repeating herself. "I'll head over there first thing. Oh, thank you, James. That was very thoughtful of you to step in and help them out like that." She stepped closer, touched my arm, and looked up into my eyes.

I looked into hers, trying to decipher what could be going on in there. "You want a drink?" I asked.

"Sure!" she said with a smile. I could see concern in her eyes over her grandparents' situation had just flown out the window.

"How about a Big Lebowski."

"You mean a White Russian?"

"Except with powdered coffee creamer instead of cream, but whatever you've got is fine."

"I'm pretty sure I don't have any powdered coffee creamer. I drink my coffee black."

"Ha, black coffee, whiskey, I'm surprised you don't smoke unfiltered cigarettes. You sure play the part of the hardboiled Humpty Bogart to the hilt." She teased.

"Humphrey, it's Humphrey Bogart." I corrected.

"Whatever. So, what made you decide to become a detective anyway? You certainly don't pay the rent for this place on a detective's pay."

"No, I have some investment income to pay the bills. I like detective work. It's kind of a hobby. Like I said, it feeds the romantic in me."

"Romantic? Creeping around, spying on people? Not this girl's idea of a fun time."

I went into the kitchen to make her a drink, but with milk as I had neither cream nor non-dairy creamer, being careful to take a whiff of the carton first to make sure it hadn't gone bad. I started to lightly quiz her about the various characters I've encountered. I scrupulously avoided any mention of Messer.

"Those cops still camped out at your place?"

"I've been at school. But I think they're still camped out at our home if that's what you mean."

"You met them when they first showed up, right? I think you complained that they interrogated you. Were either of the detectives named Bowman or Mejia? One's old with a crew cut, looks like Dick Tracy with white hair. The other guy's younger, Hispanic, kind of ugly, real scary looking dude." I queried.

"I don't remember their names, but yeah, one was Hispanic, he asked me the usual questions. Why are you asking?"

"Just curious if they were the same guys who busted me. Did I already ask you if you knew a guy named John Lee?"

"Yes, I told you he's one of my dad's old partners, and now one of his competitors. What's he got to do with anything?"

"I don't know, maybe nothing. No one mentioned to you that he was a relative, also, a distant uncle, maybe once or twice removed?"

"No. I'm sure he's not. Someone would have mentioned it if he was family."

"Doesn't matter. What about Solano Canyon? Did your dad ever talk about a casino being planned for there?"

"He may have mentioned it once or twice. I think Mr. Lee was involved in that. That was one of their disputes. Father was trying to rejuvenate the neighborhood, buy up distressed houses, and turn them around. I think Lee complained that my dad was driving up the prices."

"I think this Mr. Lee likes to play rough. When I was there earlier today, some punks drove by and put a couple slugs in my car."

So Young suddenly seems very worried, for her grandparents, for me, maybe, for herself?

I couldn't tell. She took a long draught of her drink, and the moment passed. She walked over to the front window, paused to take in her reflection, and fluffed her hair with her free hand.

"How did your mother get mixed up in all this?"

"I don't know." She answered without turning around. "Is she mixed up in it? Maybe all her visits to Halaboji and Halmi sent a wrong message to some people. I don't know."

She finished her drink, then turned to me, suggestively licking off her milk mustache.

"Maybe I should call you an Uber."

She wasn't expecting that. She turns to me with a hurt look on her face. I can't help but picture her at the Dong-Seo, though, made up like the other girls, arm in arm with Messer. I caught myself being jealous for no reason.

"The night before was a mistake. I mean, that didn't come out right. Look, I'm trying to keep this professional. I work for you, and maybe still for your mother. After this is all over. Well."

"No, you're right. I should be going. I can get my own ride." She puts down her glass and heads for the door.

"You can wait inside."

"No, I need some air."

She doesn't give me any more time to protest before she shuts the door behind her.

I make myself another drink. Rule number two – never sleep with the client until the case is closed. What have I been doing, playing the sap for her? I sure never pegged her moonlighting as a *nohrehbang* girl. Or whatever it was that she was doing. Teenage rebellion, or was it something else?

What a day.

CHAPTER

TWENTY-THREE

The next day I slept late. I reluctantly rolled out of bed and staggered to the window. The sun was well up when I pulled back the curtains to see the mystery house next door. There didn't seem to be anybody around, yet. But I didn't feel like investigating that today. I grabbed my phone off the bedside table and unplugged the charging cable.

There was no reply from Rachel; maybe she was going to finally give up on me. I should probably make a reservation for dinner just in case, I thought.

Then my phone dinged. Not Rachel. It was a text from Mrs. Shin. Mrs. Park would meet me at the same coffee shop after lunch, one o'clock. Well, there was that. I wondered how I would know her. I suppose I'm the one who's easy to spot. Have to rely on her to find me.

I was moving kind of slow this morning, but somehow managed to shower and shave, grab my new computer, still in the box, and head out for the office just the same. When I opened my front door, the heat hit me like the afterburner of an F-35. This weather had to be going on three weeks straight, twenty days of hundred-degree-plus days. On top of that, the hills north and east of Pasadena were burning, and soot was wafting through the air. It smelled like campfires. Welcome to L.A.

I grabbed my usual coffee order at Starbucks, but Jim, my goldfish guy, was not on his customary corner. Maybe the heat and the air were too toxic for him. Hope he found someplace cool and safe to breathe. Well, more coffee for me, I thought.

When I got to the office, it was still locked. Juggling a computer box and coffee tray, I managed to open up, wondering if Yana had already come and gone. I checked my phone for the n'th time, already ten o'clock. Then it dawned on me that it was Saturday. I was so disoriented.

I set down my cardboard tray of coffees and my new laptop, still in the box. I guessed I'd have a relaxing morning to myself, loading software onto my new computer. Sounded like fun. Maybe now was a good opportunity to start practicing better cybersecurity.

I cranked up the AC units in both rooms. After fumbling through various software tutorials, I decided to call Jack to come help me set everything up. No answer, so I left a message. Fussing with the laptop frustrated and annoyed me. I folded it up and headed for the diner. Jack's radar was bound to pick up on me, and he'd show within twenty minutes for a free meal, and I'd get my install done, and maybe he'd have those phone records to boot – win/win.

One hour, one tuna melt with fries and countless cups of coffee later, and I was quite buzzed from all the caffeine, but no Jack. I packed it up and headed back to the office. I put my laptop back on the desk along with my feet, and I stared out the window. With all the coffee coursing through my veins, a nap now was out of the question.

My cell phone pinged, reminding me of my appointment with Ms. Park, the Mahjong lady. I rushed out the door. Hopefully, the coffee shop would have something else besides coffee.

Driving back to Koreatown, I wondered about this pursuit of

Mimi's friends and friends of friends. Were they being honest and helpful, or was this an elaborate ploy orchestrated by Mimi to lead me astray, keep me off the trail. Their stories were all the same. Coincidence or strategy? What was I hoping to find by interviewing them?

The coffee shop was becoming quite familiar. Actually, it was more of a tea house. I arrived early and entered from the parking lot in the back. The hostess recognized me this time and showed me to my usual table by the window. I waved off ordering until my guest arrived.
I sat there quietly surveying the room. It was an odd place
with lots of little areas sectioned off by screens. Lots of plants, bonsai trees with battery-operated waterfalls, and pictures of Buddha complemented the soft drum and chime music.

A youngish woman entered and approached the front desk. The hostess pointed to me at my corner table. As she approached, I rose and offered my hand.

"Mrs. Park?" I asked.

She was not what I was expecting. Older than me, but younger than Mimi or the other ladies, she wore a brown cashmere top over blue jeans and carried a small clutch. Shoulder-length brown hair and large glasses framed an attractive face. She looked like a grad student or a librarian.

"Have you had lunch?" I asked as we sat down.

"Yes, thank you. Did you?"

"I did. Maybe dessert? They have *patbingsu*."

"Oh, no thanks. That's too much. Maybe some *songpyeon*."

We ordered tea and *songpyeon*. Those are little rice cakes filled with red bean or sesame, or some other sweet syrup. Very tasty, soft, and chewy. While we waited for our teas, I filled Ms. Park in on Mimi's disappearance. She had agreed to meet because she was concerned. Mimi had missed their weekly Mahjong date without calling and had not answered or returned any calls for the past week.

"How do you know Mimi?" I asked, starting off our interview.

"We first met through hairdresser. We discovered we are from same hometown."

"Taegu?" I asked.

"You know Taegu?"

"Only that it is the town where Mimi comes from. I've spoken to a lot of people while looking for her, and everyone seems to describe a different woman. Tell me about the Mimi you know."

"Oh, I love Mimi. She is so beautiful and smart and such a big success.

"You're the first I've met to call her smart."

"Yes, I know, she didn't go to university, but not because she was not smart. Her father was not rich. He owned an orchard, grew apples, Taegu apples are famous. He could only afford to send his first son to university, and Mimi was a girl. She was expected to marry and raise a family. But she wanted more. She wanted to be famous actress or big-time model."

"So, she went to Seoul. I guess a lot of small-town girls are drawn to the big city."

Ms. Park laughed. "Taegu is not a small town, but it is not the same as Seoul."

"Her cousin went to Seoul, too, didn't he?"

"Yes, they went together. I think he put a lot of those ideas in her head. He was not a firstborn son either, so no inheritance, no future for him at home. He was very ambitious. I think he saw Mimi's beauty as a way to help himself."

"By getting her married to some rich guy?"

"Married to an American or other foreigner. Rich Korean husbands are not going to help out the country cousin. Mimi said he always dreamed of going to America. She only realized later that her cousin was using her."

"Well, they are both here now, and both doing well. Sounds like Mimi should be happy, but I get the sense that she is not."

"No. She fell in love, but not with the husband she has now. She was never really happy after that."

"How do you mean?"

"Mimi is a romantic girl. She met her handsome American Army officer. He talked sweetly to her, made many promises about a future together. She was so in love. Then one day he was gone. Shipped out, they say. He never said anything to Mimi, just disappeared. Mimi's heart was broken. Then she found out she was pregnant."

"That's not easy in Korea, is it? Being an unwed mother."

"Terrible. Terrible. Many girls don't keep the baby, either abortion or give it up to adoption. But Mimi wanted to keep her baby. She was still in love and hoped that the father would come back someday, especially if he knew they had a child together. She had very romantic notions."

"And that's when cousin Lee brought Mr. Lachlan into the picture."

"Yes. Mimi never loved him, but she pretended to. She had no other choice."

The tea and rice cakes came. I sipped my tea and thought about all of this. It was not surprising. I had mostly pieced it together already. But who knew what was really going on with Mimi and her pursuit of

Councilman Messer? Certainly, Lee and Alistar did. They were probably scrambling to prevent her from spoiling all their real estate plans. But did Messer know? Did So Young know? And, where was Mimi now?

"I get the sense that of all the ladies who play in your Mahjong games, you are probably the closest to her. Maybe in part from you both hailing from the same hometown. Do you have any idea where she might go, who she might turn to if she was in trouble?"

Mrs. Park took a bite from a green rice cake and chewed thoughtfully, then looked up at me. "Not a clue."

On the drive home, I called my mother; she always liked to hear from me and would probably want me to come over for lunch on Sunday, if only to give me an earful about how I was botching my chances with Rachel.

Another no answer. This time I decided not to leave a message. Instead, I headed out of the office. I'd just grab my car from the lot and drive over to the club. Mom would probably be having lunch with her foursome before her afternoon round.

The club was usually crowded on weekends, tennis or golf; most members who weren't retired were workaholics or had careers to pursue during the week and would only allow themselves to come out on Saturdays or Sundays. After a stroll around the cafés and the courts, I saw no sign of my mother. I debated waiting for her at the bar, but instead I wandered into the pro shop to kill some time, flipping through the golf shirts and other merchandise.

The club pro was behind the counter, a young guy with a blond crew cut reminiscent of Palmer in his heyday.

"Mr. Gardinier, how are you doing? Going to play a round today?

Shall I call for your bag?" He called out, grabbing the phone for the caddy shack.

"Not today, Allen," I replied. "Just looking around. Do you have that new Scotty Cameron?"

"Sure. Should be one on the rack."

I walked over to the putter rack and there it was, red and white leather grip, it stood out from the rest.

"Going to put that in your bag?" Allen asked suggestively.

"No, think I'll try it out first."

"Sure thing, knock yourself out, sir."

I took the new putter out to the practice green. It was littered with fifty or so new Titleists. I kicked a few over to a clear spot and tried sinking a few long putts. I'd always found golf a good way to clear my mind and sort things out. But today, I was finding that I had precious little new information to sort, I looked at the different scenarios until my head spun. I was stuck, no idea which way to go. I gave up and headed for the parking lot.

As I fished around in my coat for the valet ticket, I pulled a business card. It was Ted Carmady's, the one Jack gave me the last time we were at the Brasher. I turned it over.

Ted Carmady – carmadyscity@blogspot.com, it read in typewriter font on newsprint light grey stock. Cute.
On the reverse side were an email address and a phone number. I called Ted, explaining my connection to Jack and interest in the Casino business, and asked him to meet me at the Brasher for a drink that evening.

The valet brought my car around. A flyer was still stuck under the windshield wiper. As I yanked it out, I did a double-take. At first, I thought it said, 'No on Mimi!', but on second glance, I saw that it read 'No on M.M.!' and underneath 'Stop the Casino!' M.M. being the designation of the Casino referendum on November's ballot. Now, how did someone get on the club grounds to stick these on the windshields?

As the valet got out and held the door for me, he gently caressed the bullet holes in the door.

"You're pretty badass for a white dude." He says with a mischievous wink.

Before pulling away, I fished through the flyers on the floor before finding the one that I wanted one that I had already identified as part of John Lee's group. I didn't know where I was going with this; it was a stab in the dark. I phoned the number on the flyer. A young woman answered.

"Hi!" I started. "I saw your flyer and I am interested in looking at some property in Solano Canyon."
There was silence on the other end, then a young woman answered, somewhat confused. "Pardon me?"

"I'm looking to buy a home. I've been driving around the area, and I saw your flyers. I'd like to set up an appointment to see something in the Solano Canyon neighborhood."

"I see." She replied. "I'm sorry, but we're not that kind of real estate company. We don't sell homes; we only buy them."

I pretended to be clueless.

"I'm a big Dodger fan. It would be a dream come true to find a house where I could walk to the ballpark for a game. A fixer-upper would be fine. I noticed a couple of properties with for sale signs that looked very interesting."

"We are not real estate agents, here. You should try a traditional firm, like Coldwell Banker or Sotheby's. You can find them on the internet."

"But, your flyers…"

"We're looking for people who might be interested in selling. We're home buyers, just like yourself. I don't think you'll find what you're looking for in Solano anyway. In my opinion, it's way overpriced. You might take a look at Echo Park." She added helpfully.

Well, that was a bust. I hung up and prepared to head back to the office or home, I was undecided. Then it occurred to me that Mejia, or one of his goons was probably still tailing me, or having me tailed. I decided to check it out.

From the club, it was only two blocks up to Sunset. The neighborhood between the gates and Sunset was usually quiet, even at the busiest of times. Even the best shadow artist was going to have to show himself or risk losing me on Sunset.

Sure enough, as I waited at the traffic light for a chance to pull out onto Sunset, I saw a grey Camry approach from a side street and wait at the intersection. The light, I knew, was a short one; even so, when it turned green, I delayed, pretending to be on my phone, then as it turned yellow, I shot across the street and into the next neighborhood. In my rear-view mirror, I saw the Camry pull up to the light, stuck. He could make a right turn, or wait out the light, but by then I'd be long gone.

He knew he'd been made, and of course, anyone could pick me up in this boat. He was probably phoning ahead now for another car to be on the lookout for a turquoise and cream barge sailing east. The bullet holes in the driver's side door should have been enough ID to differentiate me from all the other '57 Marquis on the road today. I should probably have gotten those fixed, but maybe not. They were pretty rad, and I had appearances to keep up.

I took the long way home, heading west down to the coast

highway, then circling back on the freeway through downtown, and then back up to Hollywood. I took about two hours instead of one, but it was a nice day for a drive with the top down, so what the hell.

I got off on Barham and took the northern route into the neighborhood, circling past the Hollywood Reservoir and snaking through all the little-known canyon roads. I parked a few blocks up from my house and walked, taking the "Secret Stairs".

Beachwood Canyon had all these staircases connecting the winding canyon streets. They weren't really all that secret but were mostly known and used by the locals. It made for an easy shortcut, and in my case, allowed for a stealthier approach to home. As I headed down my street, I was checking out every parked car and passerby as I went. After I was convinced that the coast was clear, I ducked into the house and locked the door behind me.

There was nothing to do now but wait. I watched a little golf, Sunday finals, the kids were taking it to the seasoned pros today. Man, these guys were five years younger than me and playing like that. I was jealous.

I decided to call Yana on a whim. No answer, I left a message, but before I could even get to the kitchen for another beer, she called back.

"Hooray! Someone is out there." I cheered.

"I was beginning to think my team was abandoning me."

"Huh?" Yana didn't have a clue what I was prattling on about. "You called me."

"Just thought I'd check in, see if you had uncovered any game-changing clues about our client."

"Am I getting overtime for this?"

"Overtime? What am I paying you again?"

"Not enough."

"Not enough. Well then, of course, you'll get overtime. What have you got?"

"Nothing, just the basic student profile from the admissions office, and it wasn't easy to get that. I had to lie and tell them that she was being considered for a T.A. position."

"And…"

"Born in Seoul; will turn nineteen in November; Korean national, went to Marlborough high school; she's in her sophomore year, 3.8 GPA for her first year, majoring in city planning. Her courses this semester are…"

"Wait, hold on. Back up a little. You said Korean national. She should be American. Her birth father is American. That would be automatic."

"I think it mentioned somewhere she has permanent residency, so I guess she has her green card, but not a citizen as far as I can tell. USC is a private school, so there's probably no difference in tuition, foreign or not."

I'm racking my brain trying to remember my conversation with Lachlan. Did he say anything about marrying Mimi to give her citizenship? Or was that Lee's story?

"Hello?" Yana's voice cut through my thoughts.

"Huh?"

"I thought you hung up on me."

"Sorry, my mind kind of drifted off there for a sec."

"That's all I got so far."

"No, that's fine. Thanks. Enjoy what's left of your weekend. I'll see you on Monday."

I was so distracted I didn't even hear her say goodbye.

The golf tournament was still showing on the television. I continued watching for a while, then started flipping channels and landed on some trout fishing show. I liked watching the grace of this guy whipping his line back and forth in a balletic rhythm and then plopping that lure right where he was aiming.

As I admired his skill, a sudden thought popped into my head. Miles was into fly fishing, even tied his own flies. You go with what you know.

I scrambled out the door, ran up the block, up the 'secret stairs', not caring anymore if someone was watching. I hopped in my car, too excited to even think this train of thought through. It was a shot in the dark, but I had no other cards right now.

I was wondering if my car was bugged. I climbed out and crawled under, looking for any obvious GPS tracker, but didn't see anything. I searched the interior and found nothing there. I got back under the wheel, still not feeling secure, actually feeling foolish for that over-eager mad dash from the house. I turned my phone off, just in case they were tracking that. Of course, if they were, I realized, they would know my position by my last call just now with Yana. Too late to worry about that now. Turned the phone on again, double checked that I hadn't missed a text from Rachel. There was none. Good, now the evening was mine.

I drove quickly down to Inglewood to Miles' house. It was nearly sunset by the time I got there. The streets were pretty empty with everyone inside eating Sunday dinner or watching 60 Minutes on the telly.

I parked the Merc in the driveway. It looked like it belonged there. Going around back, I jimmied my way again into the house through the rear sliding glass door, flipped on my flashlight, and found my way into the living room. I glanced around. It didn't look like anyone had been here since my last visit.

Still on the wall were the fishing trip pictures and the pair of rods hanging on their stands. I examined again the line on one of the reels. I remembered correctly, the leader had been cut off, and the line was unspooling and tangled, totally ruined. Now, why would he do that? He wouldn't, except if his line got snarled, like in some brush or in a tree, and he couldn't free it. But a serious fisherman like Miles would have squared away his gear before heading home out of habit.

Unless he was already home and up to something out of his normal routine. I walked back to the sliding patio door and looked through it at the tree, tall and black in the shadows, with just the very top still lit gold by the setting sun.

I made my way out into the backyard.

The grass had not been mowed, and not just for the two weeks since he'd been dead. It looked like it had never been mowed and was mostly tall and burnt. Miles may have been an outdoorsman, but he wasn't much of a yard keeper. Overshadowing most of the backyard was the giant Ficus tree, the biggest one I'd ever seen. It had to be at least seventy feet tall. I shone my flashlight up and down the branches, walking in a slow circle around the base.

Just as I was thinking this was a stupid hunch, I saw it, the shiny glimmer of the wire leader, hung up high in the tree. It would have been completely invisible in the daylight.

The cut end of the line dangled about eight feet from the ground. I looked around for a patio chair to stand on and then grabbed and pulled the line. It stuck for a bit, but a good tug brought it down. At the other end, tied neatly like a prize fly was a memory stick – the pictures!

I hopped back in the convertible and headed back to my office. I hadn't forgotten my appointment with Carmady, but now I was cutting it close. I gunned it and ran a red light. I couldn't afford to be late and have him blow me off.

It was getting late; the sun had already set, and L.A. was looking her best. Salmon-colored clouds enveloped the glittering lights of skyscrapers downtown like tissue paper around a sparkly toy, all wrapped in ribbons of red and white that were the freeways. The town was gearing up for another Saturday night, and here I was alone in my car, nervously peeking over my shoulder every five minutes.

What a life.

Despite the traffic, I got there early and was nursing my second craft-brewed double IPA and picking at the remaining corned beef from my half-eaten Ruben when Ted walked in.

He was a rather short guy, five foot four, maybe five-five, pre-maturely balding with a neatly trimmed reddish beard and mustache. He wore one of those tweed sport coats with leather patched elbows over a plaid shirt.

Jack had described him as Paul Giamatti playing your typical English Lit teaching assistant, except without the pipe. He had him pegged pretty good, but I might have gone with that actor from "Close Encounters", Bob Balaban.

"Hey. You, Ted?" I asked as I swiveled around on my bar stool.

"Yes, and you must be Jimmy?" He nodded in reply.

I stifled a laugh. "My friends actually call me James. It's okay, Jack does that to me all the time."

I grabbed my beer, left the sandwich. I suddenly wasn't hungry.

We retired to a quiet corner booth.

"Can I get you a drink?" I asked.

"Scotch and soda will be fine."

I started to say something, but stopped myself. This was not the time to be a drink snob.

"Any scotch okay then?" I asked.

"Sure. They're all the same to me."

I went and got him his drink, and some top-shelf, neat, for myself, and returned.

"Thanks." He said as I handed him his drink. He took a healthy swallow as I settled opposite him.

"Jack tells me you're on a case that may involve the casino bond measure in some way." Ted began.

"I'm not sure that it is, but it sure does seem like a lot of the people I'm interested in are also interested in this casino."

"Give me some names."

"John Lee, Alistair and Mimi Lachlan, Arnold Messer for starters."

"Fringe players, the lot of them. I thought you might have turned up something new or interesting."

"It sure seemed to me they were deeply involved."

"I'm not saying they're not involved. It's just that they are playing around the edges, vying for the scraps. The Chinese are calling the shots around here."

"The Chinese?"

"The boys from Macau, I call 'em. They're in the casino business. I think they're mostly gangsters." Ted leaned forward, lacing his fingers together in a lazy prayer.

"You mean Yakuza?"

"No, that's the Japanese. In China, organized crime is generally referred to as the Triads. The biggest groups, those that control gambling, are mostly based in Hong Kong and Macau, but they have people everywhere. I'm sure there's been a group based here in Los Angeles for some time now."

"So, these Triads, they're like the Mafia? They would go so far as to kill people who get in their way?"

"Please. The Triads make those Italian mobsters look like choirboys."

"And they're backing Lee, you think?"

"More like Lee is fronting for them. They like to stay in the shadows, keep their names out of the public view. You know how it is with Americans and their views on China. If there was a whiff of Chinese involvement in this, you'd have some xenophobic politician leading a torch and pitchfork parade."

"Then you think Lee is working for the Triads?"

"Indirectly. They may or may not be paying him but they own him none-the-less. I figure they have something on him that keeps him loyal to their goals, blackmail, intimidation, who knows? They own Messer, too, though I'm not so sure about Mr. Lachlan. I haven't turned up anything on him or his wife."

"Why do you think they own Messer? He's not a developer?"

"He's their guy at City Hall. He's the councilman for the first district. That's Solano Canyon, Chinatown, parts of downtown, and half of Koreatown, all the neighborhoods they're interested in. Whatever they have over him must be pretty solid. He runs down to Malibu every Sunday to get his marching orders."

"Huh. I would have figured Messer to have more spine than that."

"Oh, don't get me wrong, Messer is a bad ass in his own right. I can give you the book on him. Army Ranger, Special Forces, secret ops, probably for the CIA, missions that they don't even give a name to. You know, like Captain Willard in Apocalypse Now. He was a person of interest in an incident up near the Joint Security Area in Korea. A bar girl was murdered, neck broken. No charges were ever filed, and the investigation by local authorities was stymied. Messer mustered out of the service shortly thereafter with the usual honors and citations. Then he did some of the usual security and mercenary gigs that guys like him always land out of the service. That's where they make their mad money. He didn't stick it out for long, though. Guess there wasn't enough action in it for him. After that, he tried his hand at competitive mixed martial arts. He was too old for that sport, but he managed to mess up one opponent pretty bad, put him in the hospital. Again, no charges were ever filed. Other than that, single, never married, no kids on record, but who knows how many he may have fathered overseas."

"How do you know all this?" I asked.

"I've been investigating these guys for over two years."

"You sound like a detective."

"I'm more than a detective. I'm a reporter."He said with more than a little pride.

"Well, Mr. Reporter. Let me buy you another drink. You should try a single malt this time, straight up."

I signaled to the barman for two more of what I was having.
I figured Ted was not a drinker. I surmised that the minute he ordered his watered-down cocktail. But if I was buying, he was drinking. On a reporter's salary, he probably didn't party much. Still, I would get what I could out of him while he was still sober and coherent.

My little visit from Detective Mejia was still on my mind, so I asked Ted if he'd ever run across his name in his digging. Turns out he had, often enough to do a little extra investigating. Sam's late partner, Miles Bowman, wasn't the only one to run afoul of Internal Affairs, but somehow Mejia had skated on whatever they had on him. Maybe he had a friend higher up, who knew? He was LA's version of Dirty Harry with more than a couple of lethal shootings on his docket. Not a cop to be messed with, as he was not one to play by the rules. But he had his supporters.

"You'd better watch your six if you're going to keep investigating these guys. Mejia's actually not a bad guy, but you gotta watch out for the Chinese. They've threatened me several times." He bragged.

"You're not worried about that?" I asked. "They've already taken a couple of shots at me."

"If they missed, it was intentional, a warning. Nah. It's bad form to go after the press. They don't want to get their names in the paper."

It was well past midnight when I walked Ted out of the bar. I tried to wait with him for his Uber, but he insisted he was sober enough to stand there unassisted until his car came, so I hurried back to my office.

I parked Lola on Ivar and cut through the alley behind my building on foot, keeping an eye out for anyone sitting in a parked car. I was able to use the dumpster to give me enough of a boost to catch the bottom rung of the fire escape. The old windows were not locked and opened onto the corridor of each floor.

The building was usually empty at this hour, but nonetheless, I was careful to survey both directions before I climbed through.

I let myself into my office, being careful not to turn on the lights like I usually do. I shut the door and listened for any sounds, either inside my office or coming up the hallway, outside. So far, total silence.

I got into my inner office and peeked through the venetian blinds to the street below.

There were a couple of cars parked on Cahuenga and in the lot across the street, but I didn't recognize them, of course, it was dark, and the only car I would know by sight would be Detective Mejia's. Well, if they were down there, I thought I slipped past them.

I had a little adrenaline pumping through me now. I didn't know if I was thrilled or scared shitless. I went to the picture of a movie poster of Bogart and Bacall that hung on my wall, a publicity still from Key Largo. It was a framed photo that swung away on a hinge, revealing a safe in the wall, probably installed there by the first tenant in this office. Nowadays, I had nothing in the safe except for a 9mm Beretta. I took it out and checked that it was loaded.

I sat down at my desk, put the pistol to one side, and pulled over my new computer. I didn't know what kind of camera this memory card came from, but I had several different USB adapters for my own equipment. I found the right one and plugged it in, and started scrolling through the pictures.

After about twenty photos of trout fishing, I spotted one of the front of the Dong-Seo at night, shot from a high angle. Was Miles on a rooftop across the street? He was clever enough to have included his phone in the frame, with date and time showing for his first pic. This series was from about two months ago.

I wondered why his camera didn't have a time and date stamp as a built-in feature. I figured it must have been either an old camera or Miles was unaware of how to use it.

There were a few more shots of the girls milling about, close-ups of one in particular that Miles must have taken a fancy to, then one of

Messer and a girl exiting the club. I stopped and looked closely. It kind of looked like So Young, but her face was turned away.

A few pics later, and I was convinced it was her. Miles had shot so many pics, flipping through them was almost like watching a video. A limo pulled up and they got in.

Following this was a group of pictures of Mimi and Lee arguing outside the club. Lee's bodyguard hovered behind him. Other shots showed a few other Asian toughs in the background, either Korean or Chinese. Then Mimi was gone, but Messer was with Lee, again in an apparent argument. What was this all about, I wondered.

Another shot of the exterior of the club, probably a different day, a little lighter, dusk, maybe? Then another, which included a phone screen grab, indicated one week later.

The angle suggested Miles had changed his stakeout spot to street level. He must have been in a car parked nearby. I could see the edge of his window frame in the shot. A few more shots of the girls; Miles' previous favorite not in the mix this time. Then there was Messer again with So Young, who this time was shielding her face, or maybe just her eyes, from the glare of the setting sun.

A few better shots followed, and I could clearly see both their faces. Another photo, and they are joined by two young Asian men in black suits and dark sunglasses. One wore some sort of Fedora, just like a 40s hood. Messer did not seem happy. Could these guys be the triad gangsters Carmady was telling me about? The limo pulled up again. Close up on the plate.

Next was a shot of a house, a typical two-story California bungalow with the Limo out front. Close up on the house number plate – 802, but no street name. It looked similar to the one Mimi's parents lived in, but definitely not the same house. More shots of shadows on the curtains, but nothing useful. Further down, shots of the same house but now with Mimi exiting the front door, getting into her little convertible, and driving off. So, this was another of Alistar's properties.

What was Mimi doing there?

Another week, to the day, no Dong-Seo this batch, but a phone-dated exterior shot of the bungalow at 802 something. Curtains opened on one window, dark figures inside, could have been Messer and So Young, but not clear. Miles had one heck of a zoom lens, but no light to work with.

I kept scrolling through, seemed to be one session every week by the dates. Alternating series of Messer and So Young, then Mimi. She must have been wise to what was happening with those two. Was she trying to catch them in the act? And who was Miles following? Who was he being paid to follow? Was he looking to blackmail Messer on the side? I looked at my own phone and calculated that these are all Thursdays. That jived with what the girls told me about "Ah Na" only working Thursdays.

Finally, I found Miles' hero shot. Deep in the roll was a picture of So Young and Messer, both naked from the waist up, nicely framed in the open window, not above the front of the house like in the others, so maybe in the back. This was the money shot, or so he thought.

This may also have been the one that got him killed.

I stared at it for a few minutes before I printed it out. I don't know if I was jealous seeing her with him like that. I hardly knew her, one night was all. Now I was sure I didn't know her at all. Or, maybe I was misunderstanding the whole thing. I found myself wanting to be with her again anyway.

Actually, now having the photos in my possession had suddenly made me paranoid again. If I thought this way, what did Messer think? Did she have him twisted around her finger, or vice versa, and to what end?

Looks like I was going to sleep on the couch tonight.

CHAPTER TWENTY-FOUR

I slept late again. My windows faced West, but even so, it was very bright in the office. I got up and split the slats of the blinds, checking the street below for any suspicious cars. The streets were predictably empty; it was Sunday. I didn't recognize any of the parked cars, but one can't be too careful.

I started for the door when I caught sight of myself in the mirror. I looked a mess, like I'd slept in my clothes. Funny that. I've got to start keeping a fresh change of clothes at the office. Maybe I should write myself a note. Another time. I peeked out the office door. The corridor was empty, of course, Sunday.

Just to be safe, I decided to take the stairs down to the garage even though I couldn't be sure that was where I'd parked my car. No Prius in the garage, so I slipped out through a back door to the alley and hoofed it back up the hill to home.

Taking my roundabout route again, I walked down from above, checking every car on the street for a stakeout. When I got to my house, the door was not locked and stood slightly ajar. I wasn't surprised. I stared at it a good long while debating with myself whether or not someone was still inside. Figuring that if anyone was lying in wait for me, they wouldn't have been careless enough to leave the door open, I pushed it open the rest of the way and walked in.

"Honey, I'm home!" I called out to no one.

The house had been ransacked. Well, someone thinks I have something to hide. Probably not Mejia, though, he would have tossed my stuff more systematically and with a warrant. At least I hoped he would have. I hoped I hadn't pushed him over the line into some extra-legal scheme.

I wandered from room to room assessing the damage. Nothing seemed broken, papers and pillows tossed on the floor into a giant heap, pictures taken down off the wall, but intact, doors and drawers left open, cushions pulled from the couch, the usual, but with a polite touch. In the bathroom, that person had taken the wash rag and half-heartedly tried to erase my lipstick diagram. Now it was just a red mess. It looked a little like a bloody massacre if I didn't know better. It would all have to stay this way for a while. I could clean up tonight.

I stripped down and took a shower. As I got out, I looked again at my mirror. Faint lines still connected my cast of suspects through the lipstick smears. I picked up the applicator and drew a connecting line between So Young and Councilman Messer.

I stared for a moment at the line between her and her father. What was wrong with that connection that she wasn't a natural-born citizen? I needed to see Lachlan again, but he wasn't going to want to see me. Maybe I could ambush him at the club. Nothing like forced decorum to keep one from making a scene.

I could use that to my advantage. But first, I had an appointment to see Messer, only he didn't know it. It had taken only a few drinks to get Ted Carmady to give up the address of the Chinese boss man in Malibu, where Messer goes for his weekly report. Either Ted was drunk, or he didn't care that some young punk detective was hell bent on getting himself killed. Maybe a little of both. He indeed turned out to be a bit of a lightweight when it came to drinking, no match for me. I could finish a fifth of scotch by myself and leave with nothing more than just a warm glow.

Malibu is a one-street town, seriously. That is, if you consider Pacific Coast Highway a street. The houses to the east of it are cute little beach bungalows sitting right on the water and starting at eight figures. To the west, in the Malibu Hills, are the bigger estates, not quite as big as Kane's Xanadu, but close.

The address that Ted had given me was for one of these, just far enough past the outskirts of Malibu proper to afford the kind of acreage that gives you plenty of privacy. I had googled it to check out the aerial view. It was quite the fortress, with guard stations at two sets of gates to go with the inner and outer perimeter fences.

I half expected to see watch towers on the corners. I knew I wasn't going to be making a frontal assault. I had also scoped the surrounding area on Google maps and was aware that a fire road ran about a half mile behind the property through one of the canyons. That would be my route in. I had packed my camera and telephoto lens, and my nine mil., though I'm not sure why.

I was planning to find a decent perch at a good safe distance and hopefully get a decent look at and photo of whomever Messer was meeting each Sunday. I remembered where I had left Lola and hiked back to Ivar with all my stuff.

I drove Sunset out to the coast, then up PCH through Malibu. I turned up the canyon road about a mile before the house. It was a good five miles up to the summit before I reached the fire road that worked its way back down.

I found a secluded spot to leave the car and hiked the rest of

the way behind the mansion property. I was quite high above the house and even though still a quarter mile away, I felt I was already too close and worried about being spotted.

There was only one fence here behind the house, which was about a couple football fields away and enclosed a mown grass yard. There was a stand of oaks along the fence line. I decided that would be a close as I dared go.

The house was not outrageously large by Malibu money standards, maybe ten thousand square feet. It had an infinity pool in front. I guess from the right angle, you could imagine yourself swimming in the same water as the ocean across the highway. There was the requisite tennis court and a large expansive patio in back. A few men in black t-shirts and black slacks lounged around. Entourage or security, I assumed. One guy, in an attempt to be stylish, sported a black Trilby at a rakish angle. I'd seen that hat before.

I made myself comfortable and set up my camera on a tripod. Scanning the back of the house, I could see the kitchen and a large game room with a pool table inside, but not much else. I hoped that Messer's audience with Mr. Big would be outside. It was a nice day, a nice day for waiting.

It was a couple of hours before Messer pulled up in his limo. The entourage met him and escorted him into the house. No sign of Mr. Big. I scanned across the back of the house, waiting for Messer to appear. At last, he showed in the game room, drink in hand, joking with the others. It all seemed pretty relaxed except for one guy who kept checking his watch.

After fifteen or twenty minutes, they started to take seats in front of a big screen television which has just been turned on.

I couldn't make out clearly what was on the screen from the angle that I was at, but shortly, a man in a suit appeared on screen sitting at a desk.

I watched them watching him. Messer appeared to be talking to the screen, gesturing occasionally. Then it dawned on me that they're Skyping with the boss. This guy, Mr. Big or whoever he was, wasn't in Malibu. He was still in Hong Kong or Macau or wherever, pulling strings long distance.

As I'm trying to get a good picture of the man on the monitor and cursing that the top half of his head is hidden by the roof, my phone vibrates. I quickly checked to see that it is Rachel.

"Do we have a problem? Thought we were going out last night?" She texted.

"Never heard back." I replied.

"Do you even check your phone?"

I scrolled up through my messages. Shit. There was her reply, and I missed it. How does that happen?

"Sorry, my fault."

"What are you doing now?"

"I'm on a stakeout."

"If you don't want to see me, just say so."

"No, seriously. I'm surveilling this crooked city councilman who's taking a secret meeting with his Chinese Triad bosses. For real."

"K."

Ooh, that burned. She's not buying it.

"This won't take long. Let's get dinner tonight."

"Let me know."

Looking back, my first mistake was not factoring in the angle of the sun. I was on the high ground and facing west. The sun was well past midday and shining down on me and reflecting off my lens to the house below – amateur mistake. My second mistake was not turning off my phone – lesson learned. Then again, I should have anticipated that they might have guards to patrol the perimeter every now and then.

I never heard him walk up behind me, the guy who knocked me out. I woke up in the game room, in front of that same television, off now. It was a nice one, sixty-five inches at least, curved screen. I was admiring it and wanting to rub the knot on the back of my head when I realized I wasn't tied up. I gingerly touched the lump and looked at my fingers; no blood.

There were two guys, the one with the Trilby and another, bald with tattoos on his arms and a cigarette dangling from his lips, playing billiards, not pocket pool, but the game with only three balls, red, yellow, and white, and no pockets. They casually noticed that I had regained consciousness but did not stop playing. I looked around the room. The place was sleek and stylish but reeked of tobacco. No one else seemed to be around. I noticed my camera equipment, smashed, wallet, and gun lying on the bar. I didn't know if I dared get up from the couch.

I tried to catch the attention of one of the pool players and motioned to him that I wanted something to drink.

"What?" the guy in the Trilby said. "You want something to drink? Whiskey, beer, water?"

I don't know what I was expecting, but I was a little surprised that he spoke English, with no accent, for that matter.

"Water would be fine," I answered.

"Dao ni la." The bald one interrupted.

"There's a fridge behind the bar. Help yourself." The first one called to me as he bent over to line up his shot.

I got up, rather unsteadily, and shuffled over to the bar, finding the refrigerator as he said. I helped myself to a small bottle of water and stood there, behind the bar, drinking. In front of me lay my gun.

"They could not be so foolish. It must be unloaded." I thought. "It would be a mistake to pick it up, though."

I stood there, drinking my water, looking at the gun. The Chinese men continued playing billiards, ignoring me like a drunken party guest who's overstayed his welcome. They didn't seem to be armed, not that I could see anyway, probably no need for my case. They were probably both expert martial artists, Kung Fu or Wing Chun; they could swat away bullets with their pool cues, then snap them in half, fly across the room, and beat me to death with their makeshift nun chucks.

I took another long drink. The water wasn't quenching my thirst. Either I was hot or scared. I noticed I was shaking a little, so I set the bottle on the counter to steady my hand.

As I tried to make sense of the scene, Messer walked in, took one look at me, and grew immediately angry.

"I thought you said you took care of this damn reporter." He snapped.

"Oh, yeah. You'll not see that guy again. This is some new guy we caught poking around with his camera. Unfortunately, the camera broke." Trilby replied.

Did they grab Carmady after I left him last night, drunk and defenseless? I thought. Was he now dead because of me?

"I trust that you are not permanently damaged as well," Messer said, turning back to me.

I felt the lump on the back of my head again. "I'll live, I guess."

"Possibly." He said ominously. "Would you mind telling me what you are doing here, sneaking around and taking pictures? I'm not usually a lure for the paparazzi."

"I'm not paparazzi. I'm a detective."

"Yes, so I gather from this cheap badge you carry around." He had picked up my wallet and was flipping through the contents.

"At first, I thought you were that Carmady kid again. It would not have gone well for you if you had been."

"Well, if you must know, I was here trying to find out what you were doing here."

"That much is obvious. I'm meeting with my constituents, if you must know."

"This is rather out of your district, isn't it, Councilman?"

"These are businessmen. They have business with the city." He said with a straight face.

"Look, councilman, I'm pretty apolitical myself. I probably should care about your dealings with these Chinese Triad guys and John Lee and the whole stinking casino scam you've got going. But I don't. And they are not really that much of a secret if you were under the misassumption that they were."

That didn't get a rise out of him.

"All of my dealings as a representative of the city are above board and public knowledge." He replied calmly.

The two Chinese pool players had now stopped and were standing, arms folded, by the patio doors. Messer motioned to Trilby, and he came over to the bar, pushing past me to retrieve another bottle of water.

As he left, I may have trembled a bit. I tried to be overly casual and picked up my wallet, being careful not to touch the camera or the gun and put the wallet in my pants pocket.

The bald guard watched all of this with intense interest. He made a point of showing he didn't like me.

"I'm here about Mimi Kim." I said, looking up.

"And who is she?"

"She was a Korean cocktail waitress at a bar you frequented in Seoul."

"Which one?"

"There were so many?"

"Sadly. Those were the years when I was about your age, when my behavior was not something I recall with much pride."

"You got her pregnant. She thought you were going to marry her and bring her back to the States. Ring a bell, now?"

"Narrows it down a bit, but no."

"She's not the one whose neck was snapped. How about now?"

That hit a nerve. Messer stared at me with those killer slits. I'm sure he wanted to snap my neck, and he just might get the chance before the day was over. But just as quickly, the calm returned.

"Did you just come here to insult me?" he asked. "Or was there something you wanted?"

"Mimi had a daughter. So Young is her name. Pretty name, don't you think? Pretty girl, too, just like her mother. Anyway, she, Mimi that is, has been trying to track you down and get you to own up to your parentage. Maybe you saw her lurking about and thought her only an obsessed fan or something. Then, about a couple of weeks ago, Mimi went missing. I figured you might know something about that. Something that might help me find her."

"I think you have that figured wrong. I don't know this woman, Mimi, and I don't know her daughter."

"Oh, you know your daughter all right, just by a different name."

As soon as those words tumbled out of my mouth, it finally sank in that Messer had been sleeping with his own daughter. My mind kind of froze on that thought, but my mouth kept going.

"She goes by Ah Na. She works at the Dong Seo on Thursdays. As I said, she's very cute. I have a picture of her, of you both."

I began patting down all of my pockets searching for the photo I had printed out. I couldn't find it, but no matter, when I looked up, Messer's demeanor had definitely soured. I don't think he knew who Ah Na was, but something must have happened that he was now putting two and two together. He was not happy. He turned around and walked out of the room quickly.

One of the guards, Trilby, followed.

The other wise guy just stood at the billiard table and gave me a leering smile, like he knew what was coming and was looking forward to it.

He motioned to me, asking if I wanted a game. I didn't know for sure what was in store for me, but I sure didn't want to hang around to find out. I gave him a vacuous smile in return. My stomach was suddenly in my throat.

"Sure, I'll play, but I have to warn you I'm not very good."

I picked up a cue that was leaning against the wall and walked over to the table. I grabbed one of the cue balls and, as Baldy bent over to place the red ball on the table, I cracked him with the cue ball on the side of the head with all my strength.

He staggered, but didn't go down. Still, it gave me enough time to smack him on the crown of his skull with the handle end of my cue stick. That knocked him out.

I quickly grabbed my camera and gun and dashed out through the open sliding glass door. Because I had been watching this side of the house for a few hours, I felt I had a good knowledge of the lay of the land. I darted around the tennis court, hoping that no one was looking outside at the moment. Then it was a sprint, uphill, over rough terrain.

I was so out of shape, the air burned my throat, but it is amazing what a shot of adrenaline will do.

About a hundred yards up, I heard voices and a couple of gunshots. Dirt kicked up at my feet, but I didn't turn to look back. I didn't even run a zigzag pattern; it was just balls out up the hill. Two hundred yards up, I reached the fence and the tree line. Now I had some cover.

I started watching for others coming to head me off. The terrain flattened out a little, and I could see the fire road and a little further up, my car. I stopped, cautious that the car might be guarded.

They took my keys, which I didn't stop to find on my way out, but I had a spare in a magnetic box under the front fender. As long as there was no one watching the car, I was good.

I was eager to run for the car, but at the same time, I needed to catch my breath and make sure no one was around guarding the car.

After a minute, I made a dash for it. Fishing the key out from underneath, I unlocked the door and flopped in, starting the car even as I closed the door. I jammed it into reverse, spun around, and got the hell out of Dodge.

My heart rate didn't return to normal until I was on the Ventura Freeway cutting through the Valley on the way back to Hollywood. I looked at my gun, lying in the passenger seat. I flipped it open. It was unloaded. Glad I wasn't tempted to go for it back there at the house. I thought I had another box of ammo in the trunk. Plenty of time later to check on that.

I came into Beachwood Canyon from the back again. Parked a block from my house and hoofed it the rest of the way. After taking at least half an hour of watching my house from a distance, I felt safe that no one else was watching it. I loitered as long as I dared until the sun dropped behind the hills and the street fell into shadows. Then I slipped into the house.

I didn't turn on any lights, but I knew my way around well enough in the dark. I walked to the back of the house and looked out. Those two young men I'd seen before, shirtless, were again lounging on the back patio, smoking and casually looking over at my house. I watched them from the dark of my house.

Were they Chinese? How could this be a coincidence? Have Messer's men really been camped next door all this time? I liked it better when I just thought they were shooting porn there.

I watched them until they put out their smokes and went back inside. I was sure I was just being paranoid, but better safe than sorry. I grabbed a bottle of scotch and loaded my gun. I made myself comfortable in the living room, back to the wall, with a clear view of the house, doors, and windows. I would just stay up all night if I had to.

Then I remembered my last call with Rachel. Shit! Why does everything always come at you all at once? Couldn't risk talking on the phone. I texted her.

"Really Sorry. In a bit of a jam. I'll call as soon as I can."

CHAPTER

TWENTY-FIVE

Note to self, if you're going to stay up all night, don't drink.

I didn't know how late I stayed awake, but I woke up in the same chair, an empty bottle at my feet.

No time to clean up. I took a quick shower, changed, and headed back to the car. I had to get downtown before the Club opens for lunch. The Founders' Club didn't open for lunch until eleven. I got there right on the dot. Henry was the regular weekday lunch maître de. I knew him pretty well. I explained to him that Alistair Lachlan left his glasses in my car and I wanted to return them. I said I thought I could leave them with him for the next time Mr. Lachlan came in. Henry offered that

Lachlan didn't come in that often, except for Tuesday's he took an early lunch before a weekly meeting he attended somewhere downtown. I pretended to fish around in my coat pocket for the glasses and then pulled out my own sunglasses.

I sheepishly told him I'd run back down to the car and get them. "Be right back," I told him as I hustled to the stairs. I knew I probably wouldn't be back until tomorrow at eleven, but Henry wouldn't think anything was amiss with that. Happens all the time, I lied to myself

So now I had a date with Lachlan, although he didn't know that. It occurred to me that it was exactly two weeks ago that Mimi, his wife, first walked into my office. I had gotten so caught up in whatever I was caught up in that I'd completely lost sight of the fact that she was missing, and I was supposed to be finding her.

I put my sunglasses in my coat pocket and found a folded piece of paper there. Pulling it out, I saw it was the picture of So Young and Messer I printed out the other night, the one I couldn't find in Malibu. Such a messed-up family. I put it away. I was certain that if Lachlan hadn't stashed his wife somewhere out of town and far away, then Mimi was still hiding out in the house with her parents, but how to prove it? I looked at the picture and realized I could do what Miles did. Play to my strengths. Stake Out!

I took the back way into the hills above Solano Canyon. It's called Elysian Park, but it was pretty much just some rolling hills with dry brown grass, scrub bushes, and a smattering of Eucalyptus and Oak trees. But it did offer a great vantage point to look down on the house. There was no place to park my car there, so I had to drive about a quarter mile further, park the car, unload my gear, and walk back.

I had brought my Canon 2600 mm telephoto lens this time, great for getting in tight from a long way away. I was certain that if I could see into the windows, I'd be able to spot whoever was in there. I found a good spot on the side of the road with a clear view of the house and set up. I wish I hadn't left my tripod back in Malibu, though.

I was in my element here. I'd gotten a little go bag with water and snacks and an old iPod loaded with Jazz. I plugged in my earbuds and settled in for a long wait. This is what I used to be good at.

I scanned up and down the street. Mimi's house was flanked on both sides by smaller stucco cottages. Further down was a house under construction. I could see over the rooftops to the street behind, and behind that was Bouvett street where Miles was killed. Maybe he was staked out there. But he wouldn't have been watching Mimi's house, would he?

I panned my camera lens to the end of the block. 802! Was that the house where So Young and Messer shacked up? Just down the street from her mom and the grandparents!

The day dragged by with no sign of any activity. As sundown approached, lights went on. This would make it easier. Nighttime shots into a lit room always turned out the best.

Then the black Lexus showed up again. Two guys get out and begin tagging the house under construction with black spray paint, writing something in Hangul. I recognized them as they were dressed like the Chinese guards from Malibu, some new guy, and the Bald One, the guy I tagged with the cue ball.

I watched them through the lens as they sprayed something in Korean letters on the house. I would make a terrible sniper, though. One of the guys turned around, and as I was studying his face, he reacted as if he had seen me. It must have been the setting sun glinting off the lens again. Damn! Anyway, he began yelling at the other guy and pointing in my direction.

Then, yet another goombah, the driver, Trilby, gets out of the Lexus and looks up toward me. He pulls out a gun from a shoulder holster.

I was still watching all this play out through the camera lens with no sense of urgency, like I'm watching a movie or something. Then the driver got back in the car and peeled out. The other two guys began running toward me, up the hill. That woke me up. I grabbed my gear and bag and took off. I'm thinking, "I've seen this movie before!"

They were a couple hundred yards away and downhill from me, so I was calculating I could get to my car easily enough, then I realized the Lexus was probably racing towards me right now. No way I could beat that.

I decided to ditch the car and run cross-country and hide. This hilltop was not the best place to find a hiding spot, though; the bushes were thin and scattered, as were the trees. I kept running uphill, away from the road. As I crested the hill and was starting down the other side, I heard the Lexus come barreling down the road. It didn't stop, and neither did I. Ahead was a thicker stand of trees and bushes. I headed for that.

As I plowed through, scratching my face and snagging my shirt, I heard the Lexus return and squeal to a stop. I stopped and listened. I could hear the car door open, and the driver was yelling in Chinese to his two friends who were still running up the hill. I quietly inched further downhill, further into the woods, and looked for a place to hide.

I could still hear the three guys talking loudly above me as I moved quietly through the brush, then suddenly I reached a precipice.

The hill dropped off at a severe angle, down to the freeway below. I was stuck, couldn't go any further in this direction, and those guys were behind me. I looked around for a better place to hide. For the next half-hour, I listened to them, now closer, then further away. The driver got back into his car and drove, too fast, up and down the roads.

Eventually, it was quiet, and then it was dark. There were no lights in the park; it was pitch black. But from my perch atop the cliff over the Five Freeway, I had a great view of the lights of downtown Glendale. I drank my water and ate the last granola bar. It was too dangerous to try to climb out of there in this darkness, not with the steepness of the terrain and the possibility of falling to my death.

I decided I'll just spend the night and hope the coyotes didn't find me.

CHAPTER

TWENTY-SIX

It was not a good night. Besides freezing, every little pebble and twig felt like a knife in the back. My coat alternated between being used as a blanket and a pillow, and neither one gave me much comfort. I have never been camping, and I don't know why people like it. Maybe a tent and sleeping bag make all the difference. I don't know what hour I finally fell asleep, but when I awoke, it seemed like midday already. The battery on my phone had died, so I had no clue to the hour.

I scrambled to my feet and hustled back up the hill to go find my car. I hoped it survived the night better than I did. I tossed my camera and bag into the trunk and started the car to find that it was already after ten in the morning. If I were going to catch Lachlan at lunch, I would have to hustle.

I rushed home for a quick shower and change of clothes. As I turned the corner for my house, I noticed a familiar car parked in front, a black '69 Type-E convertible Jaguar roadster with the top down.

"Oh, Christ!" I groaned out loud. "Not now."

It had been three weeks since that morning I left Glenda in bed at the Chateau. A lot had happened in those intervening days, and I had been dodging her calls ever since. I had never brought her home with me for any of our trysts, but there was that time we swung by my house to pick up a dinner jacket for dinner at some swanky restaurant that required one. She must have memorized the address.

I parked the car, noticing that her car was empty. I didn't see her around, but wouldn't put it past her to be hiding in the bushes, ready to spring out as I unlocked the front door.

I debated driving on and abandoning any plans to clean up or trying to sneak in before she appeared. I was still in the car, weighing the options, when her voice sang out.

"James! There you are!" She was coming up the walkway from the back of the house, apparently after trying the back door and finding it locked.

"Glenda, what are you doing here?" I answered as I reluctantly got out of the car.

"Well, you won't answer my calls, so I had to track you down."

"I'm sorry, but this isn't a good time. I have an urgent meeting downtown and I'm running late. Can we talk about this at another time?"

"I don't believe you. It can't be that important. You look a mess." She picked a leaf off my shoulder.

"I know. It's a long story. I just swung by to change clothes, and then I have to run."

"You owe me an explanation. And a make-up date." She folded her arms across her chest and planted herself in front of my door.

"Glenda, I'm serious. I have to go. Someone's life may be in danger!"

"Oh, James. Always with the drama. Seriously, you and your detective fantasies. I expect an answer as to why you have been avoiding me, and I'm not moving until I get it. Are you seeing someone else? Is that it?"

I could only roll my eyes and stare at the sky. "No. I am not seeing anyone."

"Then why don't you want to see me anymore? Am I too old, too ugly, too skinny, too flat-chested? I'll get a boob job.

"No, it's not that. It's not about you. I've been busy. I'm in the middle of a major investigation. My client has gone missing, and it looks like she was involved with or uncovered accidentally some major scandal involving City Hall and these Chinese gangsters and the new casino…"

"Oh, stop it, James. You should hear yourself sometimes. You make it sound like your life is something out of a dime novel. Who is this new client? Another soon-to-be divorcee? Is that what you're trying to tell me, James? That you're moving on."

"Forget it," I shouted, throwing up my hands. "Suit yourself. Stay here. Make yourself at home. I've got to go."

I turned around and half-walked, half ran back to my car, jumped in, started the car, and pulled away from the curb. I gave a quick glance back at Mrs. Brown to make sure she wasn't about to throw herself under the car, but she still stood there in front of my door. I couldn't tell if she had begun crying, but either way, I had to get downtown fast.

At the club, Henry took one look at me and said, "You cannot go in there looking like that. Give me your jacket, and I will give you a loaner from the coat room."

He picked a leaf out of my hair. "You might want to use the men's room to clean up a bit. I believe you might find a comb or a brush in there."

I followed his instructions and cleaned up the best I could. Upon return, Henry had a jacket ready to exchange for the crumpled mess that I was wearing.

"Oh, let me grab something from the pocket," I said as I fished out the photo of So Young and Messer.

"And the glasses?" Henry asked, looking me in the eye.

He knew. I could only hold his glance for a second before looking away guiltily. I walked past without answering.

I sat down at Lachlan's table, uninvited.

It suddenly occurred to me that this was the same table where I first saw So Young, with her mother. That scene flashed through my head again. I was at Henry's station when I was suddenly surrounded by men in suits. That was also when I first saw Messer. Funny how a man only six feet tall can seem to be head and shoulders taller than everyone else. I had lost sight of So Young. She had bent down at that moment to get something out of her purse, I guess, or was she ducking to avoid being seen by Messer? So much was going on at that moment that it flew right over my head.

Lachlan looked up at me, not recognizing my face, maybe it was the beard stubble.

"Sorry to intrude, Mr. Lachlan. James Gardiner. Do you remember me? I'm the private investigator your wife hired. I believe last time we spoke; you told me she had gone to Korea to visit her parents."

He looked at me for a good, long moment, I guess trying to decide whether or not to have me removed from his table.

"Did I? I don't recall." He said at last and then continued eating.

"I happen to know that she hasn't left the country at all."

He didn't respond, but continued a very meticulous dining habit, building identical forkfuls of steak, mashed potatoes, and green peas. Each little parfait was only a bite, no more.

"I think maybe you've got her stashed somewhere close by where you can keep an eye on her and keep her out of trouble." I pressed on.

As I talked, I watched closely for any telltale sign of a reaction. So far, none. His focus was on his plate, not me.

"Or maybe she is indeed visiting her parents, but in one of your properties in Solano Canyon, not in Seoul. See, I have already been by to see them. They are not doing well. They're alone and afraid. Without Mimi, they are floundering, since they have no friends here, not to mention, no phone and no food. But you needn't worry, I have arranged to have some groceries sent over, and I think So Young is looking after them, now, as well."

Lachlan looked up at me with an expression of innocence and bemusement.

"You are familiar with that house." I continued. "It is one of many that you own in that neighborhood, all under anonymous LLCs. See, you're in an acquisition war with your old protégé John Lee to buy up the neighborhood because you know that the fix is in with his pal Councilman Messer to throw the casino that way after the bond measure passes."

I was interrupted by the waiter. Before Lachlan could say anything, I ordered a cup of coffee.

I continued, talking as fast as I could before he could stand up and walk away. Telling him what he already knew was not making much of an impression. It was time to go fishing.

"And just for a little added insurance, you conned your daughter into posing for blackmail pictures with Mr. Messer, courtesy of Lee's man, Detective Bowman, who you turned for a few extra bucks, but who's now conveniently dead. And the pictures seem to have gone missing, except when they haven't."

I pulled the picture out of my coat pocket and slid it over to Lachlan. He turned it face down without even looking at it. I guessed he'd already seen it. This is the first thing I'd said that had gotten any reaction from him, but now he had recomposed himself and continued eating without saying a word in reply.

"Have I left anything out? Oh, yeah, except she's not really your daughter after all, is she? It's so much easier to use her that way when there's no real attachment."

Finally, Lachlan stopped eating and put down his fork. He slowly looked up at me with a very pained expression. He'd done remarkably well containing his emotions thus far, but I think I'd pushed his last button this time.

"Well, young man, I think we both know you're just saying these things to get a rise out of me, but it will avail you nothing. I am not a man who is ruled by his emotions. What is it that you really want?" He said softly.

"Well, for starters, So Young hired me to find her mother. I intend to do that. I would also like to figure out who killed Detective Bowman, if only because they tried to frame me for it and I'm still a suspect, although not really. As for the real estate scam you're into, I couldn't care less."

Lachlan carefully folded his napkin and arranged it and his utensils neatly on the empty plate. The wait staff must love him. He looked up at me and held my gaze for another long, awkward moment. "I have a meeting a few blocks from here. Let's take a walk, and I will tell you some things you need to know."

Lachlan got up and headed for the door. At clubs like these, one isn't inconvenienced by the tiresome details of waiting for a bill.

I followed. As we walked down the front steps of the club onto

Flower Street, Lachlan stopped and pointed to L.A.'s newest skyscraper.

"Do you know what that is?" He asked.

"Yes. It is the new Korean Air Building."

"It is more than a building. It is a monument to the future. It is a beachhead to the coming tide of Asian money that will soon wash over this country."

"Okay." I replied, bracing myself for the lecture to come.

"Those are the real players. Lee and I are just hustling for scraps on the sidelines."

I laughed. "You're not the first one to tell me that this week."

He turned and walked up the street. I followed.

"I first bought property in the canyon about ten years ago." He continued. "But not just there. I buy all over town, wherever I sense an opportunity. I fix up distressed properties and hold them for rentals. It's a pretty straightforward business model. Solano Canyon was just one neighborhood among many that I focused on. Then I noticed rather strange activity about three years ago. Shell companies were buying up the houses at an unusual rate and paying over market. It didn't take long to get to the bottom of it. So, I decided to strengthen my position and make a few bucks. I'm not involved in the politics; I'm just along for the ride. Nothing illegal in that. John and I have already talked, and we have an understanding."

We turned and cut through the small park adjacent to the Central Library. It was a pleasant day in Los Angeles, the sun was shining, and the air was warm but not as hot as the past two weeks. Phosphor and Hesper stared down at us from the walls of this monument to Freemasonry and all the secrecy that it invoked. Would they illuminate my mystery for me, or would I get burned? I was taken by the coincidence of the symbolism of where we stood. What would Robert Langdon think?

"As for my wife," Lachlan continued, "truthfully, I do not know where she is, but it is not the first time she has disappeared for a few days. Though this has now run on for more than a week, and I am getting worried."

"Two weeks, and you haven't filed a missing person's report." I interjected.

"My wife is bipolar." He continued.

"Involving the police has not ended well in the past; so, no - I have not reported anything as yet, not that I need to. They are quite aware of her disappearance. There's a patrol car parked outside my home twenty-four-seven. As for Detective Bowman, I have never met the man, though I know who he is. If those photos are meant for blackmail, it was not employed against me."

"You seem to know quite a lot. More than you let on." I added.

"I have had my own man following my wife." He replied. "She was harassing Mr. Messer, and there was no way I could convince him and John that I wasn't behind it. Then the pictures showed up, and they both were convinced I was playing some kind of game to get a bigger cut."

"Why would your wife be harassing Messer?"

"She claimed that he was the biological father of So Young."

That stopped me in mid-step. My mind was racing, trying to fit all the pieces together. Was Lachlan now going to confirm all that I had come to suspect?

We had stopped at the bottom of a very long flight of wide steps that curved up and around the U.S. Bank Tower.

Lachlan continued, "I first met Mimi in a bar in I-tae-wan. That's a neighborhood in Seoul that sat next to a US Army base that was there.

She was a barmaid, and like all the waitresses there, she spoke English. These bars catered to GIs and expats like myself who sought out a bar that felt like home. Mr. Lee, who worked for me at the time, first took me there because he thought all Americans liked country music. He told me his cousin worked there as a waitress. I was smitten by Mimi almost at once and began to frequent that bar just to chat with her. I think that was Lee's intention all along. But I soon came to see she only had time for me if Messer wasn't around. He was tough competition for me, tall, good-looking, with an air of danger. I think he was an officer in the Rangers. I wasn't much different than what I am now, a poor working slob, except back then I had no money. Lee tried to intervene. I think he was hoping I would marry his cousin and take her and him Stateside. Anyway, he often bragged about his gangster friends taking care of Messer if he got in the way. I never thought Lee had any ties to criminal gangs, and nothing ever came of his idle threats.

"Then one day, Messer shipped out and never showed up again. I think she really expected he would marry her and take her home with him. All the girls in those bars were husband fishing. They came from poor families, and this was a way out, even though it was very frowned upon to marry white, especially a soldier. Soldiers weren't very well thought of by the locals, only for the money they spent.

"Anyway, she was heartbroken. I let her pour out her sorrows to me, and that's when she confided that she was pregnant."

"Did she tell you it was Messer's, or did you figure that out on your own?"

"Well, I knew it wasn't mine. I had never gotten to first base with Mimi. Anyway, being pregnant and unmarried is ruinous for a girl in her position in Korea and her child. They would be ostracized for the rest of their lives. So, I offered to marry her and take her back to the States with me. She wasn't interested. She was certain Messer would return eventually. I didn't stay in Korea much longer after that. My job was ending. I headed back to the States. I don't know how Lee managed it, but he contacted me later and said Mimi had reconsidered and would accept my proposal. I was thrilled of course and arranged for a fiancé visa for her to come to L.A. to get married. So Young was born before I could arrange for her trip."

"Why didn't you adopt So Young?"

"Mimi wouldn't have it. I think she still felt that one day she would find Messer, and once he learned he had a daughter, he would immediately claim paternity and take her back as his wife. As I said before, she lives a very active fantasy life."

"Some would say she's a hopeless romantic. But - she would leave you after all you did for her. Why did you put up with that?"

"Unlike you, Mr. Gardiner, I am not much to look at. You probably never had a problem attracting the girls. And Mimi, well, you've met her. At forty, she is still a stunner; you can only imagine how attractive she was at twenty. Words do not do her justice. A guy like me would never land himself such a good-looking wife in America. Looking back, it was rather immature of me."

"And now?" I asked.

"I love her. I love them both and have for the past twenty years."

"So, when did she find her long-lost lover?"

"Several months ago. Mimi saw him at the Founder's Club of all places. I had thought it long behind her, but once she saw him, that rekindled her obsession again. Lee, Messer, and their scheme for the casino land were already in play. I remembered Mr. Messer, although I doubted he was aware of me. If Mimi suddenly popped up, well, I knew the optics on that were going to be bad."

"So, you just let it happen?"

"Mimi is a bit uncontrollable. I hired a guy to watch her. I let Lee know what was going down, but he didn't trust me. I think he had his own guy tailing her as well. We were trying to keep her away from the councilman. I don't think he was quite aware of the extent of Mimi's obsession, yet."

"And then I came along and upset the applecart, so to speak."

"I will honor whatever my wife and daughter have offered you. Please find her. Now, if you will excuse me, I have a meeting to attend."

I stood at the bottom of those stairs, watching a very tired man climb them. I looked up at the seventy-three-story building and felt a little dizzy.

I headed back to the club to retrieve my coat and car. In the car, I unplugged my phone, it seemed to be charged again. After I turned it on, a series of messages started pinging, Jack, finally returning my call. My mother, 'what does she want?'

A receipt of delivery from Shop-4-You, not too much, less than two hundred dollars. Then I noticed the address, that didn't look right. I checked the address I texted Yana a few days ago. Someone had hijacked my grocery delivery. That could only be one person, Mimi.

I checked the new address on my car's navigation screen. It was about a block away. That had to be where Mimi's been hiding out, probably another of Lachlan's properties.

CHAPTER

TWENTY-SEVEN

The house was another Craftsman, big front porch with heavy columns holding up a pitched roof, brown shingle siding with contrasting trim, but here the grass was brown, and the landscaping starved for water. The house, too, though not in bad shape, looked worse for wear, needed a little paint and TLC, not typical of any of Lachlan's properties. It was the last house on the cul-de-sac. I spotted Messer's limo in the driveway alongside the house.

I wasn't expecting that. Was he here to confront her, put an end to her harassment, one way or another? I didn't like the implications.
I parked a few houses short and walked up. The limo driver
was not in the car. I shaded my eyes and peeked in the driver's side window. The car was clean, not a trace of personal effects inside. The driver's seat was moved back a couple inches more than the passenger side. I guessed maybe Messer drove himself, adjusting the seat to his height. I guessed he gave the driver the day off so he could take care of business with no witnesses, maybe? Just how desperate was he? What lengths might he go to get rid of this distraction or potential embarrassment to his career plans?

As I was surveying the inside of the car, I heard a gunshot. It sounded like it came from inside the house. I immediately called 911. I told the operator that I heard gunshots and gave her the address, then added that I believed Councilman Messer might be at that address and that he might be in danger. That should get more than a few cars dispatched.

Now I faced my ultimate 'What Would Marlowe Do' conundrum. I hurried back to my car to retrieve the Rugar.
I didn't usually carry a gun with me, never thought I needed one for my line of work.

When things got dicey, I always scrambled.
But there was a potential killer in that house. I knew it wasn't Lachlan, I had just left him. I didn't think it was Messer, and I couldn't bring myself to believe it was Mimi. I really hoped it wasn't Detective Mejia.

I'll never understand why I walked up the steps to the porch. Maybe I had an unfounded belief in my ability to talk my way out of trouble. Maybe I thought I was really going to save someone's life and didn't give much thought to the risk. Maybe I was just pumped full of adrenaline and wasn't thinking straight. Certainly, my mouth was dry and my knees weren't working the way they should, but I kept going. My hands were sweating. I wiped them on my pants, swapping my gun hand to hand to do so. It felt heavier than usual.
The door wasn't locked. I flipped open the cylinder to triple-check that it was still loaded, closed it, and raised the gun to my shoulder. I opened the door as quietly as possible and peered in.

The afternoon light slanted through the rooms, highlighting the dust motes that hung in the air, giving the place a mystical look. The house was sparsely furnished, more likely staged for showing to buyers or renters. The front door opened into a small foyer with a small secretary table against the wall. A stack of flyers and a sign-in book are the only items visible. A living room to the right was furnished with a sectional sofa, a coffee table, and a large vase of flowers, now mostly wilted. To the left was a dining room. The round dining table had been awkwardly pushed to one wall, along with all but one chair. In the center of the room sat one high-backed wooden chair.

Messer was zip-tied to it, and duct tape covered his mouth. A wicked gash showed through his short grey hair just above the ear. Blood had trickled down and dripped onto his white dress shirt at the shoulder. Messer had apparently let himself get caught off guard.

So Young backed in through a swinging door from the kitchen, carrying a pair of candlesticks with tall, tapered white candles and one of those electric fireplace starter matches.
In her USC football sweater and matching skirt, she looked more like a cheerleader than a killer, but there she was.

When she turned around, I saw the nine-millimeter in her other hand. She didn't seem to be surprised to see me.

"Oh, Hi, James. I was wondering if you would show up. You being the smart detective and all, I would have been very disappointed in you if you didn't."

"Please put the gun down, So Young." I said, aiming my gun at her. "This doesn't have to end badly."

"What are you going to do, James? Shoot me?"

"What are you doing, So Young? That's your biological father you have tied up there."

"Oh, I know, but don't say that. Daddy will get upset." She said, setting the candlesticks on the table. "See, he's already getting upset. He doesn't like to hear that he's my real daddy. But I know. I've known for a long time now. I knew when I fucked him. But Daddy didn't. How was I Daddy? Was it as good for you as it was for me?"

I couldn't tell if Messer was afraid. If he was, he hid it well. Must be his Ranger training. His eyes were cold, and he just stared unblinking at So Young. She paced around the room, very animated. I wondered if she was on something. She waved her gun around carelessly in one hand and the electric match in the other, punctuating her remarks with it.

"No, Daddy's not happy having a little girl, 'cause his little girl's a Gook, just like her whore mother. Isn't that right Daddy? Daddy and his G.I. buddies don't like our kind much. But he does like to fuck them, especially the ones at the nohrehbang. Cause Asian girls have tight little asses. Don't they Daddy?"

"Look, I get it. He abandoned you and your mother. But, what about Allistar? You have a loving father, who brought you here and raised you as if you were his own."

"Oh, yeah, him. He loves me so much he wouldn't even adopt me!"

"I think your mother prevented that. I believe he wanted to."

"Then what a dickless little man he is, can't even stand up to his own wife. Of course, she wouldn't allow it. I was her bargaining chip to get this loser back. So, I'm neither Korean nor American. I've no country, no father, I'm just a pawn in somebody's chess game."

"Let's talk to your mother. Where is she?"

"She's downstairs, but she doesn't want to talk to you."

"There's a basement in this house?" I asked suspiciously. California houses don't usually have basements. Don't ask me why.

"I guess it's more of a crawl space." She said rather cavalierly. "But it's plenty big enough for her stinking carcass."

It took me a second to process that. "Did you kill your mother?" I asked.

"It was an accident." So Young said with a shrug, waving her gun around, not particularly remorseful. "I'm not sorry. She found the pictures, the ones that Miles took for me."

"That you were going to use against your father?" I asked.

"See, you get it. Mother didn't understand.

'How could you do that?'" She said, imitating her mother's voice.'He was your father. He was my husband. He was your father.'"

"As if." She snarked and began lighting the candles. "It didn't matter at that point what I said. She couldn't hear it. She just went ballistic. It was all I could do to protect myself. She brought the gun. She pulled it out of her purse on me."

"If it was self-defense, why didn't you call the police?"

"I wasn't finished with Daddy, silly. I still had to destroy this creep's career. And then, stupid Miles. He called Mother's cell and tried to blackmail her. It wasn't enough that I was paying him a grand a week. He got greedy. He didn't know it was me on the phone. I agreed to meet him just around the corner."

"And that's when you killed Miles."

"I didn't mean to do that, either, another accident."

"Stop it. Miles may have been an experienced detective, but he didn't have too many brains. He would have looked you up and down, Angel, and gone grinning ear to ear up that cul-de-sac with you. You could have gotten as close as you liked before you put a hole in him with the gun you had gotten from your mother."

"Well, then, he got what he deserved. "

"Sounds like things got out of control pretty fast."

"Yeah, I guess they did. I had it all planned out, and then everyone wrecked it, first mother, then that dick detective. So, I had to come up with a new plan."

"That included framing me, dropping my phone in his car, and planting the gun in my office," I added helpfully.

"What else could I do? I like you, James, but you're a rich white kid with connections. You've got white privilege coming out of your ears. You were never really going to take the fall for it."

"Is that supposed to be a compliment? You're quite the actress."

"Thank you. The girls at the nohrehbang all tell me that I should be an actress, too."

It was about this time that I noticed the smell of gas. It appeared that So Young had blown out the pilot of the old stove and turned on all the gas valves. The house was slowly filling with gas. I noticed the candles were burning brighter.

"You don't have to do this, So Young. I know you're upset, and maybe you've been abused in the past. But you can get help. Things can still work out. It doesn't have to end badly for you." I pleaded.

"Time for you to go, Jimbo. Mommy and Daddy have a date tonight, and you're not invited."

I started to move toward her, and she lowered the gun, pointing it at me.

"I may have said I liked you, Jimmy, but don't think I won't shoot you. I've shot a lot of people lately. I'm starting to get the hang of it." With that statement, she smiled and batted her eyes, then aimed without looking and shot Messer in the knee. He lurched back and tried to scream through his gag.

I started to back away, afraid to turn my back to her. She just watched, still smiling, a manic look in her eyes, waving the gun playfully. As I backed into the front door, I turned to open it. Maybe the fresh air will put out the threat of an explosion. As I grabbed the door handle and I heard a shot. I froze, but for only a moment.

I rushed back into the dining room. So Young was lying on the floor, blood streaming from her temple. I grabbed the back of Messer's chair and started dragging him, still in the chair, towards the front door. I paused just long enough to grab the door handle and fling it open. The change in air pressure from opening the front door caused the swinging kitchen door to open as well. That's when the gas caught and exploded. I went flying back, across the porch, and backwards down the front steps. Messer, in his chair, landed on top of me.

I started to push him off when a second fireball exploded through the front door, and it all went black.

CHAPTER

TWENTY-EIGHT

I woke up with little black spots swirling in front of my eyes, an oxygen mask strapped to my face, and straps across my chest and arms. I was on a gurney, wrapped in a blanket.

Red and blue lights flashed across the side of the ambulance. My ears were ringing, but I heard nothing else. Droplets of water splashed on my face. Was it raining? I turned my head to see firemen spraying foam and water in slow motion from their hoses onto the house, now fully engulfed in flame. The wind blew some of the spray back toward me. It felt good. Thick black smoke billowed up to the sky. It was all playing like a movie with the volume turned off. This movie had one high ringing note for a score. I wondered if I had ruptured my eardrums in the blast. A man and a woman crossed my field of vision, wearing matching light blue jackets with 'FBI' emblazoned on the back. Behind them were more police. They had cordoned off the street, holding back a growing crowd of looky-loos. I briefly wondered if the boys who beat me up were in the crowd. News photographers were busy snapping away at anything and everything. TV Reporters stood in front of their video cams, breathlessly relaying the unfolding event.

I turned my head to the other side and watched as another gurney was loaded into a waiting ambulance. Could that be So Young? I wondered.

A news cameraman stepped in, blocking my view. He struggled to get a clear shot of me, but was pushed away by a short stern looking policewoman. Behind her, I thought I saw Detective Mejia, hands on his hips, staring at me and slowly shaking his head in disapproval.
Two attendants lifted me up and started to slide me into the back of the ambulance.

I closed my eyes again.

Sometime later, how long I didn't know, I reopened them to the inside of a moving ambulance. One of the EMTs casually noticed that I had regained consciousness. I watched the oscilloscope with my heartbeat sliding silently across the screen. I tried to sense the pulse of my blood in my ears to see if it indeed synched up.

The EMT leaned over and pointed to her watch. I tried to read her lips, guessing.

"Five more minutes, buddy, we'll be at the hospital."

I closed my eyes again and saw a swirling pool of grey. I sank into the warmth of the codeine drip like you would a hot bath.

CHAPTER

TWENTY-NINE

I came through this pretty well, some minor burns to my face and arms, bruises and abrasions, and that's about it – a minor concussion, but no broken eardrums, thank goodness.

Messer suffered only a broken collarbone besides the burns and abrasions, and of course, the gunshot to his knee, but his political career died that day. The local press, not to mention the tabloids, had a field day: a father-daughter romance that ended with two murders and a suicide – that would be So Young. That was going to keep them juiced for months.

I wasn't surprised to hear that Messer had skipped town, never to come back. It didn't matter that he was innocent of most everything except abandoning a pregnant girlfriend twenty years ago. Well, that and possibly soliciting bribes from Lee and company.

I felt terribly confused, guilty, and embarrassed about my feelings and actions concerning So Young. I kept reliving those few times we spent together, only to push the thoughts back out of my mind. I realized I'd been played, that I didn't really know her at all, and I chalked that up to my own naiveté.

The casino would be voted down in a few weeks as well, tarred with the same brush. Sordid politicians meant shady deals to most voters.

Lee and Lachlan both would both get their fifteen minutes of fame under the microscope, and both would slip back into anonymity.

At least, I would never hear their names again. Detective Mejia's name would never get mentioned, not in connection with his old partner, Bowman, or his latest bromance with Messer. He must have friends in the newspaper.

I'll have to remember to ask Carmady about that someday. Turned out he wasn't dead. They had given him a one-way bus ticket out of town with a warning.

Now that the whole affair had blown up, Carmady would be back and writing front-page stuff again. He was probably already working up a book tell-all.

I got released later the next day. Mother and Yana had both visited that first morning, filling me in on all the details in the news. Yana brought my usual copy of the Journal, but conveniently tucked inside a copy of some tabloid from the supermarket checkout rack. Rachel stopped by also, brought me a boxed set of Raymond Chandler to read.

I spent the next few days at Mother's house, letting her baby me until I could stand it no longer. By the weekend, I had fled back to my place.

The house next door, it turned out, was not a porn film site, not a meth house, nor a Mary-jane farm. It turned out to be one of the most ubiquitous illegal operations in town, the unpermitted rehab. Those two women I first saw were house flippers. They had bought the place to do a quick remodel and resell for a profit. They had stashed a couple of illegal Chinese immigrants inside, to live in the house and do all the work for a cut rate. Of course, all the remodeling was being done without the scrutiny of the Building and Safety Department, thus all the precautions against the prying eyes of the inspectors. Now, with fresh paint and new kitchen cabinets, etc., it was back on the market.

Monday morning, I walked down to the 101, half expecting Jack to pop in. For some reason, I was extremely hungry and ordered the lumberjack special.

Norma gave me a little side-eye.

"Now, don't you go now packing on the pounds. You're quite the celebrity now, Easy Rawlins. You've got to watch your appearance and stuff."

Jack never showed, so I enjoyed a quiet breakfast alone, eating and scrolling through the news on my phone.

I walked to the office, picked up my two coffees and one Frappuccino. Jimmy was at his usual spot and welcomed the cup I brought him as always. He set it down carefully, and then just as carefully, he brought out a Tupperware container with a very beautiful fish, reddish gold and white with black markings.

"It's a Chinese Moor, note the bugged-out eyes, very delicate. You will have to be diligent in caring for this little one, but I think you are ready to move up from the garden variety goldfish." Jimmy lectured me as he handed over the plastic tub. It seemed he was branching out into exotic fish.

"How did you come to know so much about tropical fish?" I asked.

"I used to work at a pet store." He reached back into his pile of stuff and brought out a small box of fish food and a booklet.

"They like to eat, so you needn't worry too much about overfeeding him. But you'll need to watch that your tank water doesn't get too warm. It's all in the book."

"What's a fish like this set you back?"

"Twenty."

I pulled out a pair of Jacksons and handed them over.

"For the fish grub, too. Keep the change."

"Thank you, sir. If you do well with this one, I might graduate you to a saltwater tank."

"Mmm." I said, nodding my head knowingly. I wondered what I was getting myself into.

Walking down the corridor to my office felt a little strange this time. It wasn't like I had been away for a long time, only a week. I guess processing all the past few weeks' events had left me more than a little reflective. I wasn't sure if I was going to continue doing this. The divorce work no longer appealed to me, and I questioned whether I was really cut out to be any other kind of detective. It would be only fair to talk this over with Yana before I made any sudden decisions. I don't know how much she needed the job, and I didn't want to just kick her to the curb.

Entering the office, I handed Yana her drink and poured the Moor into the aquarium and watched for a second to make sure he didn't start attacking the others. Satisfied, I picked up the paper and was about to head for my office.

Yana handed me a large stack of phone messages. "You're a popular guy now. Every news outlet in the country wants an interview."
I stuffed the wad in my pocket. "Don't know if I'm ready to be a celebrity detective just yet."

"Then, how about just a regular detective. You have a potential new client waiting for you inside." Yana informed me.

I gave her a quizzical look. She just smiled and shrugged, offering no further information.

I opened the door to my office. In my guest chair sat a young girl, sixteen, maybe nineteen. I'm not as good at guessing the age of Latinas as with white girls. She was dressed in a hand-embroidered cotton dress, light blue with multi-colored flowers, now faded from too many washings, and slip-on navy canvas shoes.

She stood and offered her hand.

"Mr. Gardiner, I am Rose. Pleased to meet you." She said with a bit of an accent.

"Buenos Dias, Senorita. "I'm afraid that's about the extent of my Spanish, Rose. I can say hello and ..." I caught myself before finishing my usual spiel. "Never mind."

I walked around my desk, not taking my eyes off of her.

"What can I do for you this morning?" I inquired as I flopped down into my chair, stifling the urge to put my feet up on the desk.

She sat and composed herself.

"I was hoping you could find my brother. He was supposed to come to Los Angeles last month, but he has not contacted any of my family."

Then, almost as an afterthought, she pulls out an envelope bursting with cash, not fresh bills, but dollars no doubt pulled from a sock or a shoe box.

"I have money. I can pay. Can you help me?"

I wave away the offer of pay.

"Have you contacted the police, filed a missing person's report?"

"He is *indocumentado*." She lowers her head, slightly embarrassed. "They all say they cannot help."

Then she looks up with a face full of hope and extracts a business card from the envelope of dollars and pushes it across the desk. It was my own.

"Detective Mejia gave me your card." She continued. "He said you are a very good detective, and a very good man. He said you would help."

Coming Soon!

Another James Gardiner Mystery!

<u>SOUTH BAY</u>

James is approached by an old acquaintance from ten years ago to track down a young woman missing and presumed dead.

His investigation rekindles memories of his sybaritic summer in those beach cities before his high school senior year, memories both good and repressed.

What happened then still haunts him today, and will this case raise more questions than answers?